MANATADO

VS THE MACHINE

MA WEST

Edited by Audra Gerber
Book Cover by Stacey Lane Design

YucaiPa

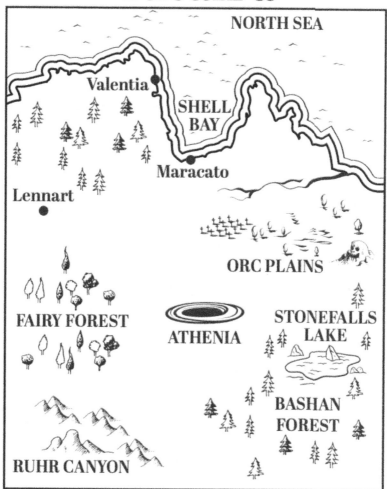

NORTH SEA

Valentia

SHELL BAY

Maracato

Lennart

ORC PLAINS

FAIRY FOREST

ATHENIA

STONEFALLS LAKE

BASHAN FOREST

RUHR CANYON

Aradoro– creature from the Gnome village

Athenia– Greatest city of all, vanished into a hole in which monsters now appear out of

Bashan– name of elven forest

Cassandra Nighttorn– AKA Archer of Valentina

Ciefraf– Malada's father

Chasm of eternity– Where Malada shield keeps the magic it's encounters

Clandine clan– Name of the Regents and Itarus clan

Davenwood– Regent of the Dwarves.

Doctor Frances– Human doctor among the dwarves

Doctor Florian– dwaren medical doctor

Ferninia– Fairy that first meets the group and escorts them to meet the queen

Itarus– Drawf who persecuted gerterma after Nicolda switched sides

Jamel of a seaborge flock– leader of the tree animals

Jalum– Mysterious older brother of Gerterma
Lennart– Gnome village of the Travelling Spirit

Malgamar– Evil Wizard who was defeated by Queen Ankinia using the shield

Eratrea– Malada's mothers name

Maracato– The name of the largest human city

Minoets– bugs that grow to the size of large dogs

Mr. Marks– old man from refugee stays in Manatado's house

Nicolda– Gerterma mentor's at the dwarven trail

Queen Ankinia– first queen of the fairies

Pennicle Rock– Malada's home town

Redleaf– Elf who is Malada's father

Ruhr Canyon– where the machine was built

Riftia– Name of monster who killed dwaren king

ShellBay– Where they play turtle backing matches

Socratea– name of the walking trees

Pennicle Rock– name of Malada hometown

Tamack and Rogers– Manatado's best friends from the village

Tammicia and Junipe– Cassandra's best friends

Traveling Spirit– Tavern at beginning of story

Turtle back (shelling) – game in which participants ride large turtles as they play

WaterWakes– Red leafs LT.

Village Valentina– name of the home village

Yucaipa– name of the continent

Prologue

Manatado steadied himself as a gust of wind tipped his giant turtle nearly sideways. His head reached out and pressed against the rising shell's side. The wind settled, as did the turtle, and Manatado could see the whole of the bay before him. Tamack was to Manatado's left while Rogers was to the right. It was a positioning arrangement they had practiced a dozen times.

Manatado handed the ball over to Rogers. He then raised his flag to catch the wind and speed up ahead of him. The other team, a group of girls, was led by a girl named Cassandra, who was an excellent turtle backer—her teammates, not so much.

One of Cassandra's teammates, Juniper, was moving into position to jump at Rogers. Manatado rode the wind until he saw the wave break, at which point he dropped the sail and flattened down on the turtle. The wave lifted him and the turtle up, only to crash down on Juniper, knocking her from the shell and into the ocean.

Manatado righted himself and, as planned, took the ball back from Rogers, who blocked off Cassandra's third teammate, Tammicia. Manatado raised his sail and made straight for the goal. Cassandra was coming straight for him, but she couldn't defend the goal from both Tamack and him. Manatado waited for Cassandra to commit to defending one of them.

Cassandra chose Manatado and tilted the front of her turtle towards him.. Manatado smiled, for in the corner of his eye was Tamack, right where he was supposed to be. Cassandra was leaning down forward on her turtle, her sail full in the wind. Manatado made a move as if he was going to make a break for the goal. Cassandra tipped her turtle in that direction. Manatado stood up and threw the ball to Tamack.

It was a ruse. Cassandra had only made it seem as if she were heading toward Manatado. Her sail was full in the wind, the same wind that was pushing Manatado. He felt his hands go to his face, as all he could do was watch as the ball floated through the air.

Cassandra launched herself straight up into the air and grabbed the ball. Tamack tried to grab it back but ended up falling into the ocean. It had come down to Manatado and Cassandra, the last two riding. Cassandra set sail for Manatado's goal while he set out to intercept her.

The two were on a collision course, staring each other down like bitter rivals. The waves were just right, and the two prepared for a crash.

A burst of warning sirens and alarm bells echoed around the bay, drowning out all other sounds. The noise brought Manatado's and Cassandra's hands to their ears. Cassandra dropped the ball into the ocean just before colliding with Manatado, and together they fell into the ocean.

Chapter 1

As if living with the other races wasn't difficult enough, now there were monsters roaming around too. "The great city of Athenia has been swallowed whole, and monsters are now appearing out of the crater." That was all the announcer said, and it made young human teenager Manatado very nervous. The human defense force was already stretched thin, and now with this news, the rumors of a draft were certain to come true.

While Manatado didn't consider himself a warrior, he liked to think of himself as at least brave and able. Having to put those traits to the test was making him apprehensive. He had done training exercises with the defense force's junior division, as all young human men do, but those were simple exercises, not life-or-death fights. A few of the other boys talked about running away, but that idea wasn't very appealing either, sleeping out in tents, always on the move, avoiding dangers and the law.

No, Manatado felt stuck like a puppet in his own life. Being called to this community meeting wasn't a relieving feeling. Currently, he stood between his two best friends, Tamack and Rogers. While they were turtle-back teammates, their true enjoyment came from watching the girls and egging each other on toward flirting with one of them.

The town prioritor, Gerterma, a gruff straight-cut warrior, a veteran of the orc wars, was known to be a serious man, and tonight he was demanding full attention. "Yes, yes, we have confirmed that monsters are now appearing out of the crater that was once Athenia. We still—"

The crowd cut him off midsentence as it roared with commotion, protest, and jeers. After several attempts to quiet the crowd, Gerterma pulled out his pistol and fired it into the air. "Now see here! I'm in contact with the regional command, and the defense force has established a perimeter to keep the monsters at bay." The crowd again started an uproar, but Gerterma was able to speak over them, furthering the conversation. "As of right now, we still don't have any idea what happened to Athenia. I can tell you, most of our—and the other races'—leadership was in Athenia. General Jalum has now taken command." A mix of cheers and jeers came at the mention of the name Jalum. We are here tonight to accomplish two things. First, all men—and I mean all men between fifteen and fifty-five—are now drafted, women volunteers accepted. Everyone affected is to report here tomorrow at daybreak."

Manatado felt his stomach sink as he heard the words. Tamack and Rogers were both silent, and together the three exchanged a look of mutual fear. Cassandra acted like an athlete being placed in a tournament while her friends suddenly went missing.

"Second, we are here to welcome some newcomers to our fine little fishing town, a collection of nice folks who have lost their homes and need our help." Jeers of protest were squashed with a scolding look by Gerterma, and he instead started a round of applause, welcoming the new arrivals. A group of about thirty people came forward from off to the side. All of them looked like hell

—except for one.

A young lady in the group caught Manatado's eye, and he was instantly smitten. The dirt gave her skin a golden-brown glow. The ragged and uncombed hair gave her a wild, untamed, beautiful look. Tamack and Rogers honed in on it and taunted him about her. "Somebody likes the dirty girl." Manatado blushed as he hit his friend on the arm.

His friends were not the only ones to pick up on it, for Cassandra displayed both jealousy and annoyance before being noticed and playing it off. Rogers and Tamack giggled at each other as well, uncertain about which girl they should encourage their friend to pursue and jealous they weren't getting any attention. The boys jumped with a start, brought back to the present as Manatado raised his arms up high and yelled, "Me, me, she can stay with me."

The overexcitement in his voice was obvious and coincided with a small chuckle from the crowd. Prioritor Gerterma smiled while soliciting places for the refugees to be housed. "Well now, young Mr. Manatado, that's a generous offer, but I wouldn't be much of a caretaker if I just let some teen girl stay alone with a teen boy." Gerterma shot a smile of reassurance toward the girl. "I don't believe that shack you live in would be very fitting anyway, but since you offered"—Gerterma moved across the stage to an elderly man—"Mr. Marks here would be very grateful to bunk at your place."

"Wait, what?" Manatado blushed at his overexuberance. His feelings had been put on display, and it was his own fault. Living in a shack, however, wasn't his fault. His father had died in the orc wars, and his mother died while giving birth to what would have been his sister. Now he lived alone, alone in a shack just outside the city. It had never bothered him before, but now that he wanted to impress this girl, he felt shame.

Mr. Marks moved slowly. All of the others quickly found hosts, showing the small town's generosity that it prided itself on. The meeting ended with a promise of yet another meeting the next night, and the crowd dispersed into a thousand different conversations amongst themselves.

Rogers and Tamack quickly collected as much as they could in the way of supplies for Mr. Marks and were more than happy to hand all of it off to Manatado before departing for their respective homes. Manatado struggled with the weight of patience more than the supplies. Mr. Marks moved slowly, and it was frustrating the young man who had plenty to think about before going to bed, and it was going to be an early morning.

A strange and unfamiliar voice called out from behind him, startling the young man, causing him to drop most of the supplies. The voice chuckled out of embarrassment and regret. "I'm sorry. I didn't mean to startle you." The voice was as heavenly as Manatado imagined, and he felt himself drifting off in her direction as she approached. Tripping over a dropped armload of supplies didn't make him feel better.

He felt her hands on his arms as she reached out to help him up. Manatado jumped to his feet and, as manly as possible, brushed off the dirt.

"My name is Malada, and I noticed you at tonight's meeting. I hope you don't mind me coming up to you."

So many thoughts raced through his mind at once that only gibberish came out of his mouth. Malada smiled in response but didn't quite know how to proceed and ended up just shifting her weight back and forth between her hips. Manatado paused, trying to decide what to do next, before putting out his hand for a shake. "Nice to me-me-meet you."

"Thank you, ugh." Malada shook his hand but stood there awkwardly afterward.

After a long moment, Manatado finally came up with a question. "Oh, so where are you staying? With which family?"

Malada put her finger in her hair. "Oh, it's a nice family. They have a girl our age—Jupitor, I think."

Manatado smiled. "It's Juniper. Yeah, they are a nice family."

After a long pause, Malada's face turned to a serious expression. "I'm going to need help. I don't think Juniper is the one to help me. After tonight's meeting, I thought maybe you might be."

Manatado's face lit up like a Christmas tree. He had never felt more pride. "Of course, of course I will help."

Malada looked at Mr. Marks, who was now waiting impatiently. "Not now. Come find me tonight after everyone has gone to sleep."

A smile both boyish and charming reached from ear to ear as Manatado's mouth dropped open while he nodded acceptance.

"Great, I will see you then." She turned and ran off toward Juniper's house.

Manatado wasn't going to get any sleep, and now he didn't care. He lingered longingly, watching her leave before Mr. Marks came upon him and knocked the back of his head with a cane. "Young love, huh? Well it's going to get you nothing but trouble. Now come along. I'm old and tired."

Manatado gathered up the supplies and gave one last look in her direction before setting out for his shack, with Mr. Marks shuffling behind.

Chapter 2

Mr. Marks certainly wasn't the type of person to hold his punches, and Manatado was losing his patience. "This shack is where you live, boy. How do you call this living?"

Manatado made a quick dinner for his unappreciative guest and then ushered out the bed and wished Mr. Marks a good night.

"It's a trap. I hope you know that, right?"

Manatado had taken enough of this old man's crochety behavior, and he wasn't going to stand for it anymore. "You don't know her. How can you stay that? All you have done is come into my home and insult my life, and now you are bashing my hopes. You are nothing but an old curmudgeon!" He stood and panted, face-to-face with Mr. Marks.

Mr. Marks made a stern face and stood slowly, meeting Manatado's eyes. "Hmm, perhaps there is hope for you after all, boy. I may have been too old for the front lines of the orc wars, but I was rear guard and I learned, just by sight, who was going to survive and who wasn't. I can still do the same now." Mr. Marks sat back down. "Go along, then. Go and find your girl, but I warn you. Girls don't just fall in love like that. If this girl asked for you, she is going to ask something of you."

Manatado, his chest still panting from the encounter, took a step back and decided against saying anything further, instead heading out to meet Malada. He crept and tiptoed, trying to avoid notice. Not to say he was doing anything wrong, he told himself, just best not to be noticed.

Manatado approached Juniper's house and paused, not sure how to proceed. Should he just walk up and knock, should he throw a rock at the window, or should he see if the door was unlocked and let himself in? After a moment, he moved forward and started feeling the ground for a small rock.

A small-but-powerful foot stepped down on his hand, pinning it to the ground. It was Cassandra, and she wasn't smiling. "You're here for her, aren't you?"

Manatado pulled his hand back, shaking out the pain. "Cassandra, what are you doing here? Shouldn't you be sleeping or training, or whatever?"

"What is it about her? You can't tell me she is prettier than me. She's all dirty and unkempt."

"It's not all about looks, you know. I can just tell, she is almost magical."

"That doesn't even mean anything." Cassandra bent her bow in frustration, nearly breaking it. "Why do boys always have to be so stupid?"

A new voice entered the conversation, and it was Malada. "Who's that out there? Manatado, is that you?" Manatado waved off Cassandra as he turned to face Malada. "Oh, it is you guys. You were making so much noise I wasn't sure." Malada hunched over, keeping a low profile as she approached the two. "Cassandra, I'm so glad you came."

Cassandra was dumbfounded when she heard her name spoken by a stranger. She found it very disarming. In fact, much about Malada was disarming. Her unkempt wild look made Cassandra feel prettier than her. Malada was slightly shorter than Cassandra, and Cassandra was more than confident she could take Malada in a fight. Malada's timid and nervous posture was also very disarming, allowing Cassandra to ease up on her anger and jealousy.

"Great, thank you both. I have an enormous favor to ask of both of you. My mother is missing, and I need help finding her." It was not the type of request either Manatado or Cassandra was expecting, and the seriousness of the request changed the tone between them. "They didn't say everything there was to know at the meeting tonight."

Cassandra and Manatado exchanged a look before focusing entirely upon Malada as she continued. "My parents were both officers in the defense force." She swallowed as if she was pushing the emotions back down into her stomach. "Athenia didn't go missing overnight like they suggested at the meeting, and they know why." Malada looked more forward than at either of them, focused on telling the story. "Recently, my parents had been hearing stories—stories about earthquakes. But more than just that . . . earthquakes that seemed to shake free terrible monsters. I guess what I'm trying to say is that Athenia has been under attack for weeks."

Malada turned around. "When the city vanished, there was something more, something terrible, something so powerful it could destroy the most powerful city on the planet."

Cassandra and Manatado exchanged a look of disbelief that confirmed they were thinking alike and then turned back toward Malada.

"And did you see this awful thing?" Cassandra asked with an unquestionable tone of skepticism.

Malada took a deep breath and composed herself. "Look, it doesn't really matter if you believe me or not. That's not why I asked for your help."

Cassandra and Manatado again exchanged a look, but this time not so disbelieving, and nodded for Malada to continue.

"My mother is missing. She was with me right up until they evacuated my town. I know the soldiers took her. I need to find out where they took her and figure out how I can get myself there."

The thought of sending Malada off into the wilderness certainly struck the right tone with Cassandra, while Manatado couldn't help but compliment Malada on her bravery. Cassandra could barely contain the rolling of her eyes as she heard him say it but again nodded for Malada to continue.

"I know this town prioritor has a long history with the defense force. If there is any place where information about where my mother might be, I bet it's in his office."

"You want to break into Gerterma's office? Are you crazy?" Manatado faced a reckoning with his own bravery earlier than he ever expected to. Seeing two girls look at him as if he were a coward, he changed his tone, coughing lightly. "I mean, you would certainly need some help for that."

"Chicken little here isn't totally wrong." Cassandra gave Manatado a look that was both teasing and insinuating. "Gerterma isn't a fool, and his office won't be easy to break into, nor will it just be out sitting on his desk. I can't break into a safe. Can you, Manatado?"

A slight reddish hue crossed his face. "Well, no, but I have been in his office before. I volunteered once to help out around the office for a couple days one time."

"You mean you and Tamack got caught stealing foodstuffs out of the public pantry at night and were forced to work it off."

Malada giggled as the two friends exchanged banter. "Look, I can take care of any safe, as long as you two can help me get in there."

Cassandra looked like she was going to question Malada further, but Manatado's look dissuaded her from doing so. Together the three teenagers snuck out to the edge of the village, where they waited for the last of the village lights to go out.

Manatado felt sleepier than he expected to, and as they lay side by side in the brush, his head become even heavier. Soon he found his body resting against the ground and then against Cassandra's body. Between the warmth of her body and the cold night air, Manatado fell asleep at a time when he wanted to be at his strongest. Gentle snores brought forth a giggle from Malada.

At first the presence of Malada kept Cassandra from a moment she normally would have rejoiced at. Yet Malada was a quiet and straightforward girl who seemed rather more interested in other things than Manatado. Cassandra relaxed and felt her body weight start to push back against Manatado's. Cassandra gently jostled him into a new position, ending his snoring.

After some time, Malada stood up and gently shook Cassandra's leg. "That's it, the last light just went out."

Cassandra easily woke and quickly regained her senses, while Manatado on the other hand rolled over and let out a furious snore, which drew the hands of both girls to his mouth. The lack of breathing woke and startled Manatado when he realized he was pinned down by two girls.

After he gave up fighting free, the girls released their hands from his mouth. Manatado stood up and wiped off the embarrassment. "Okay, girls. I was just resting my eyes." Changing the subject, he continued. " I've been thinking about this, and I think we should try to go in via the garbage chute in the back."

Cassandra gawked at Manatado. "You want us to go in the garbage? How about NO. You, the"—she let out a little cough—"man, go in through the garbage chute and unlock the front door for us ladies." She wrapped her arm around Malada, stepping to her side. Malada seemed to beam at the gesture and exchanged smiles with Cassandra.

Manatado sheepishly smiled. "Okay, I mean, I was thinking I would sneak in via the garbage chute and open the door for you girls."

Cassandra and Malada nodded their heads in approval. Manatado shuffled out, keeping hunched over and as quiet as possible. The girls watched as he made a zig-zag approach to the edge of the shrubbery. After a moment, he sprinted across an open road and the landscaping in front of the building. Finding cover under the porch, he waved for the girls to approach.

The girl reached the edge of the grass cover and waited while Manatado snuck around to the back of the building and out of their sight. Malada spoke quietly and softly as they waited. "Thank you for helping me. It's not often I can find such generous people."

Cassandra thought about her motivation and felt a tinge of guilt. "Yeah, well we haven't helped you yet. You might just want to wait and see if we even succeed before you start with the thank-yous."

"Well whatever the outcome, it still means a lot to me that you would even try."

Cassandra blushed and nodded a thank-you before the front door to Gerterma's office popped open and Manatado waved them over. The town was dark and silent. In a town as small as this, even the police station shut down at night. Manatado wore a big proud smile as he opened the door, but all he got in response was Cassandra pinching her nose as she walked by. Malada faced Manatado as she entered the door, giving him a sheepish smile before moving in.

Manatado seemed to follow behind Malada wherever she looked in the office while Cassandra stood as a lookout. First they searched the desk but found nothing. Then, after finding a key in a drawer, they searched a file cabinet. Court records, case documents, and a ton of other boring useless paperwork was all they could find, and Malada was growing uneasy, restless, and scared.

"There has to be something, anything. I have to find my mother. We've searched everywhere!" Malada again gave Manatado a puppy-dog look. "Please, I don't know what to do next. Help me."

Manatado felt a shiver flow up his spine as Malada hugged him with her tears. He started to embrace her back, when inspiration struck him. "The bathroom!"

Malada pulled back. "Yes, you do stink, but now might not be the best time to wash."

Manatado bounced up and down as he thought with excitement. "No, no, no. There's a door in the back of the bathroom. We were never allowed to go in there. That's where we should try next."

A very loud whisper came from the front of the building. "Hurry up, you two. I think I hear somebody coming."

The two teenagers exchanged a worried look and then bolted to the bathroom. They ran up to the door but found it locked. Frustrated, Manatado slammed his foot down and turned around. A bright flash caught his eye, but by the time he turned around, Malada was opening the door. Before he could question her, she was waving him inside. It was a conference room. The board displayed a map of the Yucaipa with a big X where Athenia used to be.

On the side of the board was a list of names. At the top of the list was Malada's mother's name, Eratrea. Malada froze in place as she examined the room. A flash of terror came across her face at the realization of what she was looking at. Her mother was being sent to Athenia, the heart of the monster invasion, or was she already there when it sank? Malada froze as the thoughts terrified her.

"That's it. We need to go now!" Cassandra was now in the room, grabbing the two by the wrists and pulling them as hard as she could. The three scrambled for the front door, when a deputy entered. The teens slammed against the door, pushing the deputy back down the front steps. They then all ran for the rear door.

The deputy sounded the alarm and drew his weapon as he ran back into the office. Cassandra let an arrow fly as they ran out the back room. The arrow soundly hit the wall but still forced the deputy to take cover. The teens banged into the rear door of the office, but Manatado had a hard time undoing the locks. As the door finally flew open and the kids ran out the door, a shot rang out.

Cassandra screamed out in pain but fell into Manatado's arms as the kids ran. Manatado grabbed Cassandra and put her on his back as they ran back into the brush. The deputy called out after them, signaling to the other officers which direction they were heading, but he didn't pursue them himself.

Gerterma was the first to arrive, and he immediately began questioning his deputy. "Did you see who it was? Where did they go?"

"No, sir, but they fired this arrow at me."

Gerterma grabbed the arrow and held it up to the deputy's face.

"Do you know whose arrow this is?"

The deputy gulped as the realization of what had just occurred came to his mind.

"This is one of Cassandra's arrows! Did you just shoot one of our kids?"

"But they were shooting at me!"

Gerterma moved the deputy back to where he was standing and then demonstrated how far off course the arrow was. "Go, go, and get the doctor. Have the boys light up some lanterns and start searching the brush south of here. I'm going after them myself." Gerterma paused before he left and looked back at the deputy. "You're going to need to be able to think clearer than that under duress if you want to stay in my force. By God, man, you see these kids every single day."

The deputy grew large, sad eyes as he turned about to execute his orders. Gerterma sighed and hoped for the best as he set out after the kids.

Chapter 3

They ran and ran and ran. Manatado ran until his legs gave out below him. He tumbled to the ground and laid Cassandra down as gently as he could. Malada bit her finger as her chest heaved. "This is all my fault. This is all my fault."

Manatado stepped back as he looked down at a pale, groaning Cassandra. She had always seemed so vigorous and full of life. Now she had none of that, and it scared Manatado. After a moment, the panic faded. He took his hand and placed it over her hip as he tried to stop the bleeding. Yet as the blood kept gushing away, so did Manatado's confidence. "I don't know what to do." He knelt over Cassandra and ran his hand down along her face. "Please don't die."

Cassandra opened her eyes just enough to make eye contact and smile back at him. She then began to cough and shake, sending tears down Manatado's face. He hugged her tightly when she started to feel less warm. Malada knelt beside them. She rested her hands under Manatado's and closed her eyes. She spoke inaudible words as her hands glowed bright white. The white magic traveled through Cassandra's body. The energy of Malada's magic surged through Cassandra, healing her only to then burst out into the open, shaking the air around them.

The light spread across Cassandra's body and lit the whole area around them. The white magic glowed across her skin as it closed its wound and came together. She coughed and smiled as she found herself being held by Manatado. "This isn't how I wanted to end up in your arms, Manatado."

The relief brought a genuine laugh to Manatado. He gave Cassandra a relief hug and helped her sit up. "How do you feel?" He turned his head back and forth between the two girls.

Cassandra put her hands over where her wounds were and felt them as if in disbelief. "I feel fine. In fact, I feel good." Her face showed an expression of curiosity as she reached into her pocket and fished out the bullet, held it up high, and threw it aside.

"How did you do that, young lady?" Gerterma's voice was firm and shocking, as his presence had been unknown. Malada took flight, but Gerterma was ready and faster and yanked her into his arms. "Young lady, what did I just see? How did you do that?"

"Let go of me, you enslaver!" Malada thrashed about, desperate to escape from Gerterma.

Manatado stood up, uncertain how to proceed. "What's going on, Gerterma? What are you doing?"

Gerterma kept his hold on Malada but started to speak toward the other two. "Humans are not supposed to possess the power of magic. That's what's going on."

Manatado looked longingly at Malada. "Wow, she really is magical."

Any closeness Cassandra felt she had gained with Manatado was now lost, leaving her both thankful for and jealous of Malada.

"I suspected as much. The defense force does too. That's how you ended up here in this village." Gerterma slightly loosened his grip on Malada, trying to indicate that if she stayed, he would let her go.

At the mention of the defense force, Malada became very agitated and tried to pull away. "I won't be your pawn. I won't do it. Get off me."

Gerterma pulled her back in close as she tried to pull away. " I know, I know. I'm not here to send you away with them."

"What?" Cassandra couldn't help herself. "But, Gerterma, you are always promoting the defense force, telling us to join up."

Gerterma again lightened his grip, seeing if Malada would flee. "Yes, I know they would train you two. This one, this girl's power would be used. She would be manipulated and forced into doing evil things in the name of greater good."

Malada still pulled back but with a more consistent and less urgent force. "You're not going to send me to be a soldier?"

"No, no I'm not." Gerterma released his grip, and after taking a few steps, Malada was satisfied Gerterma wouldn't chase after her and stopped. "No, I know what they would do. Those who value winning and survival above all else would weaponize her. Her entire existence would circle solely around one thing, fighting. I can't do that to another."

"What do you mean 'to another'?" Manatado blurted out.

"That doesn't matter right now. All that does matter is what happens next."

Malada finally spoke. "And what happens next? I have to save my mother. That's what happens next."

Gerterma smiled as he looked at her. "You are a brave girl, and that will serve you well, but you must not purse your mother. Do you understand me? You must never try to find her." Gerterma spoke with an authority that seemed to convey he still knew more.

Malada nodded understanding but not acceptance. Gerterma read her like a book. "The adolescents seldom do as they are told." He shook his head as if he was already regretting the words. "If you must pursue your mother, you will need help, much help. Two days' travel south of here is a gnome inn called the Traveling Spirit." Gerterma took a step back and faced the village. "You will wait two days there for me. When I arrive, we will depart for the land of the fairies."

"Why would we go there? Fairies rarely interact with the other races," Malada asked cautiously.

"True, but there are only two races still remaining that can control magic, fairies and elves. I don't know about you, but elves scare the crap out of me, and you are going to need to apprentice yourself before you start using that magic freely." Gerterma then looked at Cassandra and Manatado. "As for you two, I think I can handle your training."

The sound of shouts off in the distance ended the group discussion.

"Go now, and I shall see you in two days' time." And with that, Gerterma took off toward his deputies and townspeople. Sounds of Gerterma yelling at his deputies to head off in the wrong direction gave the kids some reassurance, but it all just seemed too unusual to be real.

The three teens looked at each other as if questioning that what had just happened had in fact really happened. After together deciding it was real, they gathered up what little they had and headed out in what they thought was south. They kept low and moved in short spurts, waiting each time to see if they were being followed.

After a couple of jaunts, the continuing sound of nature assured them Gerterma had been successful in diverting the deputies. "Why do you think Gerterma said those things about the defense force? Why did he think they would treat you differently? What kind of magic do you do?" Cassandra asked.

At first, Malada just kept walking as if she didn't realize Cassandra was talking to her. Cassandra wasn't interested in dropping it, and she ran around in front of Malada and held her bow in the standby position. Malada kept her head down but looked left and right as if she was deciding whether or not to run for it. After a moment, she sighed and spoke down toward the ground. "It's because of my mother." There was a long pause before she continued. "My mother is a half breed."

Cassandra's and Manatado's jaws dropped as they heard the news. "But that's supposed to be impossible!"

"That's just another government lie! My grandfather was an elf." Malada kept looking down, but it was obvious that her chest was pounding and her body was very tense.

"Whooow, can we see your ears?" Manatado asked with intense personal interest but total unawareness of how she would feel about the request.

At first Malada was off put by the request, but after a moment's consideration, she decided it wasn't the worst reaction to learning such news. She ran her hand through her hair, exposing an ear, and brought forth an ear-to-ear smile from Manatado.

"They look pretty normal to me, but I can't deny that I'm feeling better and no doctor did that," Cassandra said. Manatado shook his head like a puppy dog praising its owner. Cassandra rolled her eyes at his reaction and engaged Malada. "So you have power to heal. What else can you do?"

"Well that's just it. I can't really control it yet. My mother was so adamant that I not join the defense force she refused to let me ever use my magic. I'm not sure what discipline of magic I have control over."

Cassandra looked down at her bullet wound and then at Malada. "Well I'm going to call you 'Doc' from now on because you're the only doctor I ever want again."

Manatado, coming out from his lovers' trance, saw an opportunity. "And who got sick off drinking not-yet-fermented grapes from the pantry and had to get leached by the doctor for two days?"

Cassandra twisted in protest at Manatado's comment and then locked her arm with Malada's, and the two walked away side by side.

Chapter 4

It was a couple hours' walk before they realized their mistake. At first the conversation was lively and entertaining, but as their feet grew heavy, so did their conversation. The saltiness of the air should have been a sign, but they all missed it. As they passed through the final layer of scrubs, they nearly went off a short cliff running down into the ocean. They stopped at a dead end.

"Why are we at the ocean? We were supposed to be heading south," Cassandra asked.

Manatado shook his head and stepped back. He was really getting tired of being the scapegoat. "I just followed you two girls. It seemed like you knew where you were going."

Cassandra crossed her arms in protest. "Well that's just great! Weren't you listening to Gerterma? Why didn't you say something?"

Manatado stomped his foot down. "Don't throw me under the bus. Every time I've suggested something, you two girls have shot it down like it was a bad idea. I'm not in charge, so I'm not responsible."

Cassandra's fists clenched as well as her teeth, but Malada put her hand on her friend's arm, and as they made eye contact, Cassandra composed herself.

"Well maybe we should take a break in the shade and try to find some water before we start walking back."

Malada's voice was very soothing to Manatado, and he shifted his focus back to her.

"Malada, why don't you and I go look for a stream leading out onto the beach? Maybe over there. Cassandra, you stay here, or whatever."

While the "whatever" part trailed off, it was audible enough for Cassandra to hear it and become upset. She grabbed her bow, held it at the standby, and gave Manatado a menacing look.

Malada gave her friend a softening look and then walked off with Manatado. He reached out his hand to hold her, and she sheepishly jumped off to the side to avoid it. Malada's rejection of Manatado's hand holding brought about a sense of relief in Cassandra as she watch them bound down a small outcropping of rocks and land on a rocky beach.

"Not a great place for a swim, unfortunately." Manatado felt awkward but motivated to build a rapport with Malada.

"Still, the forest is such a pretty place. You have no idea how beautiful it is here."

"Well what's it like where you are from? I know not everywhere has an ocean, but surely there are trees, plants, and animals." Again, he couldn't shake the forced feeling of his conversation.

"Well yeah, of course there are trees, flowers, and animals, but instead of each tree being right next to each other, it's like they spread their arms out as far as they could and said, 'My space. Find your own.'" She raised her arms and twirled in a circle as she spoke.

Manatado was hypnotized, his head tilted and his eyes fixed on hers. "Tell me more."

She blushed at his look. "Um, let's see. I come from, I mean, I came from a town called Pennicle Rock. It lies at the foot of a mountain, and up high on this mountain is a massive stone sticking straight out of it, like a giant hand plunged a spear of rock right into the mountain."

Manatado kept his longing look but only nodded for her to continue.

"My mother and I, we would race each other there. First one always got first choice of lunch." A tear started to form as she spoke. "I always won. Whether it was a trip at the last second or her pretend twisted ankle, I always won." Malada couldn't hold back the tear, and she leaned into Manatado, who sheepishly hugged her back.

Manatado was unaccustomed to being put into the position of comforter, but as they embraced, he felt like he could do anything for her. She closed her eyes and let the tears drop down on his shoulders. The wetness didn't bother him as he focused totally on the moment.

It proved to be a huge mistake. Manatado opened his eyes and let his vision run down the beach. There, several yards away, was a large bulking mass of a bear staring hungrily at them. Manatado pulled back and started pushing Malada away with his arm as he moved in front. Malada lifted her head and cleared the tears as she saw the fear on his face.

Together the two stumbled backward before fleeing in full sprint.

"Cassandra, Cassandra!" Manatado yelled at the top of his lungs as they sprinted in her direction.

Cassandra sat fuming upon a large boulder near the forest clearing, when she noticed the two. She was quick and had her bow at the ready. The bear was fast too, and it was closing in on the two as they zoomed in on Cassandra. The first arrow flew right between the two teens and landed directly in the bear's shoulder. The animal growled at the pain and rose up on its hind feet but didn't stop.

The two teens saw a noticeable change in Cassandra's face as the arrow failed to slow the beast down much. Once they reached her, the three fled side by side. They ducked and dodged between trees, but it was no use, and the bear tripped Manatado and grabbed him up in his jaws. With its prey in hand, the bear stopped its pursuit. Cassandra quickly rounded a tree and let loose another arrow that slammed into the chest of the bear.

The bear dropped Manatado as it ripped the arrow from its skin. The bear growled at Cassandra as Malada jumped behind her. The bear, now angry with pain, charged at the girls.

Malada felt fear. As Cassandra let loose her last arrow, Malada felt something more. The fear was turning into a desire to live, and that desire to live was creating a desire to kill. Her hands grew warm, and as the bear bore down upon them, they erupted into a fire so hot it seemed to burn white.

The fire erupted into a great ball of white flames that encompassed the powerful animal. The fire scared the animal as the flames scorched its fur, and it turned away from them and fled. The bear whimpered as it charge off into the brush.

Cassandra quickly rolled over, checked herself for injury, and then turned to Malada, who lay still, her skin pale but sweaty. "Manatado, get over here. She's hurt."

Manatado winced in pain as he crawled over to Malada, his one leg sticking straight out. He dropped to a knee and put his hand on her chest. Nervous energy filled him with concern "She's alive, breathing. What do we do?"

Cassandra looked around as if hoping for a rescuer to come running out of the brush. "I don't know, I don't know!"

"Her skin is cold. Ugh, I need to warm her." Manatado started taking off his shirt.

Cassandra slapped him on the head. "Don't you dare! I will get her warm. You go make a litter."

"But I can't even walk!"

Cassandra bent sideways to get a better look at Manatado's injury. "You're telling me that you're going to let the girl you love die because your butt hurts!"

Manatado looked hurt at the accusation but gave it a second thought. "By God, you're right. Don't you worry, Malada. I'm here for you!" He stood up with great pain, straightened his leg, and rolled it forward, limping as he went off to collect the needed supplies.

Cassandra felt a jealous sadness as she watched him walk away in pain, motivated by a girl other than her—someone she now had to embrace.

She then bent down next to Malada and felt her head, ice cold. Manatado was at least genuine in his efforts to help, even if done foolheartedly. She would need to warm this girl and fast. Luckily, being an arched hunter for the village, she had plenty of experience in the wild and was able to start a small fire as Manatado returned.

"How is she? I found what I could, but I failed to find anything to tie with. I thought maybe you would have an idea."

Cassandra looked up from placing Malada next to the fire. "Yes, yes, I do know what to do." Her eyes looked sadly at Manatado, but he didn't seem to notice. Instead, his body language begged for an answer. "Just keep her near the fire without catching her on fire. Okay, can you do that?" Cassandra felt more sharpness in her words than she intended, but once again, Manatado seemed oblivious to her emotional state.

"Yes, of course. Please go do your thing. I will look after her." Manatado slid into Cassandra's spot and stroked

Malada's hair with his hand. Cassandra gathered her composure and tried not to feel ugly and unwanted. She ventured farther afield than she really had to, just to get herself some breathing room.

Guilt kept Cassandra on task, and it didn't take her very long to fashion a litter from the materials Manatado had gathered. She took a deep breath before approaching the fire. Her heart and spirit rose again. When she appeared with the litter, Manatado jumped up in excitement with a big smile on his face, hugged her, and announced, "You're awesome."

Chapter 5

The two took turns pulling Malada in the litter. Stopping for the occasional repair was all the downtime they could afford. While Malada was no longer pale and shivering, she was still flush and dry. Hour after hour passed by, as did each mile. Cassandra and Manatado had long run out of things to talk about. The two simply walked side by side in silence.

It was approaching the peak of day when Malada came about, startled by her unfamiliar surroundings. "Where are you taking me?"

Manatado nearly dropped the litter in excitement as he hurried to turn around. Cassandra hurried forward and helped Malada out of the litter as Manatado grabbed the two and hugged them both. "Malada, what happened? Are you okay?"

Malada pulled out of his hug and took a step back, running her hands over her body. "Yeah, yeah, I don't remember really what happened or how we got here, but I think I'm feeling better now."

Cassandra put her arm on Malada's forearm. "Has that ever happened before?"

Malada instantly pulled back as if on instinct. "What do you mean?"

Cassandra expressed a look of worry and nervousness. "The fire, the magic, the coma after—has any of that ever happened before?"

Malada sighed and looked down at her feet. "Well, yeah, my mother always told me never, ever to use my magic. Something about, it didn't really belong to me and there would be a price for every time I used it. I guess the coma is just the price I pay for using too strong a magic."

"You are one mysterious girl." Manatado couldn't help but smile as he tilted his head and stared at her.

Malada blushed at the comment but kept her gaze down as she noted Cassandra's displeasure. "You two are the first ones outside of my mother to ever know I had magic." Malada raised her eyes and looked at her friends. "I'm feeling both terrified and relieved now that somebody else knows."

"Don't forget Gerterma. He knows too." Manatado chimed in, excited at having something to contribute. Unfortunately, it didn't relax Malada at all.

"Can we trust Gerterma? Is he leading us into a trap?"

"Gerterma is a good man. He would never betray us."

"But you said he was a high rank in the defense force during the orc wars. How can you be sure that's not where his loyalty lies?"

Cassandra and Manatado exchanged nervous glances but gave her a reassuring look. "Gerterma may have been a soldier, but he is a servant first. I'm certain he will help us." Cassandra held out her hand to Malada and pointed her in the direction of their destination. "I thinks it's the best decision, but if you think it's a trap, I will go elsewhere with you."

"I'm with the team too." Manatado walked up and placed his arm around the girls and pointed for Malada to lead the way. She hesitated for a moment but then nodded to her friends and set out in the direction of the Traveling Spirit.

Malada laughed as she slapped Manatado on the butt, healing his wound, and then scurried up alongside Cassandra.

Chapter 6

The Traveling Spirit was the outermost building from the gnome village of Lennart. It stood multi-floored compared with the rest of the village but was barely taller than the three teens, the largest part being a tight fit for an orc or comfortable for a seated human. The building became smaller, as did the windows leading to two front entrances, each accounting for a different height in customer.

The gnome village stretched out back among the trees, down a narrow cobblestone road lined with small house stacked upon small house. White-bearded gnomes sat around a small fountain while gnome children sang and danced around them.

"What do you think? It looks normal." Cassandra spoke quietly as the three huddled together along the edge of the tree line.

"So we should just go in, right? Normal like?" Manatado felt both excited and nervous.

"Why would Gerterma send us here? It seems so . . . plain?" Malada was thankful to have something she hadn't had in a very long time: friends.

"That's exactly why he would send us here. Who would look for somebody here? It's nowhere." Manatado stood up and looked around confidently. "I think it's safe, and I'm going in."

Cassandra and Malada exchanged nervous glances but followed along. Together the three crossed out into the open, half expecting a deputy to be waiting somewhere, ready to call out their names. Yet nothing happened and they strolled into the larger of the front doors.

Two small tables filled in the space before a hallway that led to two rooms. The other side of the room had a counter with a bell on it and a view into the other half of the establishment. The room had a smoky smell, and the stink of spilled beer permeated the floor.

Manatado approached the counter and, not immediately seeing anybody, stuck his head over the top. A small fist hit his jaw, sending him backward and onto his butt.

"I suggest you mind what is your own, young human." A tough white-haired gnome wearing a black shirt and red hat rose up from behind the counter. "A trio, huh? Well there's only one room available. That will be five pence for the night." The gnome then put a bowl out on the counter to receive payment.

The two girls exchanged nervous glances, while Manatado built a slow smile, as he finally felt needed. He prepared to speak but was interrupted by Malada. "Oh, that's so generous of you to offer to pay for our room. That's very kind of you." She held the bowl out for him.

Manatado obviously had something to say but paused and changed his mind. Instead, he bent over and took off his shoe. After removing his sock, Manatado pulled out a small sack that held his coins. The girls looked at each other and spoke almost in unison. "That's where you keep your money? Eww."

Manatado ran the coins under Cassandra's nose as she winced and playfully pushed him away. The gnome accepted the money and began to turn back around before Malada called out to him. "No, wait. We are here to meet somebody. Who is in the other room?"

The gnome spoke without turning back around. "Young human, what do you know about travelers? Each of them is here doing something they rather wouldn't be. Otherwise, they would be home. I don't ask them their business, and I suggest you do the same." The gnome moved back into his hidden position behind the counter but left a key behind.

"Wait, wait. He told us to come here. His name is Gerterma." Cassandra spoke urgently but clearly.

The gnome descended behind the counter without turning back but could still be heard clearly. "Never heard of 'im."

Manatado grabbed the key and held it up proudly. "I guess we're bunking together tonight."

Malada grabbed the key right out of his hand. "Boys take first watch, thank you."

Cassandra stuck her tongue out at Manatado as the two girls unlocked the door and walked into the room, a sparse space with only a bed, a desk, and a chair. Cassandra took the chair and ushered Manatado back into the hallway with it. She then shut the door and left him in total silence.

After a minute of waiting, Manatado sighed and leaned his chair back against the door. It wasn't until the calm of the moment that he realized just how tired he was. Breaking into the office last night, followed by a bear attack and miles of marching, had worn him out, and before he knew it, his eyes had collapsed and his head lay asleep.

Chapter 7

The world before Manatado was moving quickly—so quickly, in fact, that he couldn't understand where he was until his body hit the floor. The back of his head hurt and his vision blurred for a moment, but as he opened them, he saw Malada and Cassandra looking down upon him. "No sleeping while on watch. What if somebody had tried to break in here?"

The accusatory tone in Cassandra's voice upset Manatado. "Well nobody ever came to switch. I'm not a machine, Cassandra." He stood up and looked boldly at her as he rubbed the back of his head.

Manatado's tone didn't sit right with Cassandra, and she prepared to say something before Malada recognized the situation and chimed in. "Oh, I do hope they serve breakfast here."

A strange and almost scary voice announced the presence of a tall, dark man wearing clothes that were obviously expensive but unbranded. "Ah, kids, there you are. I have been looking for you."

The hairs all over Manatado's body rose to a nervous stand. "Who are you?"

"Ah, I'm so glad you are all okay. You left Gerterma so long ago I was afraid you had gotten lost, or worse even." The man spoke as if concerned, but there was a hollowness behind the words."

"How do you know where and when we came from?" The anxiousness in Malada's voice was clear.

"Patience, young youth. I am a friend of Gerterma's. He sent me ahead to meet you and take you to where we are supposed to go."

The three teens collectively took a step back and huddled together.

"A very long time ago, back before the responsibilities of these days, I was his commanding officer." The man tilted his head up and off to the side as if reminiscing. "Now, I must implore you to hurry, as time is short." The man grabbed a bag off the floor that hadn't even been noticed before.

"How do we really know what you are saying is true?" Manatado felt the hairs on his arms rise up as he spoke.

"You simply have no other choice. I am here. I know where you need to go. Now grab your things and let us make haste." The strange and scary man took several paces toward the door but stopped when the teens didn't follow him. "Don't try my patience, young ones. I am not a man used to being disobeyed."

The girls looked at one another, and the fear and confusion was obvious. Their unspoken conversation led toward following the man, until Manatado broke in with physical bewilderment. "NO, no, and NO." Manatado looked at each person as he spoke the words. "We, I mean all of us, are going to wait here for Gerterma. Only Gerterma knows the truth."

"Truth, boy, you know nothing of truth. Now I tire of these ridiculous games. I was sent here to retrieve you kids, and that's what's going to happen." The man spun back around and stuck his face right in front of Manatado's. "Be forewarned, if you were one of my soldiers . . . you wouldn't be."

The veiled threat sent the three backward, up against the wall. The man raised his arm and the three ducked as if he were attacking, but he merely waved it back in the direction of the front door.

"I don't trust that guy. You two know Gerterma. Is this guy with him?" The fear in Malada's voice was clear.

Cassandra spoke with a shake in her voice. "He does know who we are and why we are here. Are we certain we don't know what we are doing? I have no idea what to do. Manatado, you decide!" With that, she stood up alongside Manatado but still off to the side and behind some.

Manatado swallowed his fear but couldn't keep it out of his voice. "We choose n-n-not to go."

The fake smile on the man's face vanished. An unseen force slammed shut the front door to the inn, and a darkness overtook the room. The man seemed to grow in stature and size, his chest puffing up to a warrior's size. "I am not one to be disobeyed! You will come or I will take you."

Cassandra grabbed her bow and handed Manatado a small knife that failed to intimidate. Malada sank back against the wall between the two and slid to the floor. A strange and foul wind blew across the room, and the man brought out a large, sharp blade of steel that may have weighed as much as Malada herself.

Manatado had expected to experience more fear than he currently was, and as he stepped forward brandishing his blade, he felt manly. The feeling didn't last long because the man threw his blade very expertly between the teens, sticking straight out of the wall above Malada's head. The girl sank down deeper to the floor with tears in her eye.

Seeing her distress filled Manatado with rage, and he charged at the man.

Manatado slammed to the ground with his own blade against his throat while the man's other hand grabbed Cassandra's arrow right out of the air. "Enough, children! I'm not here to hurt you, but if you don't comply, I will force you." The man's voice was solid and firm.

A new strong, commanding voice entered the room. "Put the teen down and step away slowly!"

The man removed the blade from Manatado's neck but didn't stand up or look behind him. "Ah, Gerterma. It has been too long. This is far too overdue." Without looking, the man burst toward Gerterma like a swimmer off a wall. Manatado's blade clanged and slammed against Gerterma's blade over and over again. The two men exchanged a series of blows before the room became totally dark.

A series of swinging cabinet doors along the roof of the inn echoed about. Behind each cabinet was an armed gnome as more than a dozen flaming arrows filled the inn with light. Dozens upon dozens of armed gnomes now presented themselves as ready for battle. The voice of the innkeeper rang out from an unknown source. "Human, you are not welcome here. You will depart immediately or be destroyed!"

The strange and scary man let out a gut-bursting laugh. "Hahaha, it's always such a pleasure to see you, Gerterma. It seems we will have to finish this piece of business later. Now I will be taking the children, so step aside!"

Gerterma's chest beat heavily with effort. "Unfortunately, sir, I can't say the same, and you can't have them!"

"My oh my, have we forgotten the chain of command. Now step aside!"

"Jalum, you are just as arrogant as ever, NO!"

"And just what makes you think you can stop me?"

"The gnomes weren't talking to us."

Jalum swallowed and stood up straight. "Hahaha, you always were a challenge, but don't forget who always got their way in the end." Without even physically touching it, he pulled the blade from the wall and walked out the front door. "This reunion has been . . . touching. Perhaps we should do it again real soon."

Manatado gathered himself up off the floor and, together with Cassandra, ran into Gerterma's arms for a big hug.

"Yes, yes, it is good to see you kids too. I wasn't expecting Jalum to be here so quickly. I should have known better, darn it!"

Malada cautiously approached but stayed ready to flee. "So you do know him."

Gerterma released the hug and stood in front of, but still several feet away from, Malada, "Yes, Malada, I do know him, and yes, that is why I fear him. You were right not to go with him. Whose call was it not to go with him?" Gerterma's eyes looked at Cassandra, but she looked at Manatado.

The gnomes closed up their hatches and put out their flaming arrows, allowing the regular lighting to return. "Ah, Manatado. I see you are growing. Still have a long way to go, but yes, good job. From now on when I'm not around, you will be in charge."

Manatado smiled and blushed a little as the girls looked at him. He felt the pressure of all eyes upon him. "Woohoo!"

44

Gerterma smiled and patted him on the back. "A very long ways to go. Now we have a problem, and I don't have an immediate solution. Jalum will not go far, and he will be waiting for us to leave. Have you seen any other exits?"

The three looked at each other before shrugging their shoulders collectively. Gerterma shook his head. "Ugh, then I suggest we at least wait until nightfall and use the cover of darkness to help. Perhaps we can recruit some gnomes to help give us some cover."

Again the three teens looked at each other before saying nothing. Gerterma yawned as he sat down. "For now, however, I'm tired. Perhaps we should order some breakfast."

"There's a man waiting to ambush us, and you want to stop and eat!" Malada spoke with exasperation.

"Patience, young lady. He's not going anywhere, and we are safe here for the moment. If a battle is coming, we must be at our best when it comes. So yes, it is time to eat." Gerterma gave a hand gesture to the gnome at the desk and then signaled for everyone else to sit down too.

"Who is he, Gerterma? Who is that scary man, and what did he want from us?" Cassandra spoke with a higher-than-normal level of intensity.

"From you, Cassandra, and Manatado there, nothing. He would have killed you as soon as he had her in hand." His face nodded toward Malada as he spoke. "Now who he is, is a much more complicated subject." There was a long pause as he shifted to a more comfortable position. "That might be the most powerful human on the planet. We were drafted together for the orc wars. But Jalum's abilities were far superior to my own, and he quickly gained the attention of the highest levels of the defense force command. Anyways, he was whisked away shortly after our second battle." A big sigh followed a big breath in. "Some time later, near the end of the war, we were reunited, but this time he was my commanding officer. And he was different. Jalum was always arrogant, always taking on the biggest of challenges, no matter how much Mother protested."

Gerterma raised his finger, quieting the teens' reaction to the news. "Yes, you heard that correctly. Jalum and I are brothers . . . but don't let that make you think he has any love left for me in his heart. Whatever happened, or whatever they did to him, he has lost all touch with morality and humanity."

A gnome arrived with four plates of food, each containing the same meal. It didn't take much for them to realize how hungry they were. As soon as Manatado felt that warm food on his tongue, his stomach yearned for more, much more. Cassandra and Malada weren't shy about eating either, and as Gerterma watched them eat with passion, he felt happier than he had in a very long time.

After consuming the majority of his plate, Manatado finally slowed down eating enough to mutter out some words. "So, um, Gerterma, what do we do about Jalum? Even if the gnomes help us slip by him, he's going to chase after us. Then what? Are you sure you can't talk to your own brother?"

Gerterma finished chewing before gently putting his fork and knife down. "I still believe that Jalum's intention is to protect. However, his worldview had become so self-centered that he can justify any immoral action in the name of the greater good. So I don't know. I don't think he sees me as anything more than an impediment to his goal, something standing in the way of his great victory, a victory that he sees in his own mind as a victory for all of humanity."

"Gerterma, your brother scares me." Malada looked as if she had shrunk in size as she raised her feet to her chair and crossed her arms around them.

"Me too, Malada, me too."

Chapter 8

The alarm bells rang out over and over again. Screams of gnomes and sounds of battle erupted from outside the Traveling Spirit. Cassandra instinctively grabbed her bow and threw her arrow sack back on. Malada stood behind her. Manatado stood last and longed for a weapon, shield, and armor. Instead, he looked down at the utility knife Cassandra had given him.

Gerterma snorted in disappointment at the weapon. "Here, at least use something that might be called a weapon." He pulled out a large hunter's knife and gently tossed it, handle first, to Manatado, who fumbled it. "All right, kids, whatever is out there, it is something we can handle. It might be big, it might be tough, but together we are better. All right, kids. Rules to surviving any battle, number four."

It was a well-rehearsed speech that Gerterma had given before to any number of recruits, and it was a speech Manatado had himself heard a number of times. Yet in this moment, he needed to hear it again and it made him feel better.

"Don't hesitate when you have the advantage. Kill and move on.

Three, whatever I say to do, you better be doing it as I'm say it!

Two, if someone goes down, that doesn't mean you do too. If someone gets hurt, stay in the fight. Malada will help anyone who get hurts.

And rule number one, keep Malada alive." Gerterma stared straight at Malada as he spoke. "You keep yourself out of harm's way. That's an order, young lady!"

Manatado and Cassandra exchanged a very nervous look before Gerterma confirmed they had heard what he said and turned around to walk out the front door.

Manatado came out right behind Gerterma, but as he stepped off to the side, he closed his eyes and swiped his knife violently into the air before him. Gerterma reached out and took hold of his arm.

"AHHHH, they got me, they got me." Manatado pulled away, failing to even move Gerterma's arm.

Gerterma's free hand slapped Manatado on the back of his head. "Keep your eyes open, and for the love of God, pull yourself together. We need you to man up, right now."

Manatado pouted at the remark, trying to hurry past it for the sake of the situation. A small gnome went flying across the skyline as the screams and rumbles came closer. Several gnomes were at the village's edge, already engaged in battle with the monster. It rested on all fours and had a back made of armored plates, a spiked tail, and a mouth full of predatory teeth. A long tongue reached out and wrapped itself around a fleeing gnome and devoured the gnome into its mouth.

"Listen close, gang. Here is the plan. This monster is known as an Aradoro. That beast has armored plating. We can only hurt the creature below that armor. Cassandra, as soon as that creature shakes, those armored plates are going to flap around. That's your target, under the armor. Malada, stay out of sight and only come out if someone gets hurt." Gerterma smiled at Manatado in the way that made him even more nervous. "Now, boy, it's up to us to make that thing shake."

Manatado tried to hide the terror in his voice but found it shaky anyway. "An-an-and how do we do that?"

"Ever ride a bull, son? Or do you just prefer tipping cows over and running?"

Manatado gave a slow, guilty reply. "Uh, no?"

"I'm the town sheriff. I know of all your and Tamack's shenanigans. Who do you think kept you out of trouble?"

Again Manatado could only give a guilty look in reply.

"Well now is the time to make it up to me. Show me what skills you learned and go."

Manatado gave a blank look in reply and failed to move. Cassandra kicked Manatado in the butt. "Go!" This time, Manatado moved at great speed as he raced toward the creature.

Gerterma smiled. He may not have been Manatado's father, but he sure felt proud like one. He then looked at Cassandra, her bow at the ready. Their eyes met and said it all, the fear, the pride, and the reliance they had on each other. Gerterma pointed for Cassandra to climb up on a roof and shoot from there.

The pitch in Manatado's voice changed as he started screaming in fear, and he was now running at a ninety-degree angle away from the beast as it turned to face him. Gerterma charged in at full speed, his blade at the ready. The beast took a step after Manatado, who again changed directions as he ran. Gerterma slid and thrust his blade at an upward angle. The blade came up and slipped through the armored plate of the beast, cutting it.

The beast howled out in pain and then lifted its foot in an effort to smash Gerterma. Gerterma dodged the foot with ease, running off to the side. The beast, no longer interested in Manatado, raised its giant tail and swept Gerterma off his feet. Gerterma was knocked to the ground but easily rolled out of the way of the beast's next attack. An arrow clanged as it hit the beast's armor and fell to the ground.

Manatado now came screaming as he charged at the beast, his hunter's knife in hand. The beast raised itself up onto its back legs and came crashing down in the direction of Manatado, who immediately turned back around and screamed out in terror. Cassandra tried to take advantage of the beast's exposed belly but didn't have a good angle for it. "Manatado, go left, go left!"

Sure enough, despite his cowardly scream, he did as told and ran to his left. The boy ran at top speed, never looking behind him and never pausing. Cassandra held her bow at the ready, watching the beast as it followed him, squaring up for an attack.

"Come on, open up." Cassandra spoke only to herself, almost as if in prayer.

Manatado felt the sweat streaming down his face, entering his eyes, and stinging. He held out for as long as he could. Then he suddenly stopped to wipe his eyes. The timing couldn't have been better, for as he stopped, the creature slammed down its tail precisely where he would have been.

"Manatado, attack, attack!" Gerterma yelled with all his strength but was invisible.

Manatado stood panting hard with the beast's tail rising up from the dust in front of him. He stood motionless, his fear staring him in the face. Another arrow clanked off the beast's armor and landed at his feet. The arrow snapped him out of his fear-filled daze, and he charged forth, slicing his knife at the creature's tail.

The knife struck armor plate after armor plate before sliding into the bulky mass of the tail. The beast screamed out in pain and thrashed its tail, crashing into Manatado and throwing him down onto his back several yards away. The beast then spun around 180 degrees in search of Gerterma, who was still unseen. The beast looked left, looked right, and swung its tail wildly in defense.

Gerterma roared as he flew onto the beast from a nearby rooftop, landing squarely on the beast's back. The beast shook like a wet dog, and Cassandra was ready with her bow, letting loose arrow after arrow. Two of the arrows struck below the armor, one of them staying in the shoulder of the beast. The beast howled out in pain and then bucked like a horse, throwing Gerterma off the side.

Manatado watched in horror as Gerterma landed directly on his back and bounced. He could tell instantly that he was hurt. He also knew he had to do something. So he charged. He bounced up on the beast's front elbow and jumped toward the arrow stuck in its shoulder, grabbing hold. Manatado pulled himself up onto the back of the beast. The beast raised up on its hindquarters and shook like a wet dog. Manatado screamed before he, too, was thrown off. Yet it was all Cassandra needed.

The beast's stomach was exposed, and a large volley of arrows came flying into the beast. This time, Cassandra wasn't alone, as a gathering of gnomes had joined her. The arrows drew blood, and the beast roared in pain as it charged off, out of town and into the distance.

Malada came out of her hiding spot and joined Cassandra as they ran to Manatado. He sat upright but crying. Cassandra came to a halt as she spoke. "Are you crying?"

Manatado looked over, his eyes full of tears. "Nooooo."

Cassandra and Malada exchanged a look of endearment. "You did it! Manatado, you're a hero."

He sniffled before responding. "I knowwwww."

The small group of gnomes had now grown large and started applauding and rushing the group, patting their backs, and shaking their hands. Malada looked around. "Where's Gerterma?"

A separate small gathering of gnomes huddled around the entrance to one of the village stores. The entire storefront had been collapsed in. There, in the middle of the rubble, lay Gerterma, motionless. Malada charged at the group, feeling instantly guilty. She was a healer, and Gerterma was hurt.

Some of the gnomes were removing his clothing as she approached, revealing a deeply black-and-blue side. One of the gnomes looked up to Malada. "He's bleeding inside. We cannot help him."

Guilt brought forth tears from her, and with all her heart, she readied to heal. She took a deep breath, kneeled down next to Gerterma, placed her hands on the wound, and began to speak inaudible words. Nothing happened. Malada tried again. Nothing happened. Panic started to creep into her. Again she tried, but nothing happened. Tears were now pouring down her face. Again and again she tried, but nothing happened.

Malada stood up and pulled away. How could this be happening? Cassandra and Manatado came to her side. "What's wrong? Why can't you heal him?"

"I don't know. I don't know." Malada was working herself up into a tizzy. Her feet bounced as her hands covered her face. She collapsed into Cassandra's arms. "I'm failing."

Manatado and Cassandra looked at each other with uncertainty. Manatado bent down next to Gerterma, who was shaking, his face pale. Cassandra put Malada's hands back onto Gerterma and tried to give her a reassuring look. Two harsh large coughs brought forth blood. The sight shocked Malada, who loosed a large powerful glow onto Gerterma.

The light surrounded Gerterma and started seeping into him. Back and forth, the light went through him, his eyes now wide open, and for just a moment, he looked well. Then the light continued.

Malada's eyes burned as the magic flowed out from her, but she couldn't stop it. It kept coming and coming. Gerterma went from bad to good and then back to bad. And now the light was causing him pain. He screamed as a bright light erupted from his face. Malada screamed, and together they both collapsed into the ground.

Chapter 9

Malada opened her eyes and, feeling the sting of daylight, shut them again. Her body ached, her muscles tensing from overuse, but she felt warmth. Manatado sat beside her, holding her hand. She smiled as her eyes adjusted to the light. "Are you still crying?"

"Nooo." Manatado smiled as he sniffled. "I'm so glad you're okay."

"What happened? Where's Gerterma?"

Manatado pointed to the other side of the room, to a bed where Gerterma lay upright with Cassandra by his side. They were in the Traveling Spirit.

Cassandra stood up and walked over to Malada. "How are you?"

Malada sat up with great urgency now that her memory of what happened had returned "How is he? Did I hurt him?"

"Never mind that!" Gerterma spoke loudly, even though he lay flat. "I've been through plenty in my life. This isn't anything I can't handle." Slowly he rose up and threw his leg over the side of the bed.

Malada looked at him and felt instantly guilty. Gerterma now had white hair and stood with a limp. "Oh my god, what happened?"

"Magic is a dangerous and powerful tool. I can't instruct you. We need somebody who can, and judging by my appearance, we need them sooner than later." Gerterma stood but looked uneasy as he rose. "Come now, kids, I do believe the gnomes have a present for us. Provided of course you feel up to it, Malada."

"I feel fine, just a little disoriented. I'm more concerned with you, Gerterma." She jumped out of bed and embraced Gerterma. "I'm scared. I don't want to hurt anyone."

"Good, then let us feast and make haste, for that beast will surely not be our last encounter."

Manatado froze as he heard what Gerterma said. "More monsters? When do we get to go back to the village?"

Gerterma smiled as he stood before Manatado. "I'm proud of you, boy. Keep up the good work." Gerterma then turned around and headed out the door to the main room of the Traveling Spirit. Manatado swallowed his disappointment and hung his head low. Cassandra wrapped her arm around him. "Don't worry, buddy. We're here with ya." Manatado forced a smile, but really all he wanted to do was go back to the village. He even preferred school over this.

After a large meal and short ceremonial thank-you from the gnomes, the four headed back into the forest in search of the land of the fairies. Gerterma took the lead. Malada walked right behind him. Manatado was trying to stay close to Malada, and Cassandra was trying to stay close to Manatado.

"Gerterma, I'm so sorry. Please forgive me." Malada's voice was guilt ridden.

Gerterma stopped, causing the teens to bump into each other. "Now listen here, Malada, and the rest of you. Save your guilt for ill intent. I demand that you do the best you can with the best of intentions. Don't demand perfection. Now, Malada, you saved my life. Never feel guilty about that. You are still a young lady who has yet to be trained. Don't beat yourself up over a few white hairs. Now we have a long way to go." Gerterma looked around the forest before deciding which way to go.

Manatado reached his hand out and grabbed Malada's. "I still want you to be my healer." She smiled but then pulled her hand back and turned around again. Manatado felt kinda sad about the reaction but tried not to show it, while Cassandra felt conflicted.

The four passed between two large trees so big they had to squeeze between them. "Gerterma, how do we even get to the land of the fairies? I've never seen it on a map or anything," Cassandra asked as they walked.

"Yeah, and aren't fairies even smaller than gnomes? Where are we going to stay?" Manatado rushed in with his question.

"Will a fairy really be able to help me control my magic?" Malada threw her question out there with the others.

They passed between two large trees as the kids continued their questioning.

"Do you think they can charm my bow so I never miss again?"

"Ohhh, imagine what kind of food magical people eat. Gerterma, what do they eat?"

"What if I can't find a fairy who wants to train me?"

"What if we can't find the fairies?"

"What if we can't eat their food?"

Gerterma stopped after he passed between two very large trees. "Would you kids shut up already! Only those who have been to the land of fairies can go to the land of fairies. Manatado, shut up about food already. Malada, you will be fine. Now, as for the rest of your questions, they will just have to wait. Travel is the destroyer of ignorance. We have a long way to go. Now pass through the trees so we can be on our way."

The kids passed between two of the largest trees they had ever seen and continued along for a very long time. This was a part of the forest none of the kids had ever visited before, and it was starting to look strange to them. "We must be getting close. I don't recognize this part of the forest anymore. Look at those two trees before us. I never imagined such giant trees ever existed."

"Are the trees getting bigger, or are we getting smaller?" Cassandra asked, bringing Gerterma's head around with a giant smile.

He said, "You're one sharp girl. Manatado, you could learn from her."

The remark brought a smile to Cassandra's face and a frown to Manatado's. The four walked along, flanked on each side by massive timber trees towering into the sky. The sound of running water echoed off the trees from the distance. New types of plants started to appear, and as they walked along, flowers scented the air dripping with dew.

Gerterma walked up to one of the flowers. "Wait here," he ordered. He walked up to a huge red bell-type flower, and as he stood under it, the plant swallowed him up. The kids ran to the base of the plant, bringing out their weapons.

"Halt, put those away!" a voice rang out from the forest.

The three instinctively stood back to back to back.

"I said, put your weapons away!" the voice from the forest demanded.

Manatado quickly complied, dropping his knife to the ground, and raised his hand up high. He then nudged Cassandra, who gave Manatado a look he didn't understand but followed his lead.

"Sit on the ground and wait," the forest voice now ordered.

The three sat together in a circle, and the warmth of the girls' bodies felt nice to Manatado, who relaxed back against them. There they sat for what felt like a long time. Manatado started drift off as his head became heavy, and he rested it on Cassandra's shoulder. She smiled as she felt the warmth of his comfort with her and let herself fall back against him. Malada, however, was too preoccupied with what had happened and sat impatiently waiting with nervousness.

Chapter 10

After some time, another voice rang out from the trees, startling the kids. Manatado's head jerked up, slamming into Cassandra, who was resting hers against his. He jumped up, his hand rubbing his head in pain. He was ready for anything, except maybe this. A single female fairy stood flanked between two forest dogs. The animals seemed huge, their teeth the size of his full arm. Yet they only sat there trained to obey commands.

The female fairy spoke with a strong commanding voice. "Malada, I call you forth!"

Malada slowly and nervously stood up, her chest pounding as she started to sweat.

"Don't worry, Malada. I'm here with you!" Manatado yelled out.

Cassandra smacked Manatado gently on the back on the head.

"I mean, we are here with you."

The two walked in front of her as to protect her. The fairy snapped her fingers, and instantly the dogs were upon them. Manatado barely had time to raise his hand in defense before he wound up in the mouth of one of the dogs. Cassandra was just as easily taken.

The dogs held the two firmly, but neither was harmed as Cassandra felt the teeth before her and behind her. Yet her head was still protruding from the animal's mouth, and with great effort, she could bend and twist to see what was happening.

The female fairy was still tiny in stature even compared to the now-shrunken size of Malada. The fairy may have been small in size but was anything but small in presence. The fairy flew up to Malada and examined her face closely, her wings buzzing. "Malada, you will defend yourself!" the fairy shouted before transforming her clothes into a dark-black battle outfit.

Malada looked stupidly at the fairy. Then, after just a second, the fairy attacked, landing a tough blow to her stomach. Malada bent over in pain. "I said, defend yourself!" The fairy quickly moved out of the way as Malada attempted to grab her and landed a second blow to her side.

Again Malada bent over in pain. Manatado called out in frustration from not being able to help. "Come on, Malada, you can grab her!"

Malada again reached out to grab the fairy but missed and took another blow, this time in the butt. Again the fairy called out, "I said, defend yourself!" This time, Malada changed tactic and faked a grab and sidestepped. While she didn't grab the fairy, she did dodge another blow.

The two circled each other, waiting for an opportunity. With each move the fairy made, Malada shifted away, always keeping her hands up and facing the fairy. After a couple attempts, the fairy showed a tiny smile but again demanded, "Defend yourself!" This time, the fairy vanished into thin air. Malada looked terrified, and blow after blow quickly came.

"That's not fair!" Manatado screamed as he wiggled but couldn't break free.

"Don't try to guess, Malada. Use your instincts, intuition!" Cassandra called out to her friend.

Malada closed her eyes for a second and tried to feel the fairy's presence. Malada now bounced around the area in a kind of perpetual motion. Sometimes the fairy would land a blow, other times a miss. "Is this the best you can do, girl? I said, defend yourself!" The fairy's voice echoed through the forest as she landed multiple hits in a row, dropping Malada to her knees.

"Stop. How can I fight you if I can't see you!" Malada called out into the air.

"Stop! No, there is no stopping. You have seen our realm. Either you will prove yourself worthy or you and your friends will die."

"What, that can't be, Gerterma. Gerterma, where are you?"

"I said, defend yourself!" Again, another set of blows struck Malada hard, sending her to the ground. Blood now ran down from her nose as tears of pain fogged her vision.

Malada stood up again but was quickly knocked back down. "I said, defend yourself!" The fairy appeared now, flying over Malada as she lay on the ground. "I'm sorry, young lady, but you have failed." The fairy then gave an order to the dogs, who threw Manatado and Cassandra onto the ground and held them in place under giant paws.

"Only those who are worthy can enter our realm. Those who are not must be destroyed so they cannot teach others how to find us. The three of you are not worthy." The dogs now licked their lips and tucked down their snouts as if to eat Manatado and Cassandra, who now screamed out in fear.

"Help us, Malada. Help us!" Cassandra called out in a voice of sheer terror. That was enough. Through the tears and blood, Malada dug deep, and out from within her burst forth a wave of white power that sent both the fairy and the dogs flying off into the forest.

Chapter 11

Malada awoke in a room filled with the most wonderful smell. Flowers grew in every corner and every crevice of the room. Her nose filled with scent after scent of amazing. She felt great, so good in fact she jumped out of bed and rushed to the window. There, for the first time, she experienced a fairy village. A small stream trickled down the middle of the village. To each side were large mushroom houses, with lights shining out from open windows in the tops. In between and seemingly everywhere, flowers and greenery grew.

Malada stuck her head outside, and it felt like night. Glowing, floating embers lighted the street. A beetle pulled behind it a large cart full of objects that sparkled and shined. She was so excited to start exploring that she was surprised to see Manatado asleep on the floor and Cassandra asleep on a couch in the room. She stopped herself from bolting out of the room and instead decided to sneak out so as not to disturb her friends.

Malada carefully and quietly opened and closed the door and then snuck down the hall. Approaching the main room, she heard many voices, and they were discussing her.

"We must know the girl's lineage! That is not normal magic the girl possesses."

"I can only tell you what I know." Gerterma's voice was unmistakable, but the comment sent a shiver down her spine and she stopped to hear more.

"You told us she possessed the powers of healing and fire. That—well I don't even know what kind of magic that was. My dogs are still deaf."

"I tell you she does, and she can, wield it with great intensity. Look at my hair. I tell you, she is the first human I have ever seen with such abilities. "

"And we are telling you this cannot be. Humans do not control magic."

Malada pulled back against the wall. "What if she wasn't human?"

"She is human. Her blood runs red, just as mine does."

"If what you say is true, then we are missing a large piece of this puzzle. I cannot help you, nor can I train her."

Malada gasped at the words, drawing the attention of the two in the other room. Gerterma stood up and rounded the corner. He stood before her, examining her very intently. She slowly slid down the wall and into the curled-up position. Gerterma reached down and pulled her up by the armpit.

"Well I'm glad you're feeling better. How are the other two?"

Malada froze, trying to understand what they were saying.

"Hmm, it seems snooping ears have heard more than they were ready for." Gerterma guided Malada to a table in the main room and sat her down.

"Malada, we would like to ask you some questions. Do you feel well enough to answer them?"

Malada looked like a deer in the headlights but nodded yes.

"Malada, there is no doubt that you possess the power of magic, but we cannot understand how or why. Tell us, who were your parents?"

"My father died in the orc wars. My mother, she served in the defense force."

"Yes, sweetie, we know that, but who were they?"

"I never met my father, not even once. My mother was very protective. After the war, we were constantly moving, never staying anywhere for long." Malada then trailed off with her answer.

"Tell us the whole truth, Malada. We are not going to risk our lives if you're not going to tell us everything." Gerterma spoke, still knowing more of the story. "Why were you running from the defense force?"

On instinct, Malada snapped. "I am telling the truth, and I don't have to tell you anything!"

"Why was your mother afraid of the defense force?"

Malada's body tightened up, and she clamped down.

Again Gerterma asked the question. "Why was your mother fleeing the defense force? Tell us what she told you."

She raised her arms and all the furniture with them high into the air, smashing it back down to the ground, sending wood chunks everywhere. "We will not serve those murderers!"

Gerterma and the fairy both took cover from the debris. The noise and ruckus summoned both Cassandra and Manatado, who came with weapons in hand.

"What's going on? What's happening?" Manatado instinctively approached and stood beside Malada. "Gerterma, what are you doing?"

Gerterma waited to see if there would be any more magic, but Malada seemed calmed by the presence of her friends. "Malada, calm down, calm down. We agree the defense force isn't for you." Gerterma raised his hands as if surrendering and slowly stood up. "Well, Manatado, we were trying to unwrap Malada's strange gift. It seems her type of magic is something new, and it begs the question, where is the right place for you?"

Malada was panting hard but still in control.

Manatado, however, seemed flustered. "Wait a minute, Gerterma. You were always encouraging me and Cassandra to join the defense force. What's up with that?"

Gerterma pivoted with a smile on his face as he moved to look directly as Manatado. "Hmm, let me explain it with an analogy. The defense force would treat Cassandra and you as tools, meaning that they would take care of you. When a blade needs sharping, it gets sharpened. When a rifle needs retooling, it gets retooled. However, Malada here would be treated as a weapon. Weapons are wielded, meaning they are instruments of death and destruction. Do you understand now?"

"So you mean they wouldn't treat Malada well, even though they're using her?" Manatado asked.

"Correct, I mean they would feed her well and bask her in luxury, but they would grant her no freedom and she would have no say in who she hurts with her magic."

"Um, yeah, I guess so, but what happens now? Will the fairy train Malada like we planned?"

The fairy now reappeared out of thin air in a burst of sparkling magic. "No, I'm afraid this kind of magic is much different than what I possess. I will take you to see Her Majesty, queen of the fairies. We must seek out her guidance."

"Aw, man, do we have to walk there too? How far is that? Can we have breakfast first?" Manatado complained. The three teens looked at each other in agreement: they were hungry.

Chapter 12

The village of the fairies was most beautiful. While the thick vegetation kept most of the sunlight out, shining embers floated above each pathway. Flowers and greenery grew everywhere, and as they walked, they must have passed a dozen tiny streams. The group made their way slowly, stopping to look at nearly every house they came upon. Some of the houses were inside giant mushrooms, others inside the trunks of long-passed-away trees, and yet others built directly into caves. Oohs and aahs filled the conversation, as this was a place like none of the teens had seen before.

Manatado spent most of the time trying to talk to Malada. He would approach her side as they paused along a bridge and took in the beauty of the village. "It's almost as pretty as you," he would say, while Malada would smile in return and then run off to Cassandra's side.

After this happened the second time, Gerterma picked up on it and slowed his pace to speak to Manatado. "Listen up, boy. We have real things to accomplish and real challenges to face. Don't set yourself up for failure on a challenge you don't need to take on."

"Hey, Gerterma, where is your pistol? Don't you think that would have been helpful in fighting the monster?"

Gerterma chuckled. "Now that pistol was the property of the village. Had I kept it with me while not doing the village business, that would make me a thief. No, that pistol stayed at the village. Now that's not what I'm talking about. I'm talking about things beyond your control." His head nodded in the direction of Malada.

"But, Gerterma, how do I get her to like me?"

Gerterma paused and smiled. "When it comes to women, I have no idea, but I know you're barking up the wrong tree. Malada has enough to deal with right now. Your puppy love isn't going to make things easier for her. So just give it up already."

"Wait a minute. If you left your pistol behind, doesn't that mean you gave up your job as prioritor? Does that mean we are not going home?" Manatado swallowed as the thought sank down into his stomach, making him queasy.

"What it means, boy, is that we now have new priorities in life, priorities we mustn't confuse with desires." Gerterma's body language pointed straight at Malada, without raising an arm. With that, he nodded and returned to the front of the group, while Manatado sank back and pouted. Cassandra gave Manatado a sad look, as she had overheard the two speaking.

They snaked their way uphill, passing fewer and fewer houses while the river got wider and bigger. After some time, they crested a small grassy hill, and with a pant in their breaths, they were still left breathless.

There, at the foot of the largest tree in the forest, was the entrance to the fairy castle. The castle rounded the base of the most massive tree. Its towers spread out across the great circumference. Several fairies were tending to the lush array of flowers and plants that seemed to fill in from the lawn to the sky. Floating embers bounced across the roof, giving a golden light to the entire area. The sound and smell of a waterfall greeted them as they approached the front door.

Two male fairies stood guard at the entrance. They were the same size as the females but had no wings, and each stood with a long, sharpened blade. As the group approached, they crossed their weapons and blocked the entrance.

The fairy who had challenged Malada appeared again from thin air. "Please tell Her Majesty that Ferninia is here with a most important matter for the queen. I present my caliphate for inspection." The fairy put her hands together, and with a bright light, a good-sized bouquet of flowers appeared out of thin air.

"What's a caliphate? I think I've heard that word before," Cassandra asked Gerterma as they waited.

"A caliphate is a collection of a fairy's accomplishments. You see, the fairies are a meritocracy. Just like you couldn't enter until you had proven your abilities, the queen, who is the most able and powerful of the fairies, will only see those who are worthy."

"How did they decide Manatado and I were worthy? All we did was get stuck in some dog's mouth."

Ferninia handed over her caliphate to a third male fairy, who came running out from the front door. He took the item and rushed it inside. Ferninia returned and answered Cassandra's question. "I spoke on your behalf. I could feel your strong desire to protect your friend. Your friend will need all the help and protection she can get. That is why you were determined to be worthy."

Gerterma gently kneed Manatado in his thigh and motioned with his head. Manatado looked in the direction and saw the two male fairies and, misunderstanding, asked Ferninia about them. "So yeah, why don't those fairies have wings, and why do they carry weapons?"

Gerterma leaned in toward Manatado and whispered as best he could. "You idiot, you were supposed to thank her for vouching for you."

Ferninia paused for just a moment as Manatado blushed. "Oh, well male fairies have never been able to control magic. The most gifted of them are trained as guards. The rest usually work at the house, raising children and such. For fairies, females are the dominant sex. Same is true for humans, is it not?"

"Yes."

"No."

Cassandra and Manatado had replied at the same time.

"Oh, that's cool. Now, Malada, when we approach the queen, you must follow protocol. First, you must always face Her Majesty. Turning your back to her would be considered a challenge to her authority. Second, never speak unless spoken to. And finally, you must be honest. We can only help if we know the whole truth."

Malada looked nervous and scared but nodded her head in understanding. The third male fairy returned, and as he raised his hands, the two guards raised their weapons and signaled for the group to enter.

The palace was even more amazing than the village. A stream snaked its way through the palace whose floors were covered in red petals. Small-to-medium boulders made up the walls, each covered in moss that grew in chunks. Floating embers lighted the roof, and every smell of every flower drifted throughout. At the far end of the chamber stood a large throne placed atop a large pile of stones with water running over and between them. A large pair of wings unfolded to reveal a tiny, very aged fairy.

"Come closer," a frail voice ordered.

The group with Gerterma and Malada at the front approached as far as the edge of the flower petals, where the water gathered and began its life as a stream.

"Come closer," again the voice repeated.

The fairy who had met them at the gate now appeared and used her magic to make a bridge out of two long flower stems and a giant leaf. She then signaled for Malada to proceed, sealing the bridge off to the others. A moment of fear crossed Malada's face, but Gerterma waved her onward.

Malada turned and slowly crossed the bridge approaching the throne. The face of the queen of the fairies greeted her with a large and aged smile. "Come closer, come closer. I don't see as well as I used to, now." Malada came to within arm's reach, when the fairy escort signaled for her to kneel. Malada complied, and the fairy escort created a shining ember above Malada and vanished.

The queen hopped off her throne and rolled her wings back behind her. She took slow aged steps with the use of a cane and came close enough to touch Malada with an outstretched arm. The queen pinched Malada's cheek with her fingers. "Oh, how precious. It has been too long since I last met a child."

"I am not a child, Your Majesty!" Malada seemed to take offense.

"Oh, deary me, an adolescent. It has indeed been too long." The queen released her grip on Malada's face. "Such a difficult time in life. It's the first big step between two very different worlds, between being a child and being an adult. Tell me, what is it you seek?"

Malada paused for a second. "I, I seek training for my magical ability."

The queen raised and lowered her cane, making a loud tapping noise as she did so. "That's why you are here. I want to know what you seek."

Malada paused. "I don't understand the question. I'm here to find a magic teacher."

"Humans aren't supposed to have the ability to control magic. Why you are here is not a mystery. I want to know, what is it you seek?"

Malada leaned back, almost exiting her kneeling position to look the queen in the eyes, hoping for a clue as to what she meant. "I'm afraid I will hurt somebody I want to save. I want to learn how to use my magic to help people."

The queen had a very empathetic look on her face. "Yes, sweetie, I know. I have seen your magic protect your friends, but I must know what you seek."

"I don't understand. What do you want me to say?"

"I only want the truth. What do you seek?"

"I seek nothing. I only want to be . . ." Malada trailed off as she spoke.

"Oh, deary me, deary me. Such youth is not ready for such responsibility."

"But I am ready. I am ready to learn my magic."

"But, my dear, what do you seek with it?"

"I . . . I . . . I want to save my mother."

"Ah, the truth. I can accept the truth."

The queen approached Malada and grabbed her by the cheek. "You certainly are a pretty young human. Yet . . ."

Malada's body cringed at the word, her face displaying utter fear.

"Oh, do not fear, my young lady. Whatever mystery is trapped inside you is a blessing, not a curse. The question remains, what kind of blessing do you have and how do we teach you how to use it?"

The queen opened the back end of the bridge and increased the power of the shining ember. "Come, companions of Malada, come forth. There is much to discuss." The end of the bridge unfolded to create a larger platform for Gerterma and two teens to approach and stand by Malada's side.

Chapter 13

The group stood before the queen. Gerterma knelt first and indicated for the others to as well.

"Gerterma, you told me this young lady's grandfather was an elf. You are mistaken."

"No, but it's true. My own mother told me!" Malada spoke with a new intensity, releasing very strong emotions about her mother.

"Oh my, oh my. Young lady, you will need to learn to control those emotions or they may be your undoing." The queen moved back to her throne and wiggled until she was comfortable.

"Elves are magical creatures, but each elf can only control one element of magic. Malada, you have already shown the ability to control many elements of magic. It is my belief that your grandfather was no elf, but rather a wizard."

Gerterma stood and raised his hands questioningly. "Your Majesty, how can that be? There hasn't been a wizard in all of the land since the great exodus after the uniting of the races at Athenia."

"To that end is where you must next seek your answer."

"But what about my mother? I must save her."

"How can you save her until you have learned how?" The queen gave the look of a parent reining in one of their children. "No, before you can save your mother, you must first learn to control your magic. Gerterma is a wise man to know this. No, I cannot help you. I can only tell you where you must go next."

Manatado groaned with dissatisfaction but felt the scorn of Cassandra's scowl and stopped.

"Next, you must travel farther than you ever have before, and it will not be an easy journey. In fact, I will send someone with you in order to help you on your journey, someone who could not only help you on your quest but help herself as well."

The queen then pulled out a large luxurious wand and waved it around and spoke softly. The queen waited a moment and then gave an expression of displeasure. The queen then waved her wand again, speaking the same incantation, only this time a new fairy appeared. "Ah, Mom, I was doing something. What do you want?" This new fairy was not dressed like a traditional fairy. Her clothes had holes in the pant legs, and she looked unkempt.

"Lukinia, I have had enough of your sass. I have found the perfect avenue for you to prove yourself as my daughter. These humans are undertaking a grand journey, and you will accompany them."

Lukinia's mouth dropped open. "But, Mom, I was doing something. I don't want to spend time with these creatures." She flew over and around the group, examining them, moved close to Manatado, and pinched her nose. "Eww, Mom, this one really stinks!"

Manatado began to protest, but a dark cloud was forming directly above him, and before he could speak, an intense downpour of rain was upon him.

"Lukinia, it is not your place to judge the other races! Now, for too long, I have let you have free rein. If you want to have any hope of taking my place, this is the path for you."

Lukinia started to protest but was met with a nasty look from her mother, and she ended the rain. "Mother, I have no desire to travel with these weak, pathetic creatures. Where are we going anyways?"

The queen stood and walked before the group. "You are traveling to the highest peaks of Udal Mountains. There, you will seek out the king of dwarves. It is rumored that a small band of wizards still inhabit the most isolated recesses of those mountains."

Gerterma raised his hand. "Your Majesty, that journey would take significant time. Can your magic expedite our journey?"

The queen paused. "No, I'm afraid our magic cannot, but I have a suggestion. Deep, deep in our forest, you can find a Socratea tree. Perhaps you can convince it to take you there."

"Socratea trees are REAL?" Cassandra exclaimed in excitement. Manatado and Malada both gave her a confused look. "Socratea trees can walk and talk, and are rumored to be the guardians of the forest, but I thought they were all destroyed in the race wars."

The queen brought the attention back. "Horrific things were done in those days. That's why the city of Athenia was created, to prevent the horrors of those days ever returning. The few Socratea that remained fled deep into the forest and have remained hidden ever since. It will not be easy to convince them to help you. Their trust of the other races is no more." The queen looked at Lukinia. "This, my daughter, will be your greatest challenge, the challenge that could prove your worthiness. I wish you success."

"Ah, Mom, but—" Lukinia was cut off by a powerful frown from her mother. "Fine, let me go get ready." With that, she vanished.

The queen then faced the four. "Good luck, my friends. I wish I could offer more help, but unfortunately, you are being chased. Those chasing you are nearing the village. I must ask you to leave as soon as you are ready, for we are not warriors and those who chase you are."

Gerterma looked at the kids. "Jalum."

"Yet before you go, there is one last thing." The queen spoke in a very formal tone. "As a gesture of goodwill and in hopes that your quest will be fruitful, I wish to offer you the use of a most unique item—the shield of Queen Ankinia."

The group, including Gerterma, smiled politely, not quite sure if she was done speaking. After a long moment, the queen rolled her eyes. "Queen Ankinia was the first of the fairy queens. She ascended to the throne by defeating the most evil of wizards, one who ruled this forest a thousand years ago, Malgamar. With this shield, Queen Ankinia was able to protect herself from all forms of the evil wizard's magic."

A group awe came from a collective exhale at the excitement of the story and the immensity of the gift. "Upon completion of your quest, or your unfortunate demise, Lukinia will return it to me." The queen then waved her wand, bringing sparks directly before Malada. A large oval shield nearly the size of Malada herself appeared and then fell onto her as the sparks faded. Malada fell back onto her butt as the large shield took her by surprise. Malada gathered her feet under her and raised up with the shield in hand and a smile on her face.

Chapter 14

Lukinia openly complained as the group was loading backpacks full of foodstuffs and water. "Oh, they are so slow. Look at all of the stuff they need. Well I'm not carrying anything for any of them."

The griping came with a strong look from Ferninia, but she didn't openly respond. She instead whispered to Cassandra as she helped fill it with supplies. "I'm so glad you're taking her with you guys. She drives me crazy. Nothing but lazy royalty."

"I thought you guys had a meritocracy. Isn't the queen's daughter supposed to be the next best leader?"

"Ha, just because a system has a name doesn't mean that's how it works." Ferninia leaned in close to Cassandra and brought out a crystal ball she had loaded into the backpack. With a wave of her hand, she brought forth an image. It was an image of Lukinia, and she was drunk. In the image, Lukinia was having difficulty standing up straight. She was surrounded by several other young fairies in a very untidy house. The queen then burst into the house.

Lukinia sensed they were talking about her and rushed over, and Ferninia stopped the image before she could see it. "What are you two doing? Are you ready yet? The sooner we leave, the sooner this is over."

Cassandra helped to stash the ball back inside the backpack. "Gerterma, can Jalum really reach us here? Won't the fairies be able to stop him from shrinking?"

Gerterma looked up from his packing. "Never underestimate Jalum, especially when there isn't a war going on. You see, men like him always need to feel needed. Otherwise, they wouldn't get to use special abilities and privileges. During the orc wars, Jalum became one of our most important generals. His soldiers even said that he had magic-like powers. Without a war or an enemy to fight, he has no call to use those powers."

Cassandra looked up. "What are you saying? Why does that mean he is chasing us?"

"I'm saying that if Malada's powers are superior to Jalum's, then Jalum will want those abilities at his disposal. Unfortunately, finding an enemy to go to war with is easy. All it takes is some hateful language and an example or two of bad behavior and, voilà, you have the public's backing."

This time, Manatado, who was helping Malada pack her bag, spoke. "Gerterma, you don't sound like you're very proud of being a human. Shouldn't we be proud of our race?"

Gerterma stood upright and made eye contact with each of the kids. "Be proud of the good you do in this world, seek forgiveness for the bad, and always make your decisions based on the overall good, not what's good for you. Then, when you look back at your life, you will see something to be proud of."

"Oh, this conversation is so boring. Are you not done yet. Can't we leave yet? I thought you were in a hurry. All you humans do is talk, talk, talk." Lukinia spoke as she stood at the exit door from the queen's castle.

"She is right about the need for us to hurry. Once you have the supplies loaded, arm yourselves and let's head out."

"Arm ourselves? Gerterma, I thought we were going to find a walking tree." Manatado's voice had more whine in it than he meant to convey.

Gerterma looked Manatado over. "Just be ready."

Manatado gulped and threw his bag over his shoulder and pulled out his hunter's knife. "Aw, man, I wanted to ride in a tree."

With that, the group indicated they were ready to go. Ferninia gave Cassandra a look of encouragement and then gave Malada a hug. "Best of luck." They headed out a large door opened by Lukinia, who was already outside.

Chapter 15

Malada struggled mightily with her new shield. Its length was nearly as much as her height. That plus a backpack full of supplies and it was only a matter of time before Malada took a tumble. She fell several yards down an embankment and ended up in a soft fern near the base of a large tree. Unfortunately, her shield tumbled with her and pinned her down. She struggled to move but was trapped by all the straps.

Manatado scurried after her, only to slip and fall himself. He tried to roll out of the way but failed and ended up slamming face-first into Malada's shield. Instead of impacting with it, however, Manatado found himself being pulled into it. At first it felt like he was sinking, but then he opened his eyes. A large gray chasm opened up before him, and there he saw the most wondrous and terrifying magic he could imagine: fireballs the size of houses, warriors made of dark magic, spheres that exploded with acidic ooze and then reformed themselves.

Suddenly, Manatado felt Lukinia wrap herself around his arm and pull with an unforeseeable strength. Manatado felt his entire body jolt from the power of her pull, and together they flew out of the chasm and back into the forest.

"Idiots, they're all idiots!" Lukinia screamed out into the air.

"Wow, what was that? It was terrifying and amazing." Manatado spoke with an awe in his voice.

Malada exclaimed with excitement, "What? What did you see, Manatado?"

Lukinia crackled her wand and brought all attention to her. "What were you idiots thinking? By the gods,

Malada, would you put that shield away before it actually hurts somebody? Do you—DO YOU IDIOTS have any idea how dangerous that was? That's the chasm of eternity. That's where magic that never ends is stored. Those spells are beyond the power of anyone to control. I will NOT save you again." Lukinia then turned around and ranted as she floated back up toward Gerterma. "Risk my life for a bunch of useless humans? Ugh, I feel sick already."

Cassandra suddenly quickened her speed and jumped off into the brush.

She came graciously down the embankment. "What happened?"

Malada sighed and struggled with the straps. She said nothing and kept a stern face as she was helped out. After she was free, she grabbed her shield and ran off into the forest by herself. Cassandra looked at Manatado questioningly.

"That was freaking awesome. There were fireballs, floating clouds of darkness, monsters made of metal! Wow, talk about mind blown." Manatado made a gesture with his hands and then started back up the hill, leaving Cassandra with only more questions than answers.

After giving her friend a few moments alone, Cassandra slowly headed after Malada. She found her sitting in an open patch of grass with tears streaming down her face. Cassandra wanted to run up and comfort her friend but held back, not really wanting to. Time and time again, Malada would focus on the shield as if trying to will it to do something, and time and time again, it didn't.

Cassandra announced herself with a cough. "Hey there."

Malada was very startled, and her shield expanded to completely encompass her.

"Whoa, how did you do that?"

The words came with a tone as if Malada had been crying. "I don't know, but it turns out the shield can change shape."

Chapter 16

Tension and nerves were stressed. Yet the farther along the group walked, the more the fatigue let them relax. Even Gerterma started to relax as his natural walk returned. Lukinia only appeared occasionally to correct the group's course or inform them of upcoming obstacles. She was less than inclined to stay visible and gave only the most terse of answers to Gerterma's questions.

The teens all walked together. Malada this time took to the questioning. "Cassandra, how did you get so good with a bow and arrow?"

Cassandra perked up at the question. "Oh, thank you, Malada. Actually, it was my dad who taught me. He was a defense-force sniper in the orc wars. My dad had the coolest stories about all kinds of gadgets. Rifles that shoot balls of light that can go right through armor. Rifles that would shoot another kind of light that didn't even hurt the enemy but, after a few seconds, blew them up. Yet with all those cool stories, he still said archery was by far the most important. So from that day on, every day after school or after community work time, he would train me."

Manatado's bored gaze turned into a look that Cassandra enjoyed very much. "Oh, I didn't know that."

Not sure how to proceed, Cassandra shyly resumed her story. "At first he made a little platform in a tree for me to stand on. The extra height let my daddy trick me into thinking I was shooting farther than I really was." She paused to regain emotional control.

"Do you think we will ever get back to the village? That old guy better not have stolen any of my stuff! What was that old guy's name . . . Marks?" Manatado's voice raised as his thoughts raced.

Malada changed the tone very gracefully. "Oh, Manatado." He instantly perked back up, but as she said, "and Cassandra," he perked a little back down. "Tell me about your village."

"Boring."

"Wonderful."

The two spoke at the same time and made cross-eyes at each other. Malada giggled and nodded toward Cassandra. Yet Manatado replied instead. "It's nothing but fisherman, kids, and old people. Nothing to do at all."

"That's not true. You love turtle backing, don't you?"

Manatado blushed, as she seemed to know more about him than he did her. "And think of all those matches you and Tamack used to win. I remember that smile on your face when you two won the championship."

Manatado caught just a glimpse of a smile on Malada's lips, bringing his blush to a boil and his head down and to the side. "Yeah, yeah, I guess you're right."

"What's turtle backing?" Malada's smile churned into an unexpected chuckle, which unmeaningly embarrassed Manatado.

Cassandra, eager to move the situation along, spoke quickly. "Oh, turtle backing is the most amazing sport ever. Down in the ShellBay, which is named after the really large seashells that show up there, not the turtles like everyone thinks"—she paused to take a big breath in, noticing the sheer redness of both of her friends' faces, and possibly her own—"so there are these cow-sized turtles along the shore who eat the things that live in these large seashells." This time, both of her friends' attention had started to normalize and return back to Cassandra, who now slowed her voice down to normal.

Gerterma spoke with a hushed authority that transmitted an important message. "SHUT. UP." He then drew his blade.

Chapter 17

There, nearly three hundred meters ahead of them, was a mysterious little monkey. A dark cloud seemed to brew around the creature, yet it was not visible. The monkey sat motionless, its eyes fixed on the group.

Manatado, oblivious to the mood of the situation, became excited, gave a quick tug on Cassandra's arm, and jumped forward as he went out toward the animal. "A monkey! I have always, always wanted a monkey. Coolest of all the animals." Manatado was in a gentle jog when Gerterma put out his arm to stop the girls from pursuing him.

Manatado ran with a huge smile on his face as he approached the monkey. All the stories he had heard about monkeys over the years had made him anxious for this moment for a long time. Manatado's smile turned into a look of confusion as he neared the monkey. The monkey had yet to move. Manatado had expected that he would have to chase after it.

Cassandra and Malada gave nervous looks toward Gerterma. In reply, he simply held up a finger to his mouth and then made a palm and signaled for them to get down. They then crawled off into some taller bush and tried to keep an eye on Manatado.

Manatado was now feeling nervous as the monkey stared him directly in the eyes. The eyes flashed yellow, then red, and then blackout. The monkey's head started to bob, with a hint of a flame exiting its mouth with each bob. "Wait, what?" Manatado changed his mind. He didn't want this monkey as a pet. So he turned around and started walking back, only to find his friends missing.

The monkey made a horrible noise like the screaming of a banshee. Manatado was now in a full-out sprint away from the monkey. A massive wind picked up with such fury Manatado struggled to make any progress. A powerful gust brought Manatado off his feet and pulled him to only a few feet away from the monkey.

The monkey moved forward and looked down onto Manatado, who opened his mouth to scream, but nothing happened. The monkey's eye again flashed yellow, then flashed red, and then turned to blackout.

Manatado crawled back as hard as he could but was trapped by the animal's arms and tail end. "Bad monkey. Bad monkey!"

The monkey's arms rose up and threw Manatado off into the distance as one would a Frisbee. Manatado screamed out in fear as he flew off into the air. Cassandra stood up in disbelief and fear. Gerterma stood as well, a terrible look of guilt on his face. Malada ran to Cassandra's side and placed her head into her shoulder so as not to see. A second and new voice answered Manatado's voice.

While they couldn't see it, they could hear the collision between the two voices. A strapping shirtless young man flew through the air on a vine and, with amazing speed, charged past the girls, dropping Manatado into their arms as he passed by. The weight startled the two girls, who simply dropped him. The two girls then walked off in the direction of the boy and discreetly asked each other, "Did you see who that was?"

"No, me neither, but I think I'd like to."

Gerterma rushed for the girls, who grabbed hold, and they leaped out of the way of a lightning bolt charging their way. Manatado went from rubbing his head to ducking and covering from a nearby lightning strike. Lukinia appeared in a mix of white and yellow sparks and immediately matched his place and direction. The fairy rolled her eyes but gave Manatado a warming smile even if he was starting to feel more like a pet than a companion.

Manatado was pulled into the ball of sparkles. The world around was exactly the same but only in shades of black and white. He spoke with awe. "Wow, what is THIS place? You always take me to the coolest places." Again he drew an unreadable smile from the fairy.

"This is my shield of invisibility. You see, I don't really go anywhere. I get to see each and every thing you do."

Manatado had a hard time interpreting the tone. In truth, it started to make him feel a little creeped out.

The monkey screamed out like a banshee again, only this time the sound waves from the scream exploded through the black-and-gray scale to appear as vibrant colors bouncing across the sky. Lukinia appeared next to Manatado. "You see, that monkey possesses control of natural magic, and it's quite powerful."

"So what are you going to do about it?" Manatado exclaimed.

Lukinia looked insulted, but it was a cover for her fear. "Nothing, I'm going to do nothing. He is too strong."

Manatado shook his head left and right in disbelief. The monkey held out its tail, and from it shot deafening bolts of lightning at his companions. Its vibrant blue power spread across Lukinia's invisibility barrier. Gerterma was in a full sprint zig-zagging toward the monkey. Manatado wanted desperately to help his mentor.

Bolt after bolt came from the monkey's tail. Manatado then noticed something. With each bolt, the monkey's hind feet would latch down onto the ground, drawing visible power from the ground. Manatado suspected that if this monkey was using natural power, all he had to do was disconnect them. Manatado now ran toward the monkey as it lined up its next shot.

Manatado screamed back at Lukinia as he approached the monkey, this time from behind. "I have to help! Get me out of this place and back with them. Lukinia looked hurt and confused. Why would Manatado risk himself instead of staying with her?

It took another urgent yell from Manatado before Lukinia did what was asked. "Now, now, take me back there now."

Gerterma was closing in on the monkey, but he could already tell it was a mistake. The monkey fired shot after shot in a rhythm very much like a sniper or sharpshooter. The last bolts had been nerve-rackingly close, but he sensed the next one wouldn't miss. Gerterma charged forth, ready to take the blast, when Manatado appeared out of thin air. The boy grabbed the monkey by its tail, sending the bolt meant for Gerterma down into the ground.

Gerterma had too much momentum and collided with full force into the two of them. The three tumbled off in different directions. Arrow after arrow followed after the monkey; however, the monkey was already on its feet and dodged the arrows with ease. The monkey raised its hand and brought forth a powerful wind that altered Cassandra's arrow's flight path. The arrows were now heading straight for Manatado.

Manatado screamed and curled up in a ball. The arrows flew right above him, nearly missing him. Gerterma, however, was hurt, his leg broken. The monkey saw an opportunity and aimed its tail directly at Gerterma. The thunder was so loud it seemed to echo around inside Manatado's head, and he screamed out in fear.

Gerterma saw the burst of light and knew it was over, until Malada jumped in front of the lightning bolt with her shield bowed out wide. The lightning bolt vanished into the shield, causing the monkey to let out another banshee-like call. Malada could feel the impact of the lightning onto the shield, and it sent her backward onto her rear end.

The monkey's eyes went blackout. Its hands raised up as a ball of magic formed in its hands. Everything was drawn into this ball, even the light as it seemed to turn into night. Lukinia appeared before the group. "This is very powerful magic. Run!" The fairy then started after Manatado. It was too late. The ball was sucking in everything so powerfully no one could get away, not even Lukinia.

Cassandra gulped for air, but there was none. She and everything else were being sucked in. She reached out and grabbed what she thought was a tree branch, but it was soft. She looked again, and there before her was the striking shirtless young man who had helped save Manatado. The strange boy smiled a great big smile as he pulled Cassandra close to him. He then pointed upward.

Crashing down from the sky came the root of a massive tree. The collision brought forth a fog of dirt and debris. As it cleared, a bright wave of energy traveled up the tree, where it made its leaves shine. The tree stood up tall, and after a few moments, the leaves released all the monkey's evil power harmlessly into the wind.

Chapter 18

Cassandra smiled as her eyes opened to see a most handsome young man. She was lying down as he was posed above her. His big, wide blue eyes stared back at hers, and she was certain they were sharing a moment.

His eyes were so clear and easy to read, as if they could talk and were asking, "Are you well?" His facial expressions moved like an angel's, she thought. Cassandra tried to reply, but all that came out was a big sigh.

Malada and Gerterma came rushing up to the two of them. Malada stopped dead in her tracks when she saw the young man. She tried to control her reaction but tilted her head and gave a giant smile at the young man. Gerterma grunted in annoyance. "Is everyone okay?" He held out his hand to help pull Cassandra up. She shyly accepted and unconsciously stood in between the young man and Malada.

Malada jerked her head in protest, walked around Cassandra, and held out her hand as if to shake. "My name is Malada. Thank you for helping us."

The young man looked stupidly back at Malada and then stared at her hand. Cassandra walked around Malada and grabbed the young man's hand. "I'm Cassandra. It's so nice to meet you."

Again the young man only stared back stupidly.

Manatado, closely followed by Lukinia, came running in. "Hi, everybody." He took a couple of deep breaths. "What's going on?" Lukinia seemed upset and hung back but surprisingly didn't disappear. The tension between Cassandra and Malada was palpable. At first Manatado couldn't recognize why. "What's up with you two? Why do you have such stupid fake smiles?"

The young man turned to face Manatado, examined him closely, turned around, and ran nearly straight up the trunk of the tree that had smashed down on the monkey.

"All right, kids, if we could reel in the hormones, that would be great." Gerterma spoke with annoyance. "Here we will make camp. Absolutely no fires!" He turned around and set out for their supplies.

Cassandra and Malada looked at each other, trying to decide if they were mad at one another.

Manatado broke the ice before they could make up their minds. "Who was that guy? I'm not sure I like him."

"He was an absolute dreamboat." Cassandra didn't disguise her crush-like feelings. She and Malada made eye contact, decided they were not mad, and screamed out-loud excitement together.

"I wonder who he is?"

"I wonder what his voice sounds like?"

"I wonder what else he's good at?"

"I wonder if he lives in that tree?"

"I wonder if he lives alone?" The two girls erupted into hormonal laughter.

"I wonder if he has a shirt?" Manatado chimed in but was totally ignored.

Chapter 19

The group made camp minus the fire at the base of the tree, which had not moved again since crushing the evil monkey. Gerterma approached the three teens as they rested after setting up some tents. "All right, kids, I need your attention." He took a seat on a medium boulder slightly off center from where they were sitting. "There is something I want to discuss with you all."

Cassandra and Manatado exchanged a look of worry.

"We may not receive a warm welcome by the dwarves."

Cassandra and Manatado felt a sense of relief as the words came out. "Let me guess, Gerterma, you arrested the king's son?" Manatado proposed.

Cassandra then guessed. "No, that's not it. Gerterma . . . fell in love with the queen, they ran away together, and then broke up."

Malada then guessed, joining in on the fun. "No, Gerterma stole all the king's treasure and then gave it away!"

Gerterma shook his head. "No, definitely no, and just plain no. Now shut up and stop guessing. The last time I visited the kingdom of the dwarves, I was still with the defense force. We were trying to persuade them to join us in our fight against the orcs. The dwarven king traveled to the edge of his land with a small contingent of soldiers to meet us."

Gerterma crossed his legs before continuing. "For days, Jalum and I tried to convince the king that the Athenia accords had been broken. "

Manatado then asked a question. "Gerterma, I don't understand what the Athenia accords are."

Gerterma shook his head. "Didn't they teach all of this to you in school? After the race wars resulted in so much death and destruction to all of the races, it was determined that a political mechanism must be put in place to prevent it from ever happening again."

"So it was meant to prevent war from ever happening again?" Malada asked.

Gerterma thought for a second before answering. "No, I wouldn't say that. It was more like a pact, a pact between the races that if one or two races became overly aggressive, the others would come to their defense, more like a ceiling on war as opposed to a prevention of war. So here is an example of an accord. If one of the races were to kill or injure civilians, that would be a violation of an accord and could have been brought before the council at Athenia. If the council decided that the accord had been broken, then it would have been the council's duty to mediate the dispute or join in on the side for which the accord was broken. Does that make sense?"

"What would they join in with? Did they have an army?" Manatado asked.

"No, should they have decided that they needed to take control of the war, then they would have activated the protocols and every race would have been obligated to send a medium-sized forced to fight under the council command."

Cassandra spoke next. "In school, they taught us that the accords were meant to prevent war from ever happening again."

"Well for a hundred years, it did keep the peace. Then there was the orc-human war, hence why I was meeting the dwarven king. Jalum and I tried desperately to convince him that the orcs were too dangerous and would destroy the human race."

Malada asked with great curiosity, "Why weren't you able to convince him. I heard the humans nearly lost the war."

"The king believed that the humans started the war." Gerterma's voice softened and saddened as he spoke. "For an entire light and dark cycle, I debated, elaborated, elongated, begged, pleaded, and even demanded that they honor the accords. Yet it was no use. The king was not persuaded. After they broke camp, I was distraught, fraught with the idea my failure would destroy my race."

The kids were entranced by Gerterma's story, and Malada subconsciously grabbed on to both Cassandra's and Manatado's hands. The contact brought Manatado's heart to a race, and he impatiently asked, "Why does any of this mean we won't be welcomed by the dwarves? Why didn't you say anything about Jalum when you were with the king?"

Gerterma put his hand up, expressing for him to stop, but Manatado kept asking questions. Malada squeezed his hand and nodded her head, after which Manatado was no longer able to focus on Gerterma's story and abruptly stopped asking questions. Manatado's head even sank into the direction of their hands. Gerterma approached Manatado and placed his hand on the boy's shoulder, startling him. "This is important. Shut up and pay attention."

Gerterma shook his head in annoyance, trying to keep his own adolescent days in mind. "As I said, the king and his men departed back for his castle . . . but they never made it."

Cassandra and Malada, still enthralled by the story, each made a small gasp. Gerterma heard the sounds, even if faint. "Yes, you are right. Suspicion immediately fell upon us. We were ordered to turn ourselves into the dwarven authorities, which, after much debate and guidance from our superiors, we did. They took us past the place where the king had perished, a small valley that we were told was once a mighty valley, until bits and pieces of it had come tumbling down upon the king, followed by layer after layer of valley wall hurling down upon the king's men."

Gerterma let out a big sigh. "We were taken to the regent's castle. A huge crowd of nearly every race had come to see. It was one of the few trials between species and the first to involve the death of such a high-ranking official. It was also there that I met my mentor, a dwarven officer, a noble dwarf and a man who worked diligently to prove our guilt."

"What? You mentored with a dwarf who wanted to put you in jail?" Manatado exclaimed.

"Oh, he not only wanted to put Jalum and me behind bars. He wanted to destroy us, for he believed we had done it."

Cassandra gasped. "So what happened?"

"The dwarven magistrate, Nicolda, was dead set on determining our guilt. He and his men scoured the scene where the king had fallen but could find nothing to prove we were there. He interrogated us for hours and hours, but he could still find no proof. They called in magic investigators, forensics investigators, and even local people. However, when they could find no evidence, no evidence at all, that's when Nicolda truly showed the quality of man he was. You see, everybody, and I mean everybody, wanted us to be guilty. Their king was dead, and the dwarves wanted someone to blame. Nicolda was under intense political and social pressure to put us behind bars."

Manatado added in, "It became a witch hunt, scapegoating?"

"Oh yes, just about every race had reporters at the trial. It was really something, the largest gathering of races outside of Athenia. Nicolda was a dwarf of very stern stature, never revealing any emotion outwardly at all. Yet his dedication to the job and the gusto he did it with made him a dwarf of high regard. He was chosen because he was the best, but what really set him apart was his desire to find the truth. You see, as the trial was about to begin, Nicolda had come around to the truth, that we were innocent. So on the very first day of the trial, Nicolda steps down. Then, most surprisingly, he assigns himself defender to both Jalum and me."

"Oh, no wonder you were so fond of him, but honestly, he doesn't feel like a very fun person." Malada trailed off as the spoke the second half, but Manatado noted the comment to himself for review later.

"It was neither the time nor the place for fun. Nicolda, however, was forceful and graceful with his words. The entire world was caught up in this trial, and there was an immense demand for justice. For every scenario the dwarves could come up with, Nicolda had already determined its fault. However, when it comes to emotions, facts alone are not enough to cause change. Nicolda had a flair, something I could never replicate. His stern and unemotional responses lulled the crowd until it was his time to speak. Then his voice would raise and ignite with passion. It was a thing of beauty. I have tried to emulate Nicolda for the majority of my military career. After our release, I asked him if I could work with him and learn his secrets. He told me something very strange and something that took me a very long time to figure out. He told me, 'Some gifts are given at birth, some gifts are developed, and some gifts are . . . given in the moment. Learn to appreciate all of them.'"

Gerterma then stood up and placed his hand on his weapon and walked forward, past the kids.

Chapter 20

The bushes and leaves rustled gently as the handsome boy stepped forward. Gerterma lowered his hands and walked forward to meet the young man and then bowed. "Thank you for most graciously saving us. We are in your debt."

This time, the young man had a most angry scowl on his face. While his voice was angry and stern, its sound didn't match expectations. "We have communicated with those where you call home. You are ignorant, murderous barbarians!"

Manatado stood up, insulted, looking for a fight from a guy he didn't really like. Gerterma gave Manatado a stern look, as he did with the others. He then knelt down on one knee before the boy. "What you have heard is true. We use your brethren to build our towns, we use your sick and fallen to heat our homes, and we pluck your harvests to consume for ourselves. All this we openly confess."

The boy's face was still angry, but the edge had come off. "And you are here to take yet even more for us now, are you not!"

Manatado really didn't like this boy and couldn't control his temper. "WE are not here even for you! We don't know you! How dare you accuse us of being murderous barbarians!"

Malada reached out and pulled Manatado back.

The boy looked at Manatado and returned a look of stern dislike. "Adversarial tone, this one is not welcome." The boy then pointed at Manatado. The sound of snapped branches and creaking limbs brought everyone's attention to the tree above. Two limbs quickly reached down and picked up Manatado, carrying him off into the treetops.

"No, wait. He is only an ignorant youth. Do not hurt him," Gerterma pleaded with the boy.

The handsome boy looked back at Gerterma. "We are not the barbarians!" The boy then turned about and took off up into the tree and darkness.

Cassandra and Malada approached Gerterma. "What's happening? Where is Manatado?"

Gerterma shook his head. "It's all on Manatado. It's up to him now to convince the Socratea tree to help us. All we can do is wait, so let us begin." Gerterma then sat back down and took out a piece of bread to eat.

Chapter 21

Manatado felt his stomach sink as he was thrust high up into the air. Above the tree line, he was held up by a single branch. He grabbed on as tightly as he could, fearful of a fall that would kill him. It was eerily calm as the night sky stretched out as far as he could see. Yet off in the distance, a small red-yellow light was barely visible where the horizon met the sky.

Manatado jostled as he was brought back into the center of the tree and placed butt first on a very large branch. He struggled with the angle of the branch and ended up hugging it as he tried to situate himself. After relocating his foot, Manatado turned his face around to the other side, where the handsome face of the boy was sternly looking at him. "Why, human? Why?"

Manatado's physical fear of falling and physical fear of the boy were transparent as he spoke. "I don't know. I mean, I know you don't mean . . . I don't know what you meannnn."

Again Manatado was raised up high as two branches grabbed hold of him and raised him up to look at the light shining at where the sky met the ground. After a moment, he was brought back before the handsome boy with an angry look. "Why, human, why?"

Manatado looked left and right, hoping for an idea to come to him, but all he could do was think of his fear. "I don't know what you mean."

The boy spoke in a very monotone voice with a steady-but-singular rhythm. "We demand to know why the humans are doing this? Why is life being burned?"

At least now Manatado understood what the light in the distance was. "A fire, I don't know anything about a fire."

Manatado was shaken as the boy spoke. "Confess, human."

Fear rattled through Manatado's body. "I confess, I confess. I cut off tree branches to burn. I have a stove that I burn wood in every nighttttt. I cheated on my math test. I stole cookies from the pantry. I'm sorry, I'm sorry. I won't ever burn anything again."

Manatado's tears rolled down his face as the tree gently lowered him down into a more horizontal branch. He crawled onto his knees and held up his hands together. The handsome boy approached from the far side of the branch, and while he moved swiftly and assuredly, his face was no longer angry. The young man reached out his arm and lifted Manatado up by the armpit. "We have agreed. You are in fact innocent youth."

Manatado reached out and hugged the young man, but as he wrapped his arms around him, Manatado felt something surprising. A thick branch protruded out from the young man's back. The shock sent Manatado backward, onto his heels.

Manatado gathered himself as he moved to run away. "Who is 'we'?"

The boy's face looked puzzled. "We are the one you seek?"

Manatado grumped, "How is it I can understand the words you speak but not your meaning?"

"Manatado." The young man's voice was monotone and dull. "Manatado of the village Valentina."

Manatado fell backward in disbelief. "How, how do you know my name. How do you know my language?"

The young man's head tilted toward the other shoulder. "We, we have communicated with those whose limbs have burned . . . in your . . . stove." The last word came out stretched as if imitating the sound.

Manatado gulped. "Innocent youth?"

"Agreed. Now tell us your intentions."

Manatado gulped again. "Gerterma is really better at this stuff."

The branch Manatado was standing on shook enough to bring him to his knees.

"You will tell us!"

"AAAAAAA, um, let's see. Malada, that really pretty girl . . . so, um, she got separated from her mother. We think her mother is in a very dangerous place. So, yeah, we need to find her a special trainer. So then we can have the skills we need to go get her mother." Now that Manatado had heard their own plan out loud, he suddenly felt very foolhardy.

The young man shifted the slant of his head back toward the other shoulder. "We are agreed. Innocent youth."

Manatado was starting to feel much less frightened and was finding the fact that this boy would not be competition for the girls very relieving. "Who is 'we'?"

The young man's face looked flustered. "We are the Socratea, ancient guardians of the forest. Within us live the souls of all plant life. We can travel the roots of life. Together we see all. We see the truth. You! You are a group of humans. Humans are to be judged for their crimes."

Manatado's face lost its color. "What, what crime do you think we committed?"

"Enslavement."

Manatado's face switched to confused. "What did we enslave? The trees, I wouldn't even know how to do that."

104

The young man's face filled with frustration. "All life."

"What, what, what? We most certainly could not do that! My village is only a few hundred people, only one of dozens that size. Other than the human city of Maracato, there just wouldn't be enough people to do that."

The young man's face flashed with anger, and he closed in fast, placing his hands around Manatado's neck. At first Manatado thought he was being attacked; however, the young man placed his lips upon Manatado's. Manatado jerked back as hard as he could, not once but twice, when what should have been a tongue was instead a branch. The branch forked many times, quickly filling the whole of Manatado's mouth. He tried to scream, but no sound came forth.

Instead, an image came to him, now filling the whole of his surroundings. He was on the edge of a large canyon. The heat was intense and stung Manatado's eyes, forcing them to water. The canyon glowed as a large pool of molten lava was churned by orcs turning giant wheels connected to metal stirring rods.

Above them, dressed in armor and armed to kill, were humans. The vision focused in on one of the guards. The man taunted and then kicked one of the orcs, sending them sliding dangerously close to the edge of the canyon. The vision backed out to a larger view, and Manatado could see they were making something—something big, very big, and it was getting bigger. A constant flow of raw ore was being shaped at one end. It was too big, and Manatado too unknowledgeable to recognize what it was they were making.

The scene twisted off toward the far side, where a great and dark castle had been erected. Its towers stretched high above the canyon, creating an even greater contrast. There, on a platform centrally located, stood a small group of people. Four humans with a few Minoets, bugs that grow to the size of large dogs and can be trained for various tasks, stood overseeing the operation. The vision focused in on the people. One of the women looked very familiar, and after a moment, he knew it could only be her: Malada's mother. The other woman and the two men were unknown to Manatado. The vision slowly turned all black.

The roots retracted from Manatado's mouth and retreated back into the young man's mouth. Manatado's stunned face froze in place as he tried to process everything that had just happened.

"Now you are no longer innocent youth. Now you must choose a side. We will let you confer before deciding whether or not we shall destroy you."

Manatado could only swallow in response. Two branches again rushed in and picked him up by his armpits. They gently lowered him down to ground level, where the others were waiting for him.

Malada rushed forward and wrapped her arms around Manatado, who otherwise would have relished the embrace. Manatado's cold lack of an embrace worried Malada, who pulled back and asked, "What happened to you? Are you okay?"

Manatado's blank stare oddly resembled the young man, and as he slowly turned his head to face Malada's, all he could say was, "I don't want to talk about it."

Chapter 22

Manatado, stone-faced, zombied into camp and sat stiff and upright. For a long time, he did nothing, just sat and stared. Cassandra, Malada, and even Lukinia stood side by side, nervously waiting for Manatado to do something. Gerterma waited patiently at first but erupted into an outburst of laughter as he slapped his knee. "He kissed you, didn't he?"

The unexpected remark brought girlish smiles and giggles to their faces as Cassandra and Malada exchanged looks. Lukinia responded with disgust, gave Manatado a disapproving look, and then vanished. Hearing the truth snapped Manatado out of his gaze, but after making eye contact with everyone, he simply folded his arms and repeated, "I don't want to talk about it."

Gerterma chuckled before speaking seriously. "Did they show you? Did they give you a choice?"

Manatado nodded yes to both.

"Well then, which side will you choose?"

Cassandra broke in. "Gerterma, what are you talking about, a side? What do you mean? What side versus what side? Why does only he have to choose?"

Gerterma looked at the girls and then back at Manatado. "Tell them. I don't want to put words into your mouth."

Manatado said, "But, Gerterma, is it true?"

"You experienced it. You tell me," Gerterma responded, leaving the girls hooked on a conversation they weren't understanding.

"Before we left Valentina, I always just assumed that people were good. Now I'm more scared of people like

Jalum than I am evil magic monkeys. Gerterma, am I wrong to think that?"

"What do you think makes humanity different from the other races? For instance, all races eat, drink fresh water, and sleep. All races have a system of government. They all follow varying degrees of the rule of law. They all have social and political discord. So what makes people different?"

Manatado thought for a second and then looked at the girls for help. Cassandra and Malada looked at each other before shouting out a stream of guesses.

"Our cooking."

"Our clothes."

"Human knowledge."

"Technology."

At last, Malada burst out, "Our religion," to which she got nods of impressed approval from both Cassandra and Manatado, who looked back at Gerterma. "Religion."

Gerterma rubbed his eyes. "I was asking metaphorically, but whatever. Humans are different because we have no united moral code. Some humans are capable of amazing acts of goodness and kindness, while some humans are capable of acts of great evil and anger. While other races have similar tendencies, humans have by far allowed the biggest disparity."

"So it is true. Those were real people overseeing the enslavement of the orcs."

An awed "ooh" came from the girls as they heard that.

Then Manatado asked, "What were they making?"

The girls moved their eyes back to Gerterma, awaiting his response.

"A weapon."

Everyone waited patiently, expecting Gerterma to elaborate and continue, but he didn't for a long time. Then he asked, "So now that you have seen a portion of the truth, you will have to decide. Which side of humanity are you on? Are you willing to fight the other side? These are decisions that adults struggle with. Now it is all on your shoulders."

Manatado shrugged and looked at the girls, who were staring right back at him, awaiting his response. Manatado knew the answer, but saying it out loud felt like a confession, very nerve-racking. "I, I already know which side I'm on. I'm on your side, Gerterma, the side of good."

"And just what makes you so certain I made the same choice?" Gerterma's tone was cold, but that didn't even make Manatado flinch.

"Because you are on the side of good. I wouldn't be here otherwise."

Gerterma smiled like a proud father. He then stood up, walked over to Manatado, and hugged him. Cassandra and Malada looked at each other, embarrassed, as friends joining in on the moment.

Chapter 23

The handsome young man came out from the brush. "We have witnessed the choosing. Betrayal of this choice will result in your termination. We are agreed you are no longer innocent youth."

The young man's strange mannerisms and tone of voice drew the ire of both Cassandra and Malada but brought a smug look of self-assurance from Manatado. The young man then turned to face the two girls. He approached directly and stood before Malada. She stood chest high to his shirtless body and totally lost her train of thought. To Malada, he smelled wonderfully of the forest, and her head drifted upward. Cassandra felt both happy for her friend and insanely jealous, while the look on Manatado's face made her nervous.

There was a brief pause before the young man once again directly made contact mouth-to-mouth with Malada before extending the vision's roots. Manatado felt both a sting of jealousy and the joy of laughter as Malada performed the same dance he had during the same event.

Lukinia, having chosen thus far not to participate, now appeared with a great big smile on her face. She looked at Malada, who was now experiencing the vision, and then at Cassandra. "I'll save you the trouble, plus it's never quite as funny the second time around." Lukinia then waved her wand and a screen appeared for Cassandra to watch the vision on.

Manatado walked around the vision and stood close to Cassandra; however, he was shocked to see that it was a different vision, a much more personal vision. Lukinia waved her wand and two halves of a loveseat appeared magically behind both Lukinia and Manatado, who felt compelled to sit down on it. When he did, the two halves came together and they were suddenly sitting very closely, watching a very personal vision.

The canyon was the same as before. It stretched out long wide and deep with a huge dark castle built at one end. Humans in armor and weapons oversaw massive numbers of orcs engaged in slave labor. A steady stream of molten ore poured over the cliff from the far end into a massive shaping cauldron, which was in constant motion from orcs pushing with great strain on a large wheel below it.

It was the same woman from Manatado's vision. She stood in front of three men facing the same direction as her, while before her on his knees was an orc. The creature was pleading with her, hands held together, sharing words and tears. The woman approached, placed her hand on the orc's chin, and raised its head to make eye contact. The woman then made a slicing motion and it was over.

The screen flashed and faded away, and the young man pulled back from Malada. She looked to be in total disbelief. She made eye contact with those around her before she ran off into the brush. Manatado, anxious to get away from Lukinia, jumped up off the couch and ran off after Malada.

The young man then looked at Cassandra as if about to approach and kiss her, when she raised and waved her hands and yelled, "No, no, no, I'm on your side. Really, I'm the side of good. No, NO need for a vision." Cassandra was slowly backing up as she spoke. The young man stopped and paused for a long time. Deciding they were satisfied, the young man returned to the camp and faced Gerterma.

"Human known as Gerterma. We are aware of you. We are aware of what you did for the forest kind in the war against the orcs. We will give a chance for you to explain yourself." With that, the handsome young man floated up and back into the tree trunks.

Cassandra looked at Gerterma. "Who, or I mean what, is that boy?"

Gerterma returned Cassandra's look. "That boy is no longer a boy. You see, Socratea trees are not born with any way to interact with the . . . non-plant life of this world. So when a young Socratea tree comes across a dying or disabled being, it can choose to bond with it, removing the injury or disability. It also removes the person inside it too. I have no idea whether that boy is still alive and is a voice inside the tree or not, or even something else. But no, that boy is not a person, at least not anymore."

Gerterma gave Cassandra a fatherly hug and approached the tree. Two branches descended and took Gerterma up into the treetop.

Chapter 24

Malada sat crying in the brush just as she had only a few hours prior. Yet this time, it was much different, much more intense. It couldn't be true; the vision just couldn't be true. The thought kept forcing itself into her conscious thought over and over again. Yet in her heart, she knew it was true. Was her mother really a villain? Why would she just kill that orc? Who were those other people she was standing in front of?

The more she thought about it, the more scenarios she came up with as to why her mother would do that, but nothing changed her feeling about whether she'd really done that. Malada felt betrayed, saddened, and angry all at once. She would kick and stomp on a tree before breaking down in tears and hugging it.

Manatado felt very awkward as he came near, totally unsure of what to say. At last he finally gave a cough that made Malada turn around in a fit of rage. "Why didn't you say something! Can't I have any privacy!" Malada's fist struck Manatado in the arm, and it was no big deal, but throwing one punch only made her angrier, and she threw a couple more.

Manatado took two blows before throwing her hands off to the side and started to run away. Malada was in a totally uncontrollable emotional frenzy, and she chased after Manatado and tackled him to the ground. Malada sat down on top of Manatado, pinning him to the ground, and he raised his hands up to defend against more hits, but instead Malada maneuvered her face in toward Manatado and kissed him passionately.

Manatado tried to enjoy the experience, but Malada jerked back with tears streaming down her face. It was far from the romantic first kiss he had hoped for. Malada rolled off of him and curled up into the fetal position as she cried. Manatado felt completely unprepared and had no idea what to say. "So, uh, yeah, um, what can I do to help?"

"Go away!"

Manatado stood up, totally unsure whether he was actually supposed to leave or stay and try to help his crush. The end result was, he walked in several circles as she lay there crying. At last Manatado decided he should try again.

"I never really knew my parents. I always liked to think of them as good people, but in truth, I will never know. Was my father a good man or a defense-force enslaver? My memories of my dad are few and far between and are also a mixed bag. I remember him scolding me very strictly, but I can also remember the warm embrace of his hug." A single tear came down his face. "I also know that whoever they were, it doesn't mean it's who I have to be."

"That's not why I'm crying." There was a pause as she took a big breath. "I'm crying because I'm just like her."

"Hey, hey, hey, now. I've spent some time with you, and that's NOT TRUE! You are a good person. You healed Cassandra."

"It was me who also got her shot. I asked you to break into the office. I also know what I have done. I have done bad."

"What do you mean? I'm not following."

"When we were running from the defense force." A new level of intense crying started as she spoke through the tears.

"They were chasing us, three men. I . . . I . . . I . . . I used my magic on them."

114

"But if they were chasing you, then you were just defending yourself."

"Don't you see? I'm just as capable of evil as she is!"

Manatado thought about everything he and Malada had just been through, and none of it made any sense to him. "I know that I don't know much about things, girls or history apparently, but I do know that I don't know everything. All I can say is that you don't know everything either. That includes everything about your mother and what we saw. Gerterma himself told me that what we see is only one version of the truth. What I think he means is that just because we saw something happen doesn't mean we saw why it's happening. Does that make any sense."

Malada sniffed and wiped away her tears.

"What do you mean 'we saw'?"

Manatado put his hand up to his mouth and blushed.

She smiled at Manatado and held out her hand. He felt the hairs all over his body rise up anxiously. He tried to stop his hand from shaking, but he was just so nervous. Malada placed her other hand on top of his and gently rubbed it. She looked up at Manatado. "No, I didn't understand what you said at all, but I do understand why you said it." Malada stood up to kiss Manatado, when a small rock hit him in the face.

A very angry fairy in Lukinia was throwing small pebbles directly at Manatado, and she had good aim. "You, YOU, YOU stay away from her!"

Manatado didn't really get to enjoy his first kiss with Malada, and now Lukinia was interrupting their second, which made him feel mad. "GET OUT OF HERE. I DONT LIKE YOU. I'LL NEVER LIKE YOU!"

Lukinia threw one more pebble before her face turned bright red and she vanished away in tears. Manatado stomped before turning back to Malada, but the moment had passed. His frustration mounted as the moment was further disrupted by the arrival of Gerterma and Cassandra.

Manatado rolled his eyes and gave up, throwing his hands slightly into the air. Gerterma walked straight up to Manatado and gently hit him on the back of the head "You doofus, we will need Lukinia. Go make it right with her!"

Manatado again felt dumbfounded. All he wanted to do was pursue the things he wanted, and all got in return for it was trouble. Malada nodded with her head for Manatado to go after her, and he couldn't help but notice a sense of relief in her face as he left. He ran off into the brush in the same direction she was facing as she vanished. Manatado ran several meters before coming to a screeching halt. There before him, with a blade to Lukinia's throat, was Jalum.

Chapter 25

Jalum stood tall even though his head was tilted off in another direction as if he was barely even paying attention to them. "I see by your sway with women that you are in fact Gerterma's apprentice. He could at least do okay at the more difficult skills, yet when it came to the simple things, like picking up women"—Jalum held up Lukinia by her foot as her hands were bound with a glowing thread of a restraint— "he just couldn't seem to get the simple things right. I see he has passed this on to you, as his apprentice. Defend yourself!"

Lukinia was thrown straight up into the air, and before she reached the top of the throw, Jalum had Manatado pinned down on the ground and easily caught Lukinia as she fell.

Jalum reached out and, with his huge hand, grabbed Manatado by his side and lifted him up. Manatado felt the air rush out of his lungs as the hand pinched his side hard enough to lift him up high. "Call," Jalum commanded as he shook Manatado violently in the air. "Call your master, worthless apprentice! Call him!"

Manatado tried desperately to call out, but each attempt just resulted in more pain as the airflow into his lungs was no longer under his control.

"Put him down, Jalum!" Gerterma spoke with a strong authoritarian voice.

"Ah, big brother, always giving orders." Oh, no, wait. Now I'm the one giving orders, and you're the one sleeping in the dirt, homeless. Oh, how I wish Mother could see how pathetic you are now." Jalum laughed a sad laugh.

"Strike ONE, now put the boy and fairy down. NOW!"

"Wrong again, dear brother, this is strike one." With lightning-fast speed, Jalum closed with and struck Gerterma in the face with the side of his shoe. Gerterma lurched to the ground with the pain of the strike.

After a moment reeling from the pain, Gerterma stood back up. "Strike TWO! PUT them down now."

Jalum sighed. "Aw, very well, brother. Then strike two it is." With that, he threw both Manatado and Lukinia at Gerterma. Jalum's foot followed directly behind, and both were struck so hard by Jalum's foot that they flew first into each other and then into Gerterma. "Oh my, I guess I didn't count so well. I guess that's strike three." The three lay in a pile, hurting from the blow as they collided with the base of a large tree.

Jalum looked over them to gloat. He towered over his brother and lifted his arm in preparation for a devastating blow. His mouth opened wide, and a loud yelp came out. One of Cassandra's arrows had pierced itself into Jalum's buttock. His arms pulled back and grasped the arrow, but pain prevented it from being immediately pulled out. The three quickly recovered their wind and crawled off as fast as possible.

Jalum gathered himself, pulled out the arrow, and dodged Cassandra's next shot. He threw his sword directly at Cassandra, who flinched down enough to evade the sword but raised her hand in the process, receiving a nasty deep cut on her wrist. She fell to her knee and then to the prone position as she grasped the wound with her left hand.

Jalum cursed in pain and then chased after his brother. He grabbed Gerterma by the back and the neck and, with amazing strength, lifted him up by it. Jalum moved

Gerterma so as to be face-to-face. Jalum showed no sympathy as his little brother struggled for air. "Where is she?"

Gurgling sounds came once or twice out of Gerterma before he was thrown to the ground and stepped on. After regaining his breath, he boldly spoke. "Strike three, little brother."

Jalum raised his hand and head as if searching with his eyes closed. "Where has she gone. Ugh, the Socratea tree!" He dug his heel in and pushed off hard. He landed on his brother's back and stepped on him before running off after Malada and the Socratea tree.

Gerterma grabbed some large papaya leaves and made a tourniquet for Cassandra's wrist, but she would need to keep it immobile. Lukinia vanished the moment she was free, and now Manatado was hurt. Manatado lay on his side, taking only shallow breaths, for anything more was too painful.

"I believe Manatado has a punctured lung. It will be difficult to move him."

"Can't Lukinia just use her magic to carry him?" Cassandra asked.

"Well I'm not an expert on what kinds of things fairies can and can't do. If she returns, I will most certainly ask her. In the meantime, I will need to find another method of transportation." With that, Gerterma gathered some firewood and lit a small campfire. He then dragged Manatado next to it. Gerterma then went into the forest to collect a special type of leaf to throw on the fire. The smell was heavenly to Cassandra.

Manatado, with baited breath, finally got their attention. "What . . . abou—Ma . . . la . . ."

Gerterma sat next to the fire and raised his hand for Manatado to stop. "Malada is with the Socratea tree in a desperate fight for safety from Jalum. I don't know what the final result will be. Socratea is wise, powerful, and faster than you might think. Yet against Jalum, the tree doesn't stand a chance. Now if Malada can use her magic, well then maybe they have a chance."

Manatado tried to sit up in protest but was forced back down with the pain. "Well, keep in mind, she didn't stand a chance here with the six of us. Look how quickly Jalum took out all four of us. No, her best option was to flee. Now, well now, I need to come up with a new plan. First things first, however, I need to get you all to a doctor."

Chapter 26

The giant Socratea tree balled up its giant roots and tucked in its outermost branches, and the young handsome man came up and bear hugged Malada. Then the world began to spin. The root ball would hit the ground, and momentum would swing the top around. It seemed like there was no terrain it couldn't cross this way. With each break in the trees, they would drop down to ground level but pop right back up to the tree line. It occurred to Malada that these creatures must have traveled this way for a very long time. However, at the current time, all she could do was restrain herself from puking.

Malada held out for as long as she could, but the never-ending spinning finally made her so nauseous she threw up. Unfortunately, as the spinning continued, so did her nausea. That combined with the smell of puke in her nose made her miserable. The handsome young man grabbed her around the shoulder and led her to the center of the tree. The spinning was much less there, and Malada was able to feel somewhat better. The handsome young man held her with his arm as if signaling for her to move in that direction, but all Malada saw was the tree trunk. Again the young man signaled, only this time he motioned as if opening a door.

Malada looked again at the trunk of the tree, and there in the very center was a tiny door handle. She looked back at the boy, who again suggested she open it. She opened it but immediately stepped back. The handsome young man blinked his eyes several times and then again motioned for Malada to go in. She returned his blank look in reply and shrugged her shoulders.

The handsome young man blinked several times, placed one of Malada's hands on the door handle, and slowly pushed her in. To her great amazement, Malada began to shrink as she approached the door, and as she neared it, she had already shrunk enough to enter. The light flooded into the hollowed-out tree trunk as she opened the door. Malada kept the door open, ready to flee, when she was riddled by hollers from the inside.

"In or out!"

"Close that bloody thing!"

Malada closed the door, and as the light from inside began to fill her eyes, so did Malada wonder. The room or den didn't spin at all, leading her to believe it must be the center of the tree. There, huddled in three small groups, were the animals such as chipmunks and squirrels, the insects and, in a water reservoir in the back, some very small fish.

Malada wondered what this place was all about. She tried approaching the animals, but they growled and hissed, warning her off. The insects looked gross and scary to her, so she went and sat in front of the fish tank. The hollowed-out trunk space was damp, dark, and full of terrible smells. She didn't feel comfortable in this place any more than she did out with tree boy.

Malada finally sat down in the middle of some open space, wrapped her arms around her knees, and missed her friends. She wasn't sure how long she sat there, but it felt like a long time. At first she didn't even notice the feeling, so soft was the touch. Again the feeling came, almost like a tickle on her shoulder. She placed her hand on her shoulder to brush the tickle away, when she felt a paw. Malada startled with fright.

"Sorry to have frightened you." The voice came out from behind the animals. A small bird with a red feather sticking out of its head like a cap came bouncing forward. "My name is Jamel of a seaborne flock. What's yours?" The small bird made slow, small bounces forward until it reached the front of the animals' area. "I've never seen a human in here before. In fact, I don't think I have ever seen a human as small as you. Normally, I would flee from a human at first sight, as most of my friends told me. 'But she is soooo small,' I told them, 'this human must be different.' So, human, tell me, are you here to eat us?"

Malada's face expressed shock at the question. "What on earth makes you think I'm here to eat you?"

"Humans are the world's predators. They consume or displace all they control. So, human, please tell us, are you here to eat us and take control of our forest?"

"Oh, no, no no no no." Malada exhaled as she spoke, relaxing as her intentions were not what these animals feared.

"I'm on a quest to find my mother. The Socratea tree is taking me to safety from . . ." Malada trailed off and let silence fill in the rest.

The small bird exchanged chirps with some of the animals before returning attention to Malada. "The Socratea tree is very powerful but also very old. The tree cannot take you all the way to safety. Your pursuer will overtake us, and your pursuer is more powerful than the tree. Will you ask us to sacrifice ourselves?"

Malada felt immense guilt in her stomach and strongly regretted going about any of this. "I don't want that," she whined with tears forming in her eyes. "I just wanted to find my mother. I miss chasing her along the stream and through the fields. All I want is to go to school like Manatado, go to sleep in the same place every night. I just wanted to be normal. I didn't want any of this. I want to go home. I want to go home."

The small gathering of animals parted and lined up as something larger moved in the dark behind them. The room dropped to silence with only the wind rustling between the fur of the animal as it moved forward. The animal lurched forward one slow step at a time until it entered the light. There before Malada was an aged sloth. Its gray hair ran down its sides from its head. It walked with a cane that thumped every time it hit the ground, and its rear foot seemed to drag as it walked.

As the sloth approached Malada, it blew the gray hairs in from of its face apart before it spoke. "Innocent youth. We will not ask you to ask. But please tell us what you will do when you finally meet your mother?"

Malada's heart sank even lower, and the tears again started to pour down her face. Her distress came mostly from the fact that she had never given it much thought. All Malada could think of was the image of her mother killing that orc. The sloth waited very patiently, never giving Malada the impression he would do anything other than wait.

Malada swallowed and tried to clear her mind. "When I meet my mother, I will want to hug her." She let out a wave of tears before continuing. "Then, then I would want to know the truth."

The sloth waited another long moment before seeing if Malada would speak further, but she didn't, instead gathering her emotions. The sloth brought its free hand up to its chin as if thinking, "Your words communicate both emotion and logic, but we are very wary of your ability to discern the truth."

Malada's intense emotional state brought some fire to her words. "Truth, the truth is, we all do evil. Pursuit of the good and right thing is never as easy as I want it to be. My mother said we were fleeing the defense force as an act of good. My mother did terrible things in that pursuit." Her face toned down in anger and returned to a sadder state. "Good, I want to be good, but why does being good require so much bad?"

The sloth moved its paw onto Malada's shoulder. "Now, now there, dear. The trees have a saying, one that I think you should heed well. You can only tell the nature of a tree by the fruit it produces."

Malada again wiped her face and waited for the sloth to continue. The sloth finally continued after what seemed a long time "If a tree, or a person, produces bad fruit, or in a person's case produces bad outcomes, then the tree or person is bad. Reverse is true, if a tree is good or a person is good, they have good fruit and good outcomes." The sloth smiled at her. "Please tell us here, what happened when your friend was shot?"

Malada started to perk up. "My magic saved her."

"Next tell us what happened when the bear attacked you?"

"My magic saved us."

"Did it kill the bear?"

Malada again started to perk up. "No, no it didn't."

"These are the first of your fruits. Take care to always mind your fruit. Now our time grows short, as the one who pursues us is drawing near."

Malada's face turned to fear. "What happens next?"

The sloth this time lowered its head. "A battle to the death." The sloth then raised his head. "Yet there is still a little time before then. Sit and rest while we bring you some snacks and water as we wait."

Malada smiled at the warm reception but still missed her new friends.

Chapter 27

Manatado and Cassandra both grunted in pain at the same time. Gerterma laid Manatado's stretcher at an angle against Cassandra's back, and as his weight hit the stretcher, both erupted in more grunts. Gerterma tied a band around Cassandra's shoulders and waist and then attached it to the front of the stretcher so she could carry it without using her hand.

It was slow, laborious work, and they all knew this wasn't good enough to get it done. They went on hour after hour, but at last both Cassandra and Gerterma were in need of a significant rest. Gerterma made a fire while Cassandra frustratingly prepared some of the rations they still had.

Cassandra passed Gerterma his portion and sat next to Manatado and the fire. She was kind and caring, yet she realized she had little experience at these two things. She carefully tried to give him some water, but it was immediately spit up.

"Gerterma, what are we going to do?" Nervous fear was clear in her tone of voice.

"He'll pull through. He's a tough lad. We've both seen him taking some hits playing turtle backing. We just have to keep at it until a better alternative presents itself."

"But how do you know one will? Should I run ahead and bring them back?"

"No, you're injured too. What would happen if you ran across a wild animal or, heaven forbid, a monster."

Worry came through in Cassandra's words. "Well, I, I just can't sit here and do nothing."

Gerterma took a deep breath. "We are resting. We haven't given up any hope of keeping him alive, understand?"

Cassandra nodded her head up and down.

"Secondly, I know you have feelings for young Mr. Manatado here. Don't let those feelings cloud your judgment."

Cassandra's first reaction was to deny the accusation, but she thought better of it and said nothing at all. She expected Gerterma to go on talking, but he never did, and after a long time, her thoughts finally vocalized. "I mean, I don't know. I don't think I love him, but then he gives me this smile . . . and I just want to run up to him and kiss him as hard as I can. Then I see him drooling over Malada and I just want to kill him with jealously. But then I think, Malada's my friend and she could use a good guy like Manatado. Then he does something stupid and I'm mad at him, but I can't stay mad at him so . . . it's just all so confusing."

Gerterma never interrupted her, but he did stand up and approach her, and as she finished, he signaled for her to stand up and give him a big hug. Gerterma then let out a big sigh. "I never experienced love. I was always too involved in my duties to make the time. Nor did I ever find the courage to pursue those who did catch my eye. I never had any children of my own, so I guess I feel fatherly toward you and the others. I'm not sure this is the best piece of advice I can give you, but here it is. Pursue him. Then if he chooses elsewise, forgive him and move on."

Cassandra nodded in understanding and took a moment to compose herself. "What is this all about? Why am I being shot? Why is Manatado lying here near death?

Why, why can't we just be back at the village going to school?"

Gerterma sighed and thought about his answer. "I don't believe in fate. I do believe in coincidence, and I do believe we forge our own way in life. Yet I also don't believe we do it alone."

Cassandra didn't speak, but she pointed at herself questioningly.

Gerterma shook his head left and right in response. "No, I'm not talking about companionship. I'm talking about a higher power, something that connects the magic to the science to the people to the world."

Cassandra shook her head, confused. "No, I mean, why are we even out here? I like Malada, but why shouldn't we just say that's enough help and good luck?"

"And do what?"

Cassandra replied with a blank look and then thought out loud. "I don't know, go back to the village and let me and Manatado heal."

"Then what? They will just ship you off to defense-force training as soon as you're healthy. Then you will be an ally of Jalum's, doing his bidding."

Cassandra shook her head, indicating that's not what she wanted. "Then we run off to some remote place and just wait for things to happen."

"What if when you return, the world is under Jalum's control? Think of this. Just a couple weeks ago, he was the secretary general of the defense force. Now with the bulk of the political leadership lost with Athenia, he has become the de facto head of the human race. At that point, what would you give to have an opportunity to come back here now and change that fate?"

"But we're near death. Stuck here in the middle of the forest, what could we possible do? I don't even think we can save ourselves."

"Be patient. Something will present itself. Now rest up. We have a long walk possibly ahead of us."

With that, Cassandra slowly fell onto her back and cried herself to sleep.

Chapter 28

The animals and insects presented a meal of nuts and leaves for Cassandra to eat. Salad had never been her favorite, but once she tasted fresh lettuce, she changed her mind. A loud knock from the tiny door announced the handsome boy's entrance. He entered the same size as Malada, his tree branch switching as needed. He walked up to Malada with a blank stare and no emotion on his face. "He has caught us. We must go meet him."

The handsome young man held Malada tightly as they exited the tree and were gently lowered to the ground. The two stepped in front of the Socratea tree and nervously stood before Jalum.

Jalum leaned at the hip against a cane as he stood several meters away in the middle of an open field. Jalum kept his head down as his words seemed to thunder throughout the valley. "Ah, Malada, there you are. Please come here."

Malada exchanged glances with the zombie-faced handsome young man. "I'm not a Malada. Perhaps you have the wrong tree."

Jalum shook his head as he looked up. "I might have expected something so trivial from your little puppy dog Manatado, but from the daughter of the great Eratrea, I greatly expected more from you, my dear."

Malada's demeanor greatly intensified in energy and anger. "What did you do to my mother?"

"Nothing she wasn't already predisposed to. Now with you under my thumb, it will be so much easier to control her. Now, my patience wears thin. Come here, Malada."

Malada grabbed the handsome boy's hand with one hand and her shield with the other. "Can you defeat him?"

The handsome boy looked blankly at her. "NO, he possesses the power of fire."

Malada asked, "How can he? He doesn't control magic."

"He doesn't control fire with magic but with science, and its power is devastating to us."

Malada gulped. "I will not come. How about you bring my mother here?"

Jalum flung the cane out from its resting position and removed the outer covering. There, in a cylinder, was a molten rock, and the item was shaped like a rifle. Jalum then shrugged his shoulders. "OH, well this way is more fun anyways."

Jalum raised the weapon and a burst of fiery hot lava flew through the air, but Malada was quick to react and held her shield up high and jumped in front of the blast. The lava ball vanished into the shield, but its presence horrified the Socratea tree and the young man howled. The tree slammed its roots down into the ground, and a powerful wave of energy spread out like a wave through the forest.

Jalum let loose another blast of his weapon, aiming up high this time. The lava ball burnt thought the canopy of the Socratea tree as it lit up in flames. The young man screamed out in pain and launched himself high into the tree near the flames. The tree uprooted itself and ran off.

Malada, now alone, turned and faced Jalum.

"What a pathetic showing. I knew your power was a shallow comparison to your mother's, but if this is the best you can do, then you are useless as anything other than a prisoner and motivation for your mother."

"I'm not my mother. I will never join you and your wicked ways."

"My dear, you don't seem to listen either. I don't care about you. You are nothing more than a possible remedy for your mother's irritating independence."

The comment struck Malada in a way that instantly made her feel better about her mother.

"Now if you don't want to fill your role, I have no need for another prisoner. So for the last and final time, come here, Malada."

Malada's fear was transparent, but her resolve to meet it was equal. She had no idea how to attack this man. She had no idea how to flee from this man, and as she looked around, she found nowhere that would be safe from his weapon. Her only solace was her shield. That's when it came to her, and just like in the forest, Malada fell to her knee and let the shield wrap around her.

She hugged the shield tightly, expecting Jalum to somehow grab hold and pull at it. Instead, after a few long moments, she got a verbal reply.

"Malada, won't you please come out. You can't stay in there forever."

"I can stay in here long enough!"

For another few moments, nothing happened before another verbal exchange. "I grow weary of these dreadful games and wonder if it's even worth the trouble."

Malada had no plan, no means of escape. She felt like a trapped animal. She held on to her shield as tightly as she could, expecting a pull, push, or jerk that never came. Instead, from directly below her, the dirt fell out from beneath her, and Jalum grabbed her by the ankles. She lost the shield as her body jerked with the force of his grab. He whisked away the shield and expertly reduced it to its smallest size and placed it in his pocket.

Jalum and Malada seemed to rise like magic, but as they broke back out onto the surface, the face of a large burrowing animal winced in the sun and gently dropped its master Jalum gently on the ground. The monster then scurried back away into the darkness below ground.

Jalum raised Malada up almost to the point of being eye level, so long was his reach. "Now that I have everything I need and want, I no longer believe you are worth the hassle." Jalum then threw Malada high into the sky directly above the pit.

Jalum was annoyingly surprised when the handsome young man came swinging back through, catching Malada in midair. He grunted in frustration and raised his lava gun. This time, however, to each and every side stood a large Socratea tree. To his left was a large black gorilla a Socratea tree had bonded with. To his right, a fierce-looking goblin stood with an arrow at the ready on a large stout branch.

Jalum's face mimicked a masterful poker player, his face displaying no emotion at all. "Oh well, I guess we take care of two things at once, not the most efficient use of my time but productive nonetheless. Jalum then moved to raise and fire his weapon.

Chaos erupted as tree after tree launched themselves in full attack mode. An early hit reignited the tree with Malada and the handsome boy. She was thrown to the ground as it reacted in pain. Fire, screams, and pain filled the whole area as death and smoke filled the air.

Malada couldn't stand it anymore. The thought of all this death and pain coming because of her brought forth something powerful. Her heart reached out with all its ferocity, releasing an energy wave of immense power. It spread out like a tidal wave in all directions. Nothing was left in its wake except Malada, who fell to the ground where she stood and lay completely motionless.

Chapter 29

Malada's body shook and trembled as the dust exhaled from her lungs. Cough after cough stirred her body back to life as it searched for clean air among the dust. Her eyes squinted and her body felt stiff as the dust clung to every bit of her skin. She wiped it from her face and opened her eyes again as a small creature stood before her with a broom in hand. The creature swept the broom in her direction, sending another blanket of dust on top of her.

Malada rolled over onto her knees and with difficulty spit out the words, "Stop it." She turned her head toward the small creature but was hit in the face with the broom as it started sweeping across her face. She pushed back against the broom, but it returned again and brushed across her face.

"Stop it, stop it. What are you doing?"

The creature slunk back with its posture before blinking and again started sweeping her body with the broom. This time, Malada slapped the broom away and got up to her feet. The creature moved back as if in order to run but stopped short. Malada slapped her hands against her clothes, sending a big dust ball into the air. Again the small creature scurried within arm's reach of Malada, running its broom over the side of her body.

"Stop it, stop it. What are you doing?'

This time, the creature paused, blinked, and spoke. "Dusting."

"Okay, okay, but why are you dusting me?"

"Need dusting." The creature's innocent round face bore a cute look of perplex-ion.

"What happened? Where is Jalum? Where are the Socratea trees?" Each new question came with an increased sense of urgency.

The creature looked for a long moment at her and then turned around and started sweeping in the other direction. Malada felt no threat from the little creature, so she paused to look around. The forest was gone. A large circular swath of land had been stripped of its trees and now lay barren in the middle of the forest. A thick layer of dust now covered the entirety of the area. There was no sign of anybody else.

Malada turned around in pointless circles, desperate for a sign of what to do next. Her thoughts often turned to her new friends Manatado, Cassandra, and Gerterma, and now she missed them desperately. At first, Malada was resolved to race back to them, but she had no idea which direction to go. She tried and tried but could not come up with a next step.

A tear came to her eye as she sat in the middle of a barren field, but before it could fall, a gut-wrenching cough came out from across the field. That little creature was now running its brush against something on the ground. Cough after cough sent large balls of dust into the air. Malada jumped up to her feet and starting running in their direction. She came to a screeching and disappointing halt as she recognized who it was in the dust.

It was Lukinia, and now that she had recovered some, she waved her wand and a powerful gust of wind shot down out of the sky and pushed the little creature back toward Malada.

Malada took cover for the few moments the wind held and then ran up and squatted next to Lukinia. "Oh, thank God. You came after me. I wouldn't even know what to do without you!" Swept away with relief and guilt, she moved in to hug Lukinia, who quickly dodged.

"Ah, yeah, yes. Do you have the shield still?" Lukinia asked with a hint of guilt in her voice.

"No, I was so afraid that you were mad at me because Manatado's such a little puppy dog. I mean, he's cute, but I don't know. I'm just happy you're here to help me."

"Ah, yeah, yes. Where is the shield?"

"Jalum took it. Where is everyone else? Did anyone get hurt? What do we do now?"

Lukinia's face turned red with anger. "I don't believe this. I'm sent out here with these useless stupid humans, who lose one of our most prized possessions, and now it's my responsibility to get it back." Lukinia paced back and forth before she stopped and turned to face Malada. "NO, this is all your fault. You will chase after that madman, and you will return our shield. I will be watching!"

With that, Lukinia vanished, leaving a dumbfounded and emotional Malada behind.

Chapter 30

The marching was exhausting, while the hope of success was quickly fading. Every time Cassandra would stop to protest their current state, Gerterma would reply with a scowl cutting her off. Frustration was nearing its meeting point of fatigue when Gerterma signaled for them to stop.

Together with Cassandra, Gerterma laid Manatado down softly and gently on the ground. Manatado's pale face and labored breaths pained Cassandra as she forced herself to look away. She lamented Malada's absence and missed her new friend dearly.

Gerterma motioned for Cassandra to stay low and still before he quietly got up and moved off into the brush. It was a long time before he returned, and Cassandra smelled his approach long before she heard the thunderous stomping. Cassandra stood up with fear and trepidation as Gerterma came forth, leading behind him the large Aradoro beast they had fought in the gnome village.

"Gerterma! Are you kidding me? What is that thing doing here?"

Gerterma raised his finger to his lips and rubbed the monster's face several times before it turned in a circle and lay down. Cassandra stood guard over Manatado, dumbfounded and in shock.

"But, Gerterma, didn't we just try to kill that thing a couple days ago?"

Gerterma gave a stern look at Cassandra as if to say, "Never mind!"

"Okay, okay, what's the plan?"

Gerterma pointed at Cassandra and then at Manatado's stretcher. Then he pointed at the monster's tail, indicating that it would be pulled. He then pointed at himself and then at the monster's torso when he made the riding motion. "Ever ride an Aradoro?"

Cassandra looked down at Manatado and knew that she couldn't bear to see him die, but she couldn't give up hope either. She then pointed at herself, then at the torso, and finally at Gerterma and Manatado.

Gerterma looked for a very long time at Cassandra, so long in fact that it brought tears to her eyes. Gerterma then gave her a big hug and started attaching the stretcher to the monster's tail.

Chapter 31

Malada cried into her hands until the gentle rustle of movement brought her head up. The little creature from before was now holding out his hand, palm up. Malada wiped away the tears and looked directly at it. The creature opened its mouth and blew a large handful of dust right into her face.

She coughed as she yelled, "What are you doing? Stop that! Stop that!"

The creature looked curiously at Malada. "Dusting?"

"Before, you were taking the dust off of me! What are you doing?" After a short pause, Malada answered her own question. "Ah, ha. Very funny. Now go away!"

The creature's face brightened up with a large smile. "Only one who lets oneself listen can hear the truth."

Malada wrinkled her nose, rolled her eyes, and turned away from the creature. "Go away!"

The creature's reaction was instantly one of sadness, and its head dropped as it turned to walk away. Guilt rose up in Malada after seeing the creature's reaction, but she still let the creature walk several steps away before calling out, "I'm sorry. I overreacted. Thank you for waking me."

"A big mess one makes alone. A good clean needs many hands."

"I'm sorry. I don't think I can help you . . . clean this up. I need to find my friends."

"One alone I did not find."

Malada brightened up. "Who else is here? Is it my friends?"

The creature looked dumbfounded and said nothing in reply.

"Oh, you mean Lukinia. I'm not sure she is a friend, but I don't think she is an enemy either."

The creature nodded its head. "To use the most powerful force, one doesn't diminish it. One strengthens it."

Deciphering what this creature meant was exhausting and frustrating. "What? I don't know what you mean? What is the most powerful force?"

The creature again brightened up with a smile and spoke in measured and clear tones. "A seeking mind is full of found treasure."

Uncertain what the creature meant, Malada lay back down in the dust and resumed her crying.

Chapter 32

The creature moved slowly and methodically. At each new tree junction, the creature would carefully try to avoid knocking over trees even if its sheer size made that impossible. Cassandra rode up front, her nerves and guilt preventing her from looking back.

The stretcher had been reinforced before being attached, and Gerterma was glad because the original binding was wearing thin. He knew Manatado was in a bad place physically, and he knew Cassandra was in a bad place emotionally, but he had no idea what kind of condition Malada was in. Overall, Gerterma felt like a failure. He kept his hand pressed against Manatado's chest as he heaved in and out in shallow breaths. Gerterma wished he knew how to give up. He wished he could just drop these kids off at the next village and tell them good luck and they were old enough to make up their own minds. Gerterma wished he could do many things, just like his brother.

The creature came to a halt and raised its head. The creature looked left, looked right, and was silent as if holding its breath. Gerterma wrapped his left arm around the bindings and his other arm around Manatado's waist and arm. Cassandra started wrapping the extra length of the reins around her ankles. The sound of silence took hold and dominated everything.

The Aradoro was being hunted. As any prey does, it hides until it runs.

The sound of a twig snapping started it off. The creature bolted as fast as it could through the dense forest. The creature hurtled over a large log, sending Cassandra off the creature and leaving her dangling along the side.

Gerterma braced himself and held on with all his might as the stretcher slammed into the log and shattered along his backside.

The creature dashed, skipped, and bulldozed for hundreds of meters before coming to a large clearing. The creature stopped as it neared the edge of a large field of wildflowers that ran along the foothills of the mountains. Cassandra's momentum swung her around the creature, slamming her into its armored plating headfirst. The collision knocked her unconscious as her body dangled lifelessly.

Gerterma and Manatado hit the ground and rolled without injury along the field of wildflowers. The creature turned and faced the brush as it refused to enter the open valley. After a long moment, a monstrously large troll smashed through some trees as it flung a heavy thick club. The trolled raised its club and tried to smash down on the Aradoro, but it was too quick and bolted off to the side. The troll quickly pursued the Aradoro out into the open valley.

Gerterma tried to chase after it, but he was left standing helplessly as Cassandra hung lifelessly from the Aradoro fleeing its pursuing troll.

Chapter 33

After some time, Malada cried herself out and sat up. The creature from before was now gone, along with everything else but dust. Off in the distance, she could see some rolling hills with the very tips of peaks poking out from behind. She knew they were heading for the mountains. Even if she knew nothing about dwarves, wizards, or even what to expect, it still felt like the right decision to carry on.

Walking proved to be more emotional than she had expected. Being alone with her thoughts often brought bouts of guilt, anger, sadness, and everything in between. Each new round of feelings manifested itself in Malada's body language. For anger, she would kick things or throw rocks. For sadness, she would cry or moan. Yet the most terrifying thoughts of all were of her mother. Malada finally had all the time and quiet she needed to think, but fear kept pushing it away.

The mountain snows must have been melting because Malada would frequently come across a stream or a river, often leaving her wet and cold from wading across. A few times, she even called out to Lukinia, hoping she was in fact nearby, but she never appeared.

As the distance Malada traveled grew, so did her weariness. It wasn't long before her head started to sag and her eyelids started to drop. Malada came up to a large log unexpectedly. She paused, waiting for the strength to climb over it.

With great effort, she threw her leg up onto the log but again came to a rest, her body lying against the large tree trunk. It felt like only a second she had rested her eyes when the sound of people approaching woke her. As she sat up,

Malada came face-to-face with a group of young male dwarves, all of whom were pointing weapons at her.

Chapter 34

A loud whistle brought forth a volley of nets as they crashed down upon the Aradoro. The large animal came to a sudden halt as its face crashed down and pummeled through a large pile of dirt. The flaps of its armor waved about as the massive creature crashed down.

The pursuing troll in full sprint tripped over its target and smashed down to its hands and knees. Another loud whistle blew, and another volley of nets came down, this time on the troll. The troll twisted, pulled, and yanked, but the more it moved, the more ensnarled it became.

After a long struggle, the troll grew tired and lost balance as its legs grew tired. The troll let out an anguished howl as it fell down motionless except for heavy labored breaths.

Gerterma stood dumbfounded and afraid as he watched from across the field as the Aradoro crashed down into the ground. He took several strides in that direction before retreating at the sights of the nets. Gerterma knelt next to Manatado and cursed his bad luck while fear grew in his heart.

Gerterma knew who the nets belong to, and this was the last way he wanted to be reunited. He looked down at Manatado, who was in bad shape and needed a doctor. Gerterma found his guilt pulling him in two directions, one away from the dwarves and the other toward. It was a decision Gerterma was dreading.

It was also a decision he wouldn't have to make, for before he could act on it, the whistle blew for a third time and he found himself encased in netting. Gerterma struggled with surprise but was quickly curled up and stuck.

A rugged and tough-looking dwarf approached with firm, confident steps. The dwarf made a plucking sound with his mouth before speaking. "Well look here, boys. I think today we have an answer to so many questions." The dwarf put his foot up on Gerterma's shoulder and waved close all the nearby dwarves. "Today, brothers, we have accomplished much. Not only have we captured two of the more bothersome monsters in these lands . . ." A jeer came up from the crowd. The lead dwarf continued on. "No, more than that. Today, here, we have captured the one who unleashed these beasts upon us!"

A pause of silence overtook the small crowd of dwarves before a roaring cheer of relief and accomplishment filled the whole valley. "Now, my brethren, NOW WE CAN HAVE OUR REVENGE!"

"Tell us, Itarus, who have we captured?" an anonymous voice asked from the crowd of assembled dwarven warriors.

Itarus stood as tall as a dwarf could, and pure pride shined across his face. "This, my brethren, is the instigator of it all. This human, this nasty evil beast of a creature, is the one who unleashed the dreaded Riftia upon our king, killing him. Yes, YES, this is the creature who brainwashed our beloved Nicolda! This is the creature who controls the monsters who, time after time, attack us! Yes, my brethren, we have indeed taken a large prize and perhaps even shifted the momentum of this war to our side!" Itarus raised his arm with bow in hand as he led his men in several rounds of cheers.

Chapter 35

A thick bushy-faced dwarf approached Malada with its bow and arrow at the ready. A pack of dwarves surrounded them, also with bows at the ready. She sat as still as possible, but nerves and fear required labored breath. The dwarf signaled for her to raise her hands. She raised both arms straight into the sky.

"Human, explain what happened here!" The bushy-faced dwarf had some snap in his voice as he spoke.

Malada, ever fearful of disclosing her magical abilities, instantly lied out of habit. "I don't know. I was running away from it all."

The dwarf humphed. "Explain your presence there to begin with."

Malada's eyes expressed a moment of surprise as her lie was so easily torn apart. "I was fleeing, um, I was fleeing an evil human." Her eyes again flashed with surprise as she realized the truth of her intended lie.

The dwarf approached to within an arm's reach of Malada, his face intensely studying her. "Explain, then, why this evil human was after you!" The stern voice snapped after every final syllable.

Malada was unprepared for this conversation. So many times while on the run, she had seen her mother so gracefully and smoothly disarm others. She grew frustrated at herself for not being able to do the same. Her head tilted down as she dropped eye contact. "I, I . . . I was with my mother . . . when, when they came to raid our village. I . . . I just started running."

The dwarf moved his head in even closer, bringing his eyes directly in front of Malada. "I don't believe you."

The words were harsh even if spoken softly. The dwarf took a couple steps back, bow still at the ready. Malada wiggled her arms, indicating they were tired. The dwarf kept his bow at the ready but signaled it was okay for her to relax.

A few other dwarves approached and grouped around the bushy-faced one. They spoke for a very long time, a strong sense of urgency in their tone. After several conversations, the bushy-faced dwarf again slowly approached Malada.

"We have NOT decided if we trust you. You will place yourself in the restraints we give you and will walk in the center of the group as we take you to the regent. The regent will decide for himself your role and what you know of the magic battle."

Chapter 36

The new group of dwarves rushed forward and broke the chants with news of another two humans. Commotion broke out as there was an urgent call for a doctor. Again, another call for a doctor came from across the field as some dwarves approached the Aradoro and Cassandra.

The commotion lasted a long while as Gerterma sat with his hands restrained behind him. He knew what they would think, and he knew what was about to happen. He loosened his body and readied for pain. It didn't take long either before a full-on body slam blindsided him from behind. Gerterma face planted in the dirt and coughed out some dirt as Itarus approached.

Itarus placed his hands upon Gerterma's ears. "YOU MONSTER! What did you do to these children? YOU ARE UNREDEEMABLE!"

Gerterma thought about protesting his innocence but instead resigned to his fate as rock after rock came pummeling in at him. He placed his face down in the dirt, as he didn't want them to see him cry. It was more than the pain that made Gerterma cry; it was the failure. He had promised to protect the children, and now they lay near death, and he was to blame.

"STOP IT! STOP IT! YOU'RE KILLING HIM!" Cassandra broke away from the dwarven doctor's grasp and limped at full speed to Gerterma's side. A few stray rocks pounded into Cassandra's side, but she succeeded in stopping the barrage. She placed her hands and arms around Gerterma, acting as a shield. With tears in her eyes, she turned to face the dwarves. "I thought you were a civilized society. YOU know nothing, NOTHING, and yet you throw stones."

Itarus approached with a cold, hard look on his face. "Perhaps, girl, it is you who knows nothing." Itarus stood up straight and called out his next order. "Tie them all up and place the evil one on the front of the cart so we can display our fine catch to the rest of dwarven kind.

Chapter 37

Malada was placed in the center of a cart and told very explicitly not to leave or get off the cart until told to do so. She was uncertain of what the dwarves thought of her but found it very reassuring when they gave her a loaf of bread. She didn't realize how hungry she was, and after she'd greedily consumed the first one, the dwarves offered another, and then another.

Malada had never felt so hungry, but after consuming three loaves and a bowl of buckleberries, she was too embarrassed to ask for more. The food and water was in abundance for what would normally be given to a prisoner, so Malada didn't quite feel like one. However, she was clearly not allowed to go where she wished, so in that way, she did feel like a prisoner.

The armed dwarves surrounding her tipped the scales in favor of prison, and Malada started to take on that mindset. Now that she had eaten and rested some, Malada finally found her mind able to think again. Her thoughts raced about all of the sudden unknowns she may never find out about. Would she ever see Manatado and Cassandra again? What happened to the Socratea tree and the handsome boy? What happened to Jalum?

The cart ride was long, but the dwarves were skilled animal trainers and frequently swapped out tired animals for fresh ones as they progressed up the ever-steepening mountains. The road was not in very good shape, and the group often had to find ways around rock slides and collapsed tunnels.

At one point, a young dwarven guard came within earshot of Malada, who had become so bored and nervous she needed someone to talk to. "What happened here?" She tried to whisper as she asked.

The guard looked at her with a frustrated growl, but after a moment or two, it softened. "Riftia." Malada looked carefully for the body language to encourage further conversation but received a cold, hard shoulder and spiteful words. "The monster humans unleashed upon us."

Malada thought about protesting, but the guard was back in formation and growling at her. The guard's body language softened as the cart crested a hill, and there before them, stretching out for the entire valley, were dwarven huts spread around hundreds of campfires. The guard from before approached Malada and spoke with a harsh tone. "The homeless, the lost, and the forgotten. All of it is the humans' fault!"

Itarus approached in quick strides and pushed the guard back into formation. "Human found in the woods, this is your destination. This is where your fate will be decided. This is the home of Davenwood, regent of the dwarves.

Chapter 38

It was a long, uncomfortable ride. Gerterma was tied with his hands bound to his ankles behind his back. His back ached, and every bump brought discomfort or pain. The road they were traveling on was in bad shape. Rock slides, disabled vehicles, and missing bridges all slowed down the group.

Cassandra was placed on a separate cart loaded with supplies and meat from the animals they had hunted. Even with the large amount of salt they put on, it still stank. Cassandra was tied up but in a much more comfortable position. The dwarves did not interact with her much. Yet they did go out of their way to torture Gerterma. Every time after going over a large pothole or rock, they would intentionally reverse back over it just to bounce him around.

The final approach to their destination was illuminated by a steady increase in the number of campfires along the way. Dirty children sang songs as worn-out and ragged females tended to pots of thin, sparse soup. Few if any buildings remained. The empty frames of magnificent buildings from not long ago still scattered about were now nothing more than a skeleton of the past.

Two large columns of fire flanked either side of a large cave entrance, the flames reaching almost high enough to escape the nearby mountaintops. A large gathering of warrior dwarves had gathered about and was cheering praise for Itarus and his men.

At last, the cart came to a stop at the mouth of the cave. Silence came over the dwarves as a finely dressed gray-haired dwarf approached from out of the cave. The regent approached Gerterma and bent down to look him in the eyes. A roar of laughter came out from the warriors as finally a dwarf looked down on a human.

The regent then got on top of the cart and invited Itarus to join him. Together they raised their hands, and a joyous roar came from the crowd. The regent then used his hands to quiet the crowd.

"Itarus has brought the Clandine Clan much honor here today!"

Again the assembled dwarves hollered out in joy.

"Riftia destroyed first our king, then our kingdom! But now at long last, Itarus has brought us the very one who unleashed that terrible monster upon us."

Cheers came out from the crowd.

"Tonight we celebrate, for there is much honor to be bestowed! Then, tomorrow, we have our revenge!"

Chapter 39

Malada was brought to the center of a massive hollowed-out cave. Thick pillages lined the edges as huge support beams for the ceiling of rock above. The room was dark, with only a few torches keeping the light along the edges of the great hall. A scattered handful of guards stood at the far edges, attending to each and every exit.

The hall was desperately quiet, the guards motionless with a practiced and attentive hand. An ominous roar of a faraway crowd made Malada very nervous. The roar came again and again but eventually broke off into a steady stream of a party as music gently filled in the spaces.

A cold wind brought forth a dark silhouette of a dwarf's figure now standing before Malada. The dwarf was covered with a hoodie and seemed to move without any motion on the ground. The temperature in the hall dropped quickly, and Malada felt a deep chill in her bones.

The breath blew white with frost as the dwarf figure spoke. "Who is your master?"

Malada felt fear but, like a cornered animal, she was ready to fight. "I serve no master!"

The temperature dropped even more, and Malada shivered uncontrollably. The dwarf figure slid to her left, but again there was no motion. This time, however, Malada noticed something at the dwarf's feet: ice. The floor froze before the dwarf slid effortlessly across it.

A strong, cold wind twisted down from the ceiling above, knocking Malada out of her stance and onto a knee. "WHO IS YOUR MASTER!"

Malada's fear was starting to overtake her resolve, but she still managed to repeat the words. "I . . . serve no . . . master."

This time, lightning came with the freezing wind. "WHO IS YOUR MASTER!"

Malada felt the hairs on her arms and neck jump, and with it her fear. "Mommy, I want my mommy!" She fell to her knees, covered her ears, and started crying.

Again, deafening bolts of lightning preceded the words. "You admit your master is Eratrea!"

The mention of her mother's name unleashed a flood of tears. Malada didn't even know what to say. Then she said the truth. "No, she is my mother. I am her daughter."

Two large columns of flames exploded on each side of the great hall, but as the flames retreated, the light stayed and the room warmed quickly. The dwarf figure approached Malada and drew back their hoodie.

Malada looked up and fought back the tears. The figure wasn't a dwarf at all. It was the benign creature from the field.

This time, the creature smiled a big warm smile at her. "Then we have much to discuss." The creature approached, embracing her, and Malada felt a sense of warmth and comfort she had never experienced before. The creature then pulled back, looking at the entrance to the hall. The rattling of chains indicated the opening of a large door. The creature looked at Malada. "Virtues are only earned. Take heed and we shall meet again."

The flames of the torches running alongside the hall dimmed or were extinguished with the return of the cool wind. Malada turned her head as the door creaked back closed. She turned her body about but noticed that the little creature was gone—along with any evidence it was ever there.

Two guards entered and stood to each side of the door. A finely dressed white-haired dwarf removed his hood as he approached Malada. She was on her knees but adjusted her feet in case she needed to jump away. The dwarf raised both his arms and waved his finger. A group of dwarven warriors rushed the room and grabbed hold of Malada. She tried to fight them off but was outnumbered and outmuscled.

Malada fought against them, but her strength was insufficient. The finely dressed dwarf walked in front of her and looked deep into her eyes. "You are a mysterious human. I am the regent of the dwarves. I am regent because YOUR KIND unleashed a terrible foe upon us." The regent started to walked a slow circle around Malada.

"It must just be some amazing consequence that shortly after our last city has fallen, three humans just happened to show up."

Malada reacted to the news about three humans. Who were the three? Malada held out hope he meant Cassandra, Manatado, and Gerterma.

"Are you part of the human scouting party sent here to determine what force is necessary to destroy us?"

Malada looked dumbfounded. Gerterma certainly had a way of leaving behind strong and diverging opinions about him just about everywhere he ever went. Malada's pause wasn't taken well by the regent, who signaled one of the warriors, who slowly started bending her arm in a way that brought pain.

"Ow, ow, OW, THAT HURTS. STOP IT!"

"Confess you are with the humans!"

"No, no, well yes, but no, it's not what you think!" A sense of panic rose up in her voice.

"Gibberish and LIES! Where will the humans attack from?"

Malada swung her head back and forth. "NO, NO, NO!"

The warrior dwarf continued to twist her arm, and it was nearly breaking.

The regent signaled for the dwarf to lighten up the pressure but not cease. The regent finished his first circle around Malada. "Then you have much to explain. Let's start with a simple question. Are you human?"

Chapter 40

Gerterma's head was placed in a black sack, and he was rolled onto a stretcher, his arms and legs still bound behind him. The dwarves chanted songs of victory as they carried him down deep into the dungeon. "Where the orcs' bland lay, the dwarves' name they shall make! Humans lay maimed, hero we have made!"

Cassandra was taken to a different room. She tried desperately to see what they were doing with Manatado but was hurried along. A second pack of dwarven warriors escorted her to a large barren room and didn't hesitate to poke her with tips of their sharp arrows in order to move her along. On the far side of the room, three large boulders were equally spread out. Cassandra was led to a pit in the center of the room, where she was made to wait in the darkest, deepest part of the room.

The pack of warriors spread out throughout the room, each armed with bow and arrow. While Cassandra was kept in place, a tremendous amount of commotion was going around about her. Whispers turned into shouts, but from her position, Cassandra couldn't hear the words clearly. Worries over Manatado, Gerterma, and of course Malada seemed to overshadow her fear about what would happen to her.

After some time, a loud chime rang out three times, summoning all the voices to silence. The room dimmed to a level just a little brighter than in Malada's pit. A bright-yellow light burst into life, shining down upon one of the large boulders. A second whistle, shriller than the first, announced the arrival of an elderly, white-haired dwarf. Elegantly dressed, he slowly made his way to the top of the nearest boulder.

Another whistle and light screamed its arrival as another elegantly dressed and elderly dwarf made his way to the top of the far boulder, leaving the middle one empty until a third whistle coincided with the arrival of the light above the last boulder. This time, an elderly and finely dressed female dwarf made her way to the top of the middle boulder. Together the three looked at each other and then bowed toward the darkness of the room.

A blinding bright light exploded above Cassandra as she dropped to her knees with the power of the light. A stream of boos and hisses came at her from the darkness. A loud voice speaking in dwarven began reading an announcement. Cassandra couldn't understand a word of it, and after her eyes adjusted, she stood up and—to her great shock—found a white-haired dwarf standing alongside her.

Cassandra jumped back into the corner of her pit as the light broke apart into two, one shining down upon each of them. After a pause in the reading, the dwarf next to Cassandra stood up straight and spoke in Malada's language with a booming voice. "I, Nicolda, stand ready to defend the accused, and we proclaim our innocence."

Chapter 41

Manatado opened his eyes with great strain. He was in an all-white tiled room. Two fluorescent lights paralleled above him, illuminating the room. The electronic sounds of beeping and buzzing gave the place the feel of a hospital. After his eyes had adjusted, he turned his head as three people rushed into the room. The first was a dwarven warrior armed with bow and arrow at the ready. Second came an older dwarf wearing a white clock, and closely behind him came a young human male also dressed in a white cloak.

Manatado ran his eyes toward some movement at the foot of the bed, where he saw Lukinia, and she didn't look happy. The young human doctor knelt at the side of the bed and grabbed Manatado's wrist and was squeezing it while counting. A gentle-but-noticeable prickling feeling climbed along Manatado's body as Lukinia walked atop him.

Lukinia approached Manatado's face while waving her finger at him. "You are by far the worst trophy boyfriend I have ever had! Look at you! You look like death. What girl would want a boy like that? NOT THIS ONE!"

Manatado tilted his head toward the human doctor. "Please tell me I'm going to die."

The human doctor finished his counting and then looked up and shook his head while giving the thumbs-up sign.

Manatado felt his head tug back toward Lukinia, who was holding on to his chin. "I'm talking to you! Now I'm going to have to lay some new ground rules or this is never going to work. First off, you are never to be alone with either of those two girls again! Second, you are to be at my beck and call always. And you will clean yourself up and get out of this dirty, gross place right AWAY!"

Manatado shook his head throughout Lukinia speaking, but she didn't even notice, and after finishing, she turned around and started walking away.

It took effort and caused pain in his ribs, but Manatado forced it out. "No, no, no, Lukinia."

Lukinia stopped dead in her tracks. "What did you say?"

"No." Manatado coughed. "I won't be your trophy boy. I'm not a thing."

Lukinia approached him and spoke with a sinister voice. "You're cute when you stand up for yourself. NEVER DO IT AGAIN!"

Manatado shook his head again. "NO, no, Lukinia."

Lukinia looked angrily into Manatado's eyes. She then enlarged herself to be a similar size to Malada as she sat on top of him. She then bent down and kissed Manatado. Once she finished, she pulled back and slapped him very hard across his face. "YOU, you and those pathetic friends of yours will return the shield or you will pay!" Lukinia then whispered into his ear. "And if I want you, I will have you."

Lukinia then disappeared, leaving Manatado and the young human doctor with dumbfounded looks.

Chapter 42

An unseen crowd jeered and hollered as Nicolda announced his name.

"Human lover!"

"Traitor!"

"BOOO!"

Yet there were other cheers mixed in with applause as well.

"We believe in you!"

"You're my hero!"

The intensity of the crowd made for an electric emotional mix in the large chamber.

The female dwarf at the center boulder slammed a stone down against the top of the boulder, echoing out both sound and sparks. After a moment, the crowd silenced. "The guilt of the human known as Gerterma has been determined in absentia." Again the crowd erupted into a chorus of jeers and applause.

Three times, the female judge had to slam her stone down in order to hush the crowd. "We are here today, ONLY to determine the nature and connection of this human present here to the traitor Gerterma."

Nicolda took two steps forward and raised his arms to hush the crowd. "We do not accept the court's absentia decision and protest to this entire proceeding!" A round of applause came from unseen supporters, but they seemed far fewer in number than the others.

Again the female judge slammed her stone down. "Enough, you will proceed with your defense or we shall rule summarily!"

Nicolda sent a nasty look only a second long, but long enough for the female judge to see it. "Again the evidence will show that this trial is nothing more than the same witch hunt as the first, with the primary object to be finding a scapegoat for the failures of the political leadership!"

A bolt of electricity shook Nicolda's body as he fell to the floor. The female judge spoke loudly, her voice echoing off the wall. "Need I remind you again, counsel, that you are already in our custody for your outspokenness? This will be your last chance."

Nicolda fell to a knee, composed himself, and stood up tall and proud. "Very well, Your Majesty, I will proceed with the questioning." He turned to face down into the pit where Cassandra sat with her hands tied in her lap. A bright spotlight blinded her, and her hand reactively rose to block out the light. Nicolda approached the edge of the pit and spoke outwardly toward the unseen crowd.

"Please rise and begin by telling the magistrates your name and race." Nicolda then tilted his head down and looked firmly at Cassandra.

Cassandra struggled to get up with her hands bound but eventually managed, though a few smirks and giggles could be heard throughout. Cassandra cleared her throat and spoke but was interrupted by Nicolda, who asked her to speak up.

"Uh, um, YES, I am Cassandra Nighttorn, and I am a human from Valentina."

Nicolda paused for a long second. "Now tell us your age and occupation."

Cassandra took a moment to realize what they were asking. "I'm, I'm fifteen and I go to school. Or at least I used to."

Nicolda nodded approval of her answer. "And what did you study at that school?"

"A little of everything. I like to think I'm pretty good with math, but I don't know."

"And who did you study from at this school?"

"Oh, many teachers. There was Mrs. Randell, Mrs. Jamel—"

The female judge smashed her stone, interrupting. "Get to the point, already!"

"Did you ever study under the human known as Gerterma?"

The air left the room at the question, but Cassandra didn't notice and boldly spoke the truth. "Yes, I have learned many things traveling with Gerterma, but—"

Before she could finish her answer, the room burst out in uproar. The female judge deliberately let the crowd vent out in uproar before she slammed her stone, restoring order. "It seems your case has just been made against you. She admits association with the bringer of death!"

Chapter 43

Malada's shoulder hurt as the warrior dwarf twisted it and her into submission. The regent grabbed her by the face and moved her hair out of the way so as to examine her ears. The question terrified Malada, and her thoughts froze. Did she even know the answer to that basic question, are you human?

The regent let go of her hair but slowly turned her face toward his. "Speak, girl, or I might just rip out your tongue and get my answers from the other one. Malada's fear doubled at the mention of one of her friends. "My, my . . . my grandfather was an elf."

"Lie, your ears are not those of an elf descendant. Now that you have proven your lack of truthfulness, I have no need for deception. TAKE HER AWAY!" The dwarven warrior twisted her arm, forcing Malada to turn and start walking.

Malada fought against the pain and yelled out, "NO, no, don't hurt my friends. I'll tell you. I'll tell you everything I know."

The regent raised his hand, halting the warrior. "Answer the question, are you human?"

Malada looked around desperately and then hung her head. "I, I, I don't know. We were traveling to the mountains, hoping to find the last of the wizard tribe."

The regent brought his hand to his face and, after rubbing his chin and beard, signaled for the guard to release her and for her to sit down. Malada moved before the regent and then sat cross-legged, at eye level with the dwarf. The regent repositioned himself to a more comfortable standing position but never let himself get lower than Malada.

"My parents didn't want to fight in the orc wars. So they ran. Then one day they found us. My father fought them off while my mother and I escaped. We never saw him again." Malada brought a tear to her eye as she spoke, trying to say as little as possible."

"What were you doing in that field all alone?"

Malada paused, trying to decide if she wanted to be affiliated with Gerterma. He said he was hated by the dwarves, but he was also the one bringing them there. The regent raised his hands for the guards.

"I was fleeing!" In an instant and without conscious thought, Malada made her choice.

"What were you fleeing? Were you alone?"

Malada's eyes bounced back and forth as she tried to think. "I saw a magic battle in the distance. I was afraid."

"Who are the other humans?"

"I don't know."

"But you said they are your friends." The regent looked her over and then nodded his head. "TAKE HER AWAY! Place her in the dungeon until her execution tomorrow."

Malada pulled back against the guards as they came to collect her. "NO, WAIT. My mother, Eratrea, will be very angry."

The regent paused dead in his tracks and turned around with a look of terror on his face. "What name did you just say?"

"Eratrea, my mother is Eratrea." Now that it had been said out loud, Malada instantly regretted it.

The regent's look of terror remained as he now signaled for the guards to back off. He then walked up to Malada. "No one is supposed to know that name. My empress has sent you to test me." The regent then fell to a knee. "I salute Her Royal Magistracy and pledge my loyalty to the one who can deliver us from Riftia."

Chapter 44

"I don't know what you think Gerterma has done, but he is no bringer of death. He is a good man!" Cassandra found her anger overcoming her anxiety and fear.

The unseen crowd again burst out into a mix of yells and cheers. Nicolda tilted his head and raised his fist, encouraging Cassandra to go on.

"Gerterma has been a selfless leader to my village since he left the defense force." The crowd burst out into boos at the mention of the defense force. "Gerterma and my father fought together, and he would be ashamed of how you are tarnishing a good man's name!" Cassandra felt alive with energy as she came to her father's defense. The crowd responded again with a mix of applause and jeers.

The female magistrate slammed her stone down. "Order, order! Human, you will not speak unless spoken to."

"You can't take away my rights. YOU CAN'T BADMOUTH GERT."

Again the stone came slamming down, over and over again. This time, Nicolda lowered his fist, and his body signaled for Cassandra to calm down. Cassandra, on the other hand, found herself getting carried away and thought about climbing up out of her pit.

Nicolda raised his hands and quieted the room. He then very calmly and steadfastly turned around and again began asking questions. "Have you ever heard of Riftia?"

Cassandra took a second, clenched her teeth, and then relaxed, as she had in fact heard that name before. "Yes, ah, yeah, one of the dwarves guarding me mentioned that name when I asked about all the destroyed buildings."

"Did you know that there are many, even those here now, who believe the fact that Riftia arrived almost immediately after our king denied the human request is proof of his guilt?"

Cassandra looked a little dumbfounded, as she didn't quite understand what he wanted her to say. "Um, yeah, I guess I can agree that looks suspicious. BUT Gerterma could never do such a thing."

"OH, and why is that?"

Cassandra looked down at her hands before answering "Because Gerterma isn't really that good a warrior. He was nearly killed by one of those . . . Aradoros? I just don't see how he could do such a thing. Now Jalum, yeah, I could see him being capable of doing such things. That guy is scary powerful."

The female magistrate slammed her stone down a single time, pausing the proceeding, and together with the other two judges, they huddled together and spoke in hushed tones. The crowd remained oddly silent at the mention of Jalum's name. After a few minutes, the judges returned and signaled for Nicolda to come closer. After receiving some instruction, he nodded and returned to Cassandra.

"Now, that name is also familiar to us. Nicolda, you will now get the witness to reveal what she knows of this name."

Nicolda bowed respectfully and turned back to Cassandra. "Please begin by telling us who Jalum is to you."

Cassandra felt like placing the blame on Jalum would be helpful, so she did. "Jalum is a very powerful and determined man. He is, or I mean he was, Gerterma's commanding officer and his younger . . ." She paused but then decided to say no more. She was nervous and had no idea what was at stake or whom to trust.

Nicolda saw her hesitation and acted fast by quickly asking a follow-up question in another direction. "What sort of powers and skill does this man have that makes him so dreadful?"

Cassandra's bound hands rose to her face as she thought, he can use science to control fire. I saw him use a weapon of fire to destroy many Socratea trees. That's what burned down the forest. Cassandra knew she was tiptoeing around the truth and knew she wasn't very good at it, but she also knew she had to protect her friends.

"And it was him that you were fleeing from with Gerterma and the others."

Cassandra nodded. "Yes."

"Tell us, then, what happened to the third in your party? How did he sustain such terrible injuries?"

"Before the battle, um, Jalum caught up with us. We delayed him while our friend . . . the Socratea tree escaped. Jalum injured Manatado and me as we attempted to delay him."

Nicolda looked back at the three judges as they conferred. After a long discussion, the female judge turned back toward the room. "We have heard enough. There is evidence enough to place this one in custody for further questioning. We will relocate to private quarters before continuing."

With that, Nicolda bowed, turned a little toward Cassandra, and gave her a smile and nod of approval that was very reassuring.

Chapter 45

Lukinia vanished after running her hand down along Manatado's face and chest. He felt totally dumbfounded, and he was noticing a connection to that feeling and the women in his life.

After a long moment, a human doctor coughed before speaking. "I'm, um, not quite sure how to transition from something like that. Let me, I guess, begin by saying, I'm Dr. Frances." Frances then waved his hands toward the elderly dwarven doctor barely visible from his position on the bed. "This is Dr. Florian. He is the dwarven expert on humans."

Manatado shifted upward and then nodded his head toward the little doctor. There was then a long pause before he continued. "Oh, yes, so as to your prognosis." Dr. Frances then looked down and began reading off a chart. "It seems you took a forceful blow to the chest and some of your ribs punctured your lung."

Manatado's hand ran to his chest. "Am I okay?"

"Oh, um, yes, skipping ahead, internal bleeding, broken ribs, hypoxia, but, um, yes, we were able to stabilize you, and we do believe you will make a full or nearly full recovery."

"Nearly?"

"Oh, to elaborate some, I would say there is a chance the lung may not fully recover, but that remains to be seen. This is only a temporary facility. We were quite limited in equipment and experience in humans."

"But aren't you a human doctor?"

"Oh, well, uh, yeah, I am a human and I did go to doctor school, to say, but I am a specialist in dwarves."

Manatado clenched his hand hard to his chest. "Are you sure you fixed me?"

The dwarf doctor Florian crossed his arms in protest and his temperament changed. Dr. Frances placed his hand on his comrade's shoulder. "I assure you, Dr. Florian is the very best, and none here can match his experience."

Manatado relaxed a little. "Whew, so how many human patients have you had?"

Dr. Frances's body tightened up as the two made eye contact and he spoke the first word very softly. "None. Now as for your rehabilitation, it will take several weeks."

Manatado clenched up, but his mind changed over to the idea of him being stuck in this room for several weeks. "Weeks? Can you just use some magic?"

Both doctors burst out with a chuckle. "A magic healer. He thinks we have a magic healer! I don't know where you come from, but there hasn't been a magic healer since the wizards left. The ability to heal is the rarest form of magic. But you don't need magic when you have Dr. Frances and Dr. Florian." The doctor's forced smile and patient rapport certainly needed work, but Manatado was thankful to be alive. "Well thank you, guys. I'm still happy to be alive regardless. Where are my friends?"

Dr. Frances pulled at his collar very nervously. "Well, um, we tended to your female companion . . . then she, um, was put on trial. Now tell us, how are you feeling?"

The verbal trick didn't work a second time, and Manatado reacted strongly. "ON TRIAL? For what?"

Dr. Frances now looked up at the room's cavern ceiling. "So, um, to that, you two were found with the traitor Gerterma, so she is on trial as an accomplice. Now, how are you feeling?"

Manatado's instinct was to jump out of bed, but something in his memory held him back. He tried to remember back to the story that Gerterma told, but all he could remember was holding Malada's hand. "Why do you think Gerterma is a traitor?"

This time, Dr. Frances's face became more stern and he looked directly at Manatado. "It was no mere coincidence that the very day our king denied Gerterma's request, the evil monster Riftia arrived to destroy our king. NO, I WAS HERE!" Dr. Frances took a big breath before continuing. "That was evidence enough. Then there was the second event."

"A second event?"

Dr. Frances looked Manatado up and down. "How old are you, boy?"

Manatado blushed a little bit. "I just turned fifteen a couple weeks ago."

"Well then, now that you're a man by human standards, don't you find it odd that as our regent was approaching Athenia to ask the other races for help, Riftia again appeared . . . and who was left outside the danger zone but Gerterma? And who, now, is the second-most powerful political figure left alive for humanity? Gerterma." Dr. Frances moved his clipboard behind his back. I'm a doctor. I use clues every day to find the source of the problem. In this case, it's not hard to see it's Gerterma."

Manatado wanted to defend Gerterma, but he really didn't know how to. Gerterma was the town prioritor, the town leader, yes, but Valentina wasn't even an important city. "I don't think I'm understanding what you're accusing Gerterma of."

"Are you dull, boy? Gerterma somehow has acquired the power to control the monsters, and he is using them to destroy all leadership but his own."

Manatado paused as he tried to absorb this information. "I can't believe what you are saying. I would like to speak at Cassandra's trial."

Dr. Frances looked down at Dr. Florian, who nodded approval. Dr. Frances walked up to the bed, unhooked a drip line, and helped Manatado into a wheelchair. Then he headed off into the corridor.

Chapter 46

The regent clapped his hands and a group of attendants came and immediately brought forth all necessities and luxuries they still had to offer. Eight dwarves walking in unison approached carrying a human-sized sedan chair. They then lined up and bowed, creating a formal pathway for Malada to sit on the chair.

Malada felt perplexed at what all this might mean—who was her mother? In this place, she was revered as a hero. Malada felt like she knew so little about her mother. When was her mother even here? Malada was too tired to refuse the offer, and as she sat on the most comfortable chair she ever had, she felt her body relax.

The dwarves placed lotions, oils, and fruits into the cups along the sedan chair. As they walked, a slew of female dwarves brought forth and placed on the moving chair elegant dresses, flowery accessories, and lavish decorated shoes. Malada had never felt like a princess before, and she was feeling a little guilty about how much she was starting to enjoy it.

They walked down a long corridor and then turned into a large dining hall. A large group of attendants was quickly decorating and preparing a large table in the middle of the hall. Malada felt guilt creep up again, as there were many unfinished plates left in front of empty seats.

The sedan chair came to a halt only a step or two away from a large throne-sized chair. Malada took her place at the head of a very large and empty table. As she sat down in her new seat, music erupted from some unseen corner of the hall, and attendant after attendant brought forth the most diverse and wonderful courses of food. There was wild mountain boar with potatoes and gravy, greens from the king's garden, and the freshest catch of sea bass along with plates holding mounds of fruits and nuts.

Malada hadn't had a proper meal since she last used her magic, and once she had tasted that incredible food, she couldn't get enough of it. Handful after handful of food stuffed itself into her mouth. Wines, juices, and spring water only washed it down smoother. By the time she was done, Malada had nearly eaten herself into a food coma.

Upon seeing her satisfaction, the regent once again appeared and bowed before Malada. "My lady's lady. I do hope everything has been to your satisfaction. When you are ready, we are ready to take you to the canyon, and I do believe my lady will be most satisfied with the results. The orc workers have been a true blessing."

The word "blessing" struck a cold chord in Malada's heart. The image of her mother killing that orc immediately began to replay itself in her mind over and over again.

The regent paused for just a moment, unsure of how to take the change in Malada at the mention of the orcs. "We have followed Lord Jalum's instructions as best we could. We did from time to time have to improvise . . . but, but I do believe my lady will be most satisfied."

Malada was feeling most perplexed, and her fatigue wasn't making it easy to sort things out. She thought about just asking for a room and a nap, but she also needed answers, and this might provide some. "I'm very tired, but due to the urgency of the situation, I do believe it better that we go sooner than later." Malada didn't really feel comfortable in this new role. Running through the forest with Manatado was so much easier, no deception, no manipulation. Here, she found it difficult to know who knew what. How far could she push it without really knowing her mother's true intentions?

Malada stood up, and as she did so, the regent rushed in with the sedan chair and its group of hosts. The regent then clapped his hands together. "To the Ruhr Canyon!"

Chapter 47

A group of warrior dwarves surrounded Cassandra and Nicolda as they were led down a corridor and entered a formal office. What would have been a very large desk for a dwarf lined the room, breaking it in two halves. Three chairs were placed in front of the desk, and another round of attendants brought in three lavish chairs and placed them behind the desk.

Nicolda sat at the first seat and motioned for Cassandra to do the same. After a long wait, the three dwarven judges entered the room and sat in the lavish chairs. The female judge started off first. "Well, Nicolda, you certainly seem to know how to muddy a clear situation. Gerterma was so furious with our king's denial that he went behind Jalum's back and summoned Riftia. Jalum, in his guilt, summons the lady of a hidden name, a woman so powerful she might be the only one who can stop Riftia. The price we paid to that woman was very high. Now, Nicolda, tell me how our narrative is wrong."

Nicolda cleared his throat. "Imagine, Your Honor, that instead of Gerterma being the one who unleashed Riftia, it was in fact Jalum." Nicolda paused for effect. "Isn't it just very convenient that Jalum would just happen to know the one person who could destroy the beast? Now, isn't it also unfortunate that she had just used up all of her magic in another fight and needed a great amount of resources to create a weapon? We demolished our building, vehicles, our industries to make a weapon that they never intended to use to help us."

Nicolda paused and turned around as if thinking while speaking. "Then, after we had given so much, wasn't it just too unfortunate that Riftia had grown more powerful, so much that nearly our entire kingdom was needed to build a weapon to destroy the beast?" Nicolda stood up and walked behind his chair. "I assert that we have been swindled by con artists who can no more destroy Riftia than we can."

The female judge replied, "Now that is a disturbing thought indeed. What proof of this theory can this girl provide?"

Nicolda slowly turned his head to look at Cassandra. "Well?"

Cassandra felt a strong sense of panic. "I, I, I don't know. I have been traveling with Gerterma . . . from the village.

The female judge snapped at Cassandra. "Enough of the omissions and lies. YOU WILL SPEAK CLEARLY AND TRUTHFULLY! Do I make myself clear?"

Cassandra nodded. "Yes, yes you do. I first met Gerterma when he came to my house to tell my family the news about my father." A tear started to form on her face, and a quiver formed in her voice. "He said my father died bravely, fending off an orc attack that saved his life. Gerterma said he would always do anything he could for me. He said I could always trust him to be my father now."

An unexpected knocking at the door startled everyone. The female magistrate shouted out, "You were told no interruptions."

The door opened and a warrior dwarf appeared, bowed, and then reported, "Yes, ma'am. This pertains to the situation at hand. As requested, the other human is feeling healthy enough to join his companion in interrogation."

The female judge replied, "Oh, yes, well of course, of course, send him and the doctor in."

The two walked in. Manatado, moving very slowly and gingerly, agreed to take the third seat. Dr. Frances helped his patient to the chair and then bowed and left the room.

The female magistrate continued along. "We are here now trying to ascertain the feasibility that the dwarves have been betrayed by one known as Jalum. Tell us, what do you say, who is the villain, Gerterma or Jalum?"

Manatado gave a quick glance at Cassandra, smiling with genuine happiness to see her. "Jalum. It was he who gave me these injuries."

"And how did he come to injure you?"

"Oh, he kicked me hard and broke some of my ribs."

"No, no, I mean by what circumstance did he come to attack you?"

Manatado felt confused by the legal nature of the question. "Uh, I don't have much fighting experience. I guess I didn't block his kick."

"No, no, no . . . what were you in the process of doing when he came across you to begin with."

Again Manatado misunderstood the question. "Oh, the first time I saw him was in the tavern, right before the Aradoro attack on the gnome village."

The female judge looked at Nicolda. "You seem to communicate better with the humans. Get me a clear understanding of what they were doing."

Manatado felt his heart light up a little at the smile Cassandra gave him, He could tell she was holding herself back from jumping up and giving him a big hug, and it was a feeling Manatado liked.

Nicolda looked at Manatado. "What the heck were you doing when Jalum kicked your butt?" The sharpness of Nicolda's voice was much different than his lawyer tone.

182

Cassandra tried to tell Manatado not to mention Malada, but he spoke before understanding. "We were taking Malada to see the wizards."

Cassandra ducked her head down as the scornful gaze of all three judge bore down upon her. Nicolda continued. "And who is Malada?"

Manatado now understood he had made a mistake, but he wasn't sure what it was. "Oh, um, yeah, we were . . . recruiting. Yeah, we were going to try to recruit the wizards for . . ." Manatado looked at Cassandra, hoping for help. Cassandra knew she wasn't any good at this either, so she just looked sad and said nothing.

Nicolda and the judges exchanged a nervous glance. "Recruit them like you recruited the dwarves?"

Manatado's face turned to a blank stare. "Um, yes . . . but without, you know, the death of the king stuff." His hand reached up and rubbed the back of his neck.

This time, another knock at the door provided a great sense of relief. Again the dwarf warrior entered and bowed. "Your Magistrates. The regent has announced the arrival of the Supreme Lady's representative, and you are all requested to meet them."

The dwarf then rose from his bow and exited. The three judges conferred for a long time before breaking up and returning to their lavish seats. Again the female magistrate spoke. "Nicolda, it has been decided that your witnesses can provide no evidence to support your theory, and they are ordered to join Gerterma in his execution."

Nicolda exploded in rage. "YOU CAN'T DO THAT. THAT'S PREPOSTEROUS. WHAT HAVE THEY DONE TO MERIT SUCH A PUNISHMENT!"

The female judge banged against the wall and a large group of dwarven warriors rushed into the room and placed all three in restraints. "Take them to Ruhr Canyon. It's time for the traitor Gerterma and his accomplices to pay for their crimes."

Nicolda again exploded in anger. "This was a farce, the whole time just an exercise in futility! You don't care about the truth at all, just politics!"

The female judge stood up and slammed a stone down on the desk. "Order, order, you will restrain yourself, counsel. You had an opportunity to prove your crackpot theory, and all you can give us is two lying human teenagers. No, sir, that is a poor, poor showing for one who used to be considered a most notable leader for our people. It is our decision that these two were traveling with the traitor in hopes of convincing the wizards to join them in their quests of conquest. No, it is our lady who will deliver us from Riftia, not some duped, lying teenagers."

"Where is your proof? Where is your proof?"

The female judge was angry. "If you persist in this insubordination, you can join these humans you seem so much to care about!"

"I would rather die with my honor than serve a false master!"

In a fury, the female judge slammed her stone down over and over again. "Very well, it is decided that you will share their fate. Now take them away."

Cassandra and Manatado looked at each other. Neither understood what was going on, but being labeled an accomplice to a traitor couldn't be a good thing. Cassandra's smile turned to a frown, and Manatado was scared. Together they reached out for each other and, without conscious thought, found themselves in a tight embrace.

Cassandra twisted and yelled in Nicolda's direction even if she couldn't fully see him. She could see a tussle between him and the guards. Nicolda roared out in a fury. "Politics. This is all about politics. Now that our political leader has made a decision, the search for the truth comes to a halt. Traitors! You are the traitors. Traitors to the truth!"

The judge again and again slammed her stone down on the desk, sparks and bangs seeming to fill the room. At the first break in Nicolda's rant, the female judge yelled back. "It is you, sir, who are the traitor. It is you, sir, who have time and time again turned against your clan. You lecture us about loyalty. You have no legs to stand on, sir. If you cannot accept the judgment of this court, then we shall let you share in it."

The guards started pulling Nicolda away, as they did Cassandra and Manatado.

"What if the regent's wrong? Will you blindly follow him to your graves? What if the lady of unspoken name is the bringer of our doom?"

That last remark was too much, and one of the male judges made a signal to the guards, who then hit Nicolda on the head and started to drag him out of the room.

Chapter 48

Malada was moved from the sedan chair onto a very comfortable horse-drawn cart. She sat nervously as an even-larger group of dwarves seemed to join the group. Some came in waves, others singles, but by the time Malada's cart started to move, there seemed to be an entire city in convoy with her. She thought back to the vision the trees had shown her. Could it have been fake?

Malada didn't like not knowing the truth. Was her mother a villain, a hero, or something else? What was she? Malada never answered the Socratea tree. What side was she on? The Socratea tree seemed to think that Gerterma was on the side of good. Gerterma fought against his own brother, Jalum, who didn't feel like good.

A stout, thick dwarf on a large horse came alongside Malada's cart and announced himself very loudly. "Daughter of our Lady of the Canyon. My name is Itarus, and I will be commanding the journey. In the event we encounter the monster Riftia, please follow any instructions I give you, as they will be for your own safety. My primary mission is to see you safely to our destination. I, Itarus, have never failed, and I assure you, my lady, that today is no different. The journey will take several hours. We hope to travel overnight while the monster slumbers, but we must be diligent, for the monster will awaken hungry." Itarus bowed and pulled off with his horse.

The convoy twisted and winded its way along steep mountains and sliding rocks. The path was in poor condition, and progress often came to a halt as a large crew of dwarven workers and engineers would need to repair or replace a bridge. From time to time, Malada found herself drifting off into sleep. She felt guilty and wanted to volunteer to walk, but she still didn't feel fully recovered from using her magic. That combined with a full belly made Malada drift off for most of the night.

"Wake, wake, young one. Now is not the time for sleep." The words were soft, so soft it was as if they were coming from inside her own head. "Wake, wake, wake, my child."

Malada pulled her head out from its comfortable wedge. She shook her head and at first didn't see him. She had to shake out of fogginess of her sleep before she could see him. There, somehow sitting next to her, was the little creature from the field and dwarven prison hall.

"Where did, where did you come from?"

The creature gave her a perplexed looked. "I am very old. It seems now I have almost forgotten where I came from. Now that we have a moment, let me talk to you."

"Who are you?"

The creature put his hand to his chin. "You know, I have had so many names over the many years I seem to have forgotten this as well. How about you call me Ciefraf?"

"Are you here to hurt me?"

Ciefraf smiled at her and laughed. "Oh, oh, oh, no, my dear. No, I am here because an unfair burden has been placed upon you."

Malada sat up straighter. "What does that mean? What is my burden?"

Ciefraf said, "First, tell me of your mother."

Malada pulled back. "My mother. You need to know nothing about her."

"Hmm, you are very protective of her. I hope that is because you love her."

Malada was feeling very uncomfortable with this conversation. "What does that mean? What do you know of my mother?"

"A great deal more than you. I know your childhood must have been difficult. Please tell me of her as a mother."

Malada did not like this creature or its questions. "We spend most of our time on the run from authorities, criminals, and hooligans. I advise you not to mess with her. She is a powerful woman."

"Oh, of that I'm sure. She was always passionate. When I first met her, I was much older than her. She had the ability to mix youthful exuberance with a passion for service. I knew she would be one who could change the world. That, that was back before the weight of this world bore too much for her to bear."

Malada's head tilted. "Who are you?"

Ciefraf looked at her and smiled. "Don't you recognize me, my child?"

Chapter 49

Malada threw her arms across the cart and fell forward. The image of her father vanished as she tried to grab hold. She pulled back in fear she had done something wrong. Malada prepared to call out, when the image suddenly reappeared.

"Oh, my dear, how I long to hold you in my arms again. However, my body is merely a shell of what it once was. No, it is by my magic that I can see you now."

"I thought my father was an elf."

Ciefraf's face fumed for a second. "I know this elf." He took a deep breath. "He held your mother after I was no longer able."

"What happened? What are you saying?"

Ciefraf sighed. "Your mother's path and mine crashed into each other. They then broke apart. I wish I could have reached her. I wish I could have convinced her, but she is too resistant, too stubborn. You see, it was my fault. I gave her power she wasn't ready for. While I do believe she meant to use it for the best, the fruits of her labors were sour."

"Is mother evil? I have seen things, things I can't ignore. I also have memories, memories of her caring for me, encouraging me, protecting me. I don't know what to do."

"My poor dear, what a burden has been placed upon you—one that never should have been."

Malada didn't quite understand, and a quiver came with her voice. "You mean I shouldn't exist?"

"No, no, no, my dear. You should be at school, learning new skills, meeting new friends, going on first dates. It is I who have failed. All these years and I still have so much to do. At first I really thought it was your mother who would help me complete my tasks. She had such conviction, such passion. I just knew she could change the world, only I was wrong in which way she would change it."

"So Mommy is evil?"

"Evil, evil. Um, no, that's too strong a word. Your mother has been . . . burdened by this world, manipulated by its ethics, and tempted by its treasures. No, I would not say your mother is evil, but she is only of this world now, and this world only cares for itself."

"What tasks were you talking about?" Malada felt panic rise inside her as her father's image was about to once again leave her. "Daddy, don't go. Where have you been?"

Ciefraf smiled. "Tasks beyond any . . ." His image started to become fuzzy, his face started to become flush red, and his body seemed to tense up as if expecting pain.

"What's happening?"

Ciefraf tried to respond but couldn't. His body turned translucent, a flash of light burst across the cart, and his image was gone.

Malada ran her hands across the seat, along the walls, and looked all around. He was gone, and she still had so many questions.

After a few long moments, a pale frailer version of Ciefraf returned. Malada's heart sank at the sight of her weakened father. "What happened?"

Ciefraf slowly turned his head toward Malada and spoke a little slower. "Your mother, she is using my magic."

"Your magic! Mother always told me my magic was not my own. Do I hurt you when I use my magic?"

Ciefraf smiled weakly. "No, your mother was wrong. Her magic is not her own but mine. You see, I am bound to her, and she to me. When a wizard binds to another, it is for life. Unfortunately, the same is not true for humans." He again winced in pain and vanished from sight.

Malada cried out again. "No, Daddy, no, I can't do this alone."

While no body returned, Ciefraf's voice returned. "One alone I did not find."

"What do you mean? Lukinia? I don't understand."

A circle appeared where Ciefraf's body would have been, and in it came a vision. It was Malada with Cassandra and Manatado waiting to break into Gerterma's office. Then it was them fleeing the bear and then them fighting the Aradoro. Manatado's horrified face as he ran away from the monkey in the forest brought a laugh to Malada. Then the circle vanished and the vision ended.

The blare of trumpets with the thunder of lightning announcing the convoy's arrival startled Malada out of her shock. She stuck her head outside the carriage, and before it lay the most massive gates she had ever seen, stretching from the ground to above the canyon walls. Malada was impressed, for she had never seen such a feat of engineering before. The amount of steel, iron, and other metals that must have been used to make such gates was unimaginable.

A return of the trumpets from the top of the gates came with a massive groaning sound as the gates slowly slid across the ground. The doors slowly opened outward, revealing numerous sets of chains running along large prongs that came out from the bottom of the gates. Attached to the chains, pulling and pushing the massive prongs, were large groups of orcs. The orcs labored as they side by side pulled or pushed with all their might. There behind them were the masters, humans with whips that crackled with electricity.

The orcs labored, encouraged by their masters' whips, to open the door enough for the convoy to enter. Satisfied, they gave the signal to the orcs, who collapsed in exhaustion as they waited to labor the gates back closed again. Malada's cart entered first, now flanked by uniformed dwarven warriors. At first they passed tent after tent of orc slaves, but after a while the tents gave way to workshop after workshop. They lined the canyon floors with tents stuffed behind them, piled high with machine parts of every kind and shape.

The sound of pounding metal being shaped and the sizzle of boiling water as it met iron and steel filled Malada's ears. Each workshop was busy with craftsmen pounding away at flaming metals. Yet her cart turned up a path that ran along and up the wall. The road was narrow, and the escorts went either before or behind. Each dwarf had a rope connect them to the cart and vice versa. The rest of the convoy behind Malada filled in the gaps of the canyon as everyone tried to squeeze inside.

Malada now recognized this canyon as the one from the Socratea tree's vision. She felt her stomach sink as the memory once again came to the forefront of her mind. The air became ever denser with industrial fumes. She even found herself coughing at times.

The closer they got, the farther down the canyon Malada could see. At the far end stood an enormous castle towering over everything in sight. Its tall dark walls were pitted with gargoyle statues and sharp spires. A dark cloud seemed to hang over the castle, blacking out the sky.

A stream of molten metal poured down from each side of the castle down into the canyon. Malada couldn't quite make out the overall shape, but it was enormous and it was being molded into something specific.

At the top of the canyon, Malada's cart came to a large flat ledge. The cart stopped in the middle of it, and the dwarven escorts once again surrounded Malada. The door of the cart opened, and the dwarves formed a line to each side of the door. She took a deep breath and stepped out. A large blue tent with the sides open stood proudly over the canyon at its center point. A large throne was in the middle of the tent with several tables and a desk surrounding it. There, standing up from the throne, was Malada's mother, Eratrea. Eratrea stood up with a wave of her arm, flinging the excess materials of her lavish dress off to the side. An intense scowl was upon her face.

Malada slowly made her way toward her mother. She had seen her mother angry many times, but this was the first time she was on the receiving end. Malada wanted to rush up to her mother and hug her as strongly as she could, and she also wanted to attack her mother and make her tell the truth.

Eratrea approached Malada, keeping the scowl at full intensity the whole way. Eratrea wrapped her arms around her daughter and hugged her with all her might. Malada felt a tear drop from her eye as she returned the hug.

After a long embrace, Eratrea pulled back and spoke with a sternness Malada had never heard before. "You stupid girl. I told you to run. You have no idea how difficult you have just made this situation for me."

Malada fought back the tears changing from joy to sorrow. "I'm here to save you, Mom. Aren't you happy?"

Eratrea's eyes softened if her scowl and voice didn't. "Save me? No, now you have put me in a compromised situation. The stakes are bigger than just our little family. I wish you hadn't come here. Now I must betray both my daughter and myself." Eratrea hugged Malada and whispered into her ear, "Do exactly what I say. We are both in great danger."

Eratrea pulled back and turned around to face the tent. "My esteemed colleagues, I would like to introduce one of my closest aides, the lady Malada."

A cold breeze blew as a dark shadowy figure emerged from the tent. Malada felt her stomach sink and her heart grow cold with fear, for out of the tent walked Jalum. "Ah, yes, Malada, I have been expecting you."

Chapter 50

Jalum stood tall, his arms crossed, with Malada's shield neatly tucked away in his belt. He glanced in Eratrea's direction, and she gave and held a slight bow while she stood back and to his side. "What a good girl you have been, coming all the way to us. I was afraid after our little, um, miscommunication in the forest. I was afraid you might not come. But I'm always so foolish with my emotions. Sometimes they just get the best of me. Especially disappointment. Oh, how disappointment . . . angers me."

Jalum turned around, grabbed something off the ground and, as he turned back around, threw the thing at Malada's feet. A thick, turned-to-stone, lifeless Lukinia now lay at Malada's feet, her face frozen in fear. "If only I had the time, I would show some compassion and restraint, but alas, I don't have the time." Jalum took long, slow steps and was quickly bent over, looking down face-to-face at Malada.

Malada swallowed and tried to hold back her fear. She knew how powerful a man he was. His breath smelled like fire and ice, burning her nose while freezing her soul. "Now, sweetheart, that you have come to us, we can take our last conversation and put it to practical application." Jalum leaned and turned his back to Malada. "My dear Eratrea, would you please tell young Malada what we were just discussing?"

Eratrea sent a look of fear toward her daughter before turning toward Jalum and bowing. "Yes, of course, my lord. We were just speculating as to whose magic was more powerful, Malada's or my own."

Jalum smiled widely. "And how did we propose to answer that question?"

Eratrea gave a very pleading look to Jalum, who seemed to relish in her agony. He gave her a stern look as she lowered her head and answered. "In battle against each other."

Jalum smiled a wicked smile. "Seems logical. If you need to determine which is the strongest warrior, pit them against each other. Does that make sense to you as well, my lovely Eratrea?" He put his hand on her chin and raised her head.

A tear shed down Eratrea's face as she nodded yes. Malada shared her mother's fear, but still the words came out of her anyway. "Not if you want two warriors, it doesn't!" Malada wasn't even quite sure what she meant, but she knew she was on her mother's side against Jalum.

Jalum twirled around and shot Malada a nasty look before smiling again. "Oh, how wonderful a thought. To have two magical warriors, but such a thing feels greedy. It must be tested before committed to. Now let me think of a test."

After a long moment, screams, trumpets, and drums all started to ring out with echoes of fear. Jalum looked up from his thoughts. "How wonderful, things just keep seeming to line up perfectly for me."

Malada turned back toward the canyon and the commotion. The back end of the convoy that had brought her to this place was stampeding to get behind the enormous gates. The ground rumbled and shook with force. Jalum waved his hand and whispered something into a nearby attendant's ear, after which the attendant sped off.

"Oh, how wonderful would it be if I could only believe you, Malada? You would willingly become my soldier. With you on our side, the evil of this world wouldn't stand a chance."

Malada turned back and snapped. "You are the evil of this world!"

Jalum laughed vigorously. "Hahaha, did you hear that? She thinks we are the evil of this world. Such ignorant youth." He walked back to Eratrea. "How could you let your daughter think such a thing? Oh, I know, maybe it was because you kept killing all the escorts I sent after you. I think it's time you corrected your daughter."

Eratrea stepped forward and next to Jalum but kept her head low. "Malada, you don't understand what we are doing here. We are saving races, cultures, lives here."

The vision the Socratea tree showed Malada returned to her mind. "By enslaving and killing orcs! By consuming the whole of the dwarf empire!"

"Saving the world doesn't come for free!" Jalum's rage seemed even more intense as the ground shook when he spoke. "If this world were capable of saving itself, it would. But it's not. Can you save? Can she? NO, NO, NO, only I am capable of saving it, and those who can are rewarded for doing so."

A group of dwarven warriors escorted in a bloodied and beaten Gerterma, a frightened Cassandra, and a terrified Manatado. Jalum motioned and the three were thrown to the ground and held firmly in place there. Each of them had been tied up tightly with balls placed in their mouths.

"Now, Malada, you may not like it. You may not even truly believe it yet, but we are fighting to save the world here. Just because saving the world doesn't look as nice and neat as you want it to doesn't mean it doesn't need to get done. So here are your options. You can, A, fight your mother and determine who in fact does have the strongest magic. You could, B, and I do believe this is what you are currently leaning toward, try to get your mother to turn on me and you both end up dead. You could, C, choose to prove your loyalty by sending these three to their sentenced deaths."

Jalum gave a long pause before looking at Malada. "So, my dear, which one do you choose?"

Chapter 51

"Of course she will choose C, my lord." Eratrea spoke so quickly Malada didn't even have time to reply. "We gladly acknowledge the cause and the sacrifices that must be made. You yourself, my lord, are so giving you would even sacrifice your own brother. What leadership, my lord."

Eratrea moved as she spoke, placing herself between Malada and Jalum, dropping down into a head-touching-the-ground bow. Malada stepped back as fear and anger erupted into an emotional outpouring of tears. What was her mother doing? Was her mother really willing to kill her friends?

Jalum bent over and lifted Eratrea's face off the ground, but she looked away, afraid to make eye contact. "I know you too well, Eratrea. Your willingness to comply only makes me doubt your intentions further." He turned around and spoke with his back to Eratrea. "Prove to me your genuineness by starting my machine."

A look of terror crossed Eratrea's face. "Oh, oh, but, my lord, are you sure it's finished? There are still so many untested systems and . . . unwritten software. These dwarves are excellent metallurgists, but they know nothing of science."

Jalum brought out his blade and ran it with such amazing speed and precision that it only cut a lock of hair off Eratrea's forehead. She froze in place, her breath so loud with fear it echoed about.

Malada finally found her voice and tiptoed closer to her mother. "Mom, Mom, what's going on? What is this machine?"

Eratrea turned and sent Malada a look of fury. "Mind your place, girl, and do what your mother tells you to do. Send them to their fate. Do it now, now, NOW!"

Jalum and Eratrea both stared deeply into Malada as she stood back with terror on her face. "I don't know what cause you think you're fighting for, Mom, but killing my friends is wrong. I won't do it!"

Malada grabbed a handful of dirt and threw it at Jalum as she charged at him. It was a feeble attempt, and Malada was down on her back with a blade to her throat almost instantly. Manatado wiggled and tried to break free, but he and Cassandra could only offer fearful eyes in assistance.

"Pity, I really thought your presence would put your mother in line. Oh well, now that I'm wrong, I certainly won't be needing you anymore."

Malada felt the blade start to press against her skin, when Eratrea cried out, "I'll do it. I'll start your machine. Just, just leave my daughter alone."

Jalum pulled the blade back, smiled, and nodded his head, allowing Malada to hug her mother. "Ah, such a touching moment. Family reunions are always the most touching. In fact, Gerterma, Gerterma, why don't you get over here, you big buffoon?"

Gerterma kept his head down as he got on one knee and then slowly rose up. He kept his head down as he approached his younger brother, Jalum. Jalum smiled as he cut free the restraint and handed his blade over to Gerterma. Jalum then stood in front of Gerterma, allowing him the full opportunity to attack him, but he did not, instead very discreetly cutting off Malada's shield from his belt. "Thank you, brother. You played along very well. You not only helped me discover the extent of young Malada's powers, but you also brought her right to me. Well done, well done."

Gerterma gave a sad, guilty look toward Malada and then walked to her side and readied the weapon to attack if given the order. Malada couldn't even position herself to fight back. She felt her entire will to live leaving her. Her mother and Gerterma—the two closest adults in her life—were evil, and there was nothing she could do about it.

Jalum walked over to Eratrea and waved his hand, indicating where she was to move to. Together they walked over to the cliff wall. The ground again shook as the monster Riftia slammed its body into the giant metal cliff doors. Eratrea regained her footing and stood tall along the cliff face. She rubbed her hands together and started speaking inaudible words. The air around her started to glow. A yellow light started shining from within Eratrea. Then the light shot straight up into the sky.

After a long moment, a thunderous roar screamed its way down from the sky. Bolt after bolt of lightning blasted down into the canyon to where Malada couldn't see. A dozen blasts came from the sky before Eratrea fell to the ground in exhaustion.

Jalum raised his hands into the sky and roared out in a sinister laugh. "It's mine, it's finally mine." Again the ground shook, this time so strongly the edges of the cliff started to collapse in places. The ground moved differently this time as if swaying left and right.

A giant mechanical hand shot up from the canyon and slammed down next to Jalum. The sounds of metal creaking and groaning echoed through the canyon as an enormous mechanical robot rose up out from the canyon bed. Long steel arms came out from a boxy iron hulk of a torso.

The torso turned and a door popped open, extending a gate out before Jalum.

Jalum turned and held his blade at bay. He signaled for Gerterma to go on first, and with a lowered head, Gerterma complied, but as he passed behind Jalum, something rolled across the ground. "Hmm, now let me think. Now I have my wonderful machine, a machine more powerful than any magic, stronger than any monster, and it's MINE, ALL MINE!" Jalum took a small skip up the ramp and then turned back. "Gee, guess I won't be needing a magician anymore." He then entered through the door, closing it immediately behind him.

A moment later, Jalum appeared in the window at the top of the torso. The machine whizzed and hummed oddly before a loud burst of smoke deafened the entire area. For just a moment, the machine stopped.

Then, with a huge plume of thick dark smoke, it roared back to life. As the smoke cleared, the machine moved forward like a tank on two metal tracks. The machine rolled forward through the canyon, sending dwarf after dwarf upon each other as they hurried out of its way. The machine cared not for what was below, for it smashed many of the workspaces, storehouses, and living quarters as it went.

The machine rumbled toward the massive canyon gates, raising its arms up as it plowed forward. The doors burst open, slamming the monster Riftia into the canyon walls. The monster lay motionless for a long second, but instead of attacking it, the machine tumbled on away from the canyon and the monster.

The entirety of the canyon held its collective breath. Not a sound could be heard. It was the most silent any of the three teenagers had ever heard it in their lives. It all changed at once as Riftia shook it off and roared in anger. Riftia looked at the fleeing machine before turning back and finding the canyon doors wide open.

Chapter 52

Eratrea fell to a knee and then to her butt, a desperate look of despair across her face. Malada took a step in her direction but then rerouted toward her friends Manatado and Cassandra. Malada tried and failed to untie the very tightly wound knots.

The ground shook and screams raced out of the canyon as Riftia bulldozed all that stood in their way. The dwarves climbed upon one another, forming a ladder of dwarves every few yards down the canyon. The dwarves seemed to scatter as they spread out into the wilderness away from the canyon.

The dwarven regent and a few assistants labored their way up the canyon to Eratrea's side. "MY lady, what is happening. Where does the machine go?" Eratrea didn't move. Even when the regent shook her, she fell flat and started crying on her side. "My lady, MY lady, what do we do? You promised us your machine would protect us. Where does it go?"

Eratrea spoke through tear-filled words. "It was stolen. Gerterma has taken the machine."

Malada froze from her work as she heard the words. She took hold of the anger she had at her mother for lying, and as her thoughts turned angry, so did her hands. Without conscious effort, Malada had used her own hands to burn right through her friends' restraints. Manatado and Cassandra both jumped up and into her arms. They pulled out the balls that had been placed in their mouths.

"Malada, are you okay?" Manatado asked with angst.

"What's going on? What was that thing?" Cassandra asked, exasperated.

Malada pulled back from the hug and, after giving them a large smile, turned and faced Eratrea. The dwarven regent was tugging on her shoulder, pleading for her to do something. Eratrea just sat with a blank look on her face. Malada kneeled before her mother and pushed the regent away, placing her hands on her mother's face, causing tears to fall from her face. "Mom, what's going on? What do we do now?"

Eratrea shook her head no. "There's nothing we can do. The world's most powerful villain now has the world's most powerful machine." She now placed her hands on her daughter's. "I'm so sorry I failed. I'm so, so sorry. It's all over now, and it's all my fault." Eratrea now placed both sets of hands on her face as the tears came down.

The ground shook and Malada fell to both knees. A warm, stinky wind drew their attention as Riftia now stood at the cliff face. Manatado looked around. The canyon had been deserted or destroyed, and everyone but this small group had fled. Manatado ran up to Malada. "We need to run!"

"It's too late," Eratrea bemoaned.

"Then we need a plan to fight." Manatado couldn't believe he had just spoken those words, and the realization brought a smile of pride to his face.

"I can't destroy Riftia. He is too powerful for me."

Manatado lost his smile and looked to Malada for what to do next. Riftia slammed his tail into the canyon floor, and after rising up, the monster came straight down like a bird to prey. Cassandra grabbed as many bodies as she could and pushed the group as hard as possible, leaving only the regent behind.

The group tumbled and rolled. Malada landed on her side on the cliff's edge. Then Riftia slammed down into the ground, eating the regent. The vibration shook so strongly Malada now rolled backward and down the cliff.

Chapter 53

Manatado lunged forward from his knees and reached out, grabbing whatever he could get ahold of. Malada's leg was all he could grab and, under other circumstances, would have brought a blush to his face. It was enough, however, and Cassandra was able to reach over and grab hold of Malada's armpits and pull them both back. Together the three tumbled away from the cliff.

The ground shook with ferocity as Riftia crawled his way through the rock and back out into the canyon. A large hole in the ground next to the three teenagers was starting to give way and collapse outward. The three were able to scoot back fast enough to avoid falling into the new pit. While they were doing so, Malada noticed something on the far side closest to the canyon edge. It was her shield. It gave her an idea.

Malada jumped up and started running along the edge of the pit's rim, but it started to fall apart and she had to jump away. Cassandra saw the shield as Malada went after it, and as she saw Malada fail to retrieve it, she knew it was important even if not why. Cassandra acted purely on instinct, and as she pulled Manatado up off the ground, she starting twirling him as they spun in circles.

Neither Cassandra nor Manatado could believe what was happening, and the look on Manatado's face as Cassandra let him go would never be forgotten. He curled up in a ball and landed hard on his side as he crossed over the pit, landing right next to Malada's shield. Cassandra cried out in pain as she reinjured her wrist in the action.

After a bounce, Manatado saw the shield as it started sliding down into the pit. He reached out for it, bringing it in close to his chest. The warm, stinky breath of Riftia signaled the monster was about to make another attack. Manatado did nothing, and for a long moment, it seemed as if time had stopped.

The moment was broken as Riftia slammed his tail down into the ground and flung himself up into the air for his diving attack. Malada dove onto Manatado just a second before the monster slammed down upon them, swallowing them whole. Riftia's outer teeth burrowed through the ground while its inner teeth tried to chew. Riftia finished its hole and again came out into the canyon, but this time at a slow speed.

Riftia stretched out longways and then curled up in pain. The monster bent over in agony once, and then again. On the third time, the monster puked out a large ball of pus. The ball rolled off to the side as the monster lay down in pain.

The ball came to a slow stop a few feet away from the canyon wall. For several minutes, the ball stayed motionless. The slime surrounding the ball started to drip off and collect in a pool below the ball. The ball started to sink into the ground as the slime began melting the ground away. The ground hissed and steamed for another long minute before coming to a stop after having sunk nearly a foot.

The ball retracted, and there in the middle was Malada holding Manatado in her arms. Cassandra's heart both sank and rejoiced at the sight. The two flinched at the bright light of day as they waited for their eyes to adjust.

Riftia again spewed out a large amount of pus, cratering the canyon before it regained its composure and stood back up. Cassandra yelled out in warning for her friends to start running in her direction. They complied but found it difficult to make progress being nearly blind. The movement drew the attention of Riftia, who was positioning itself for an attack.

Cassandra was at a loss, with no way of attacking Riftia like she could the bear back in the forest. Yet the memory gave her an idea, and as she looked around, she spotted a single large tree left at the top of this now-barren plateau. Cassandra picked up the biggest rock she could throw with her good arm and chucked it at the monster.

The stone hit Riftia right on the tooth in its mouth. The monster cringed in pain and then turned to face Cassandra. Cassandra's face froze as the realization of what she had just committed herself to sank in. Riftia lowered its tail, and Cassandra snapped out into a full sprint. Her wrist hurt furiously as her arm swung in motion with the running. The pain and fear brought tears to her eyes, but she just kept running.

Riftia shook the ground, wobbling Cassandra's path, as it launched itself into the air. Cassandra was approaching the tree but didn't know how the timing was going to work out. She just had to hope. Sweat dripped down and collected with the tears as her body screamed out in fatigue, but she didn't stop. Cassandra felt the shadow of the monster closing down upon her.

Cassandra's legs hurt and begged her to stop, but she kept going. Cassandra could feel the shadow of the monster overtaking the tree's shadow. It was going to be very close on the timing, and Cassandra closed her eyes as she put all her effort into running as fast as possible.

Cassandra caught a whiff of flowers as she sprinted underneath the tree's canopy. Cassandra was not more than a few feet past the tree when Riftia came crashing down directly onto the tree. Riftia burrowed down a few feet before the rest of its body came crashing down, squishing the monster. Riftia's body bounced back to normal length and then fell off to the side.

The monster's long body fell, crashing into the ground before Eratrea. Her body shook with the ground but otherwise didn't move. Manatado and Malada rushed to Eratrea's side, fearing the worst. Malada grabbed her mother, placed her head in her lap, and ran her hand down the side of her face, moving the hair out of the way. Malada expected her mother to be hurt, but she just lay there like a lump of clay.

"Mother, Mother, we need you." Malada's voice carried worry and fear.

"It's too late. We can do nothing. Just give up." Eratrea's eyes looked far beyond her daughter as she spoke.

"Please use your magic to destroy the monster while its hurt!" Manatado pleaded to one, either, or both of them.

Eratrea looked at Manatado with blank eyes. "I cannot defeat this beast."

Manatado threw his hands up in frustration at not one but both of them. He then turned and ran off.

Malada screamed out, "Nooo," and then bent herself over her mother.

Riftia's body convulsed over and over again, shaking the canyon ground, even causing a nearby ledge to collapse. Malada's grip on her mother grew tighter and tighter. As Eratrea lost the ability to breathe, she reacted out of instinct and pushed Malada away as she jumped to her feet. Malada's eyes showed the pain of her mother's rejection. After another convulsion from Riftia, the monster's body stopped shaking and curled like a snake around Malada and her mother.

This time, Eratrea reached out and held her daughter close. "I'm so, so, so sorry. It's all my fault. I tried so hard to protect you, and now I'm going to fail you at that too."

Malada repositioned and embraced her mother tightly. "I love you, Mother, and I forgive you."

Riftia's skin started to compress as it wrapped around the two. Malada and her mother huddled together from head to toe. The light went out for them as the monster's body curled up like a snake squeezing the two, taking their breath away. Just as the light was cut off, Cassandra's voice cut through the darkness. "Manatado, NO, STOP!"

The darkness covered everything. There was not a sound to be heard. There was no air to breathe. There was no room to scream. There was only fear. Then there was light. Then there was air. Then there was a roar as Manatado yelled out in a furious rage.

Malada and Eratrea fell a foot downward before hitting the ground. Riftia's body shook left, then right, then up, and back down as if it were a bull being ridden by a rider it didn't like. Riftia's tail slammed down feet away from Cassandra, who was flung backward and landed on her bad wrist, adding to the injury.

Malada and Eratrea held each other as the ground shook violently around them. In a last desperate move, Riftia flung its head backward, launching Manatado straight up into the air. His arms and legs seemed to reach out into the air, grasping for something, anything. But it wasn't only Manatado. There was something in the air with him, and as Malada looked closer, she could see it was a long, large branch from the tree. Manatado's leg hooked the branch, and as he started to fall back toward Riftia, he brought the branch close to his body and together they vanished into the monster's mouth.

After just having recovered her breath, Malada again felt it leave her as she saw Manatado get eaten. But she was wrong. Manatado had used the branch to pry open the monster's mouth. He looked like a gymnast as his body flew around the branch and his body tumbled into the air and fell the entire distance of the monster's height.

Manatado screamed out in pain as his legs hit the ground.

Riftia swung its head back and forth, and after the sound of the branch cracking came a roar of pain from the monster. Drips of red pus poured out the side of the creature's mouth as it cringed in pain and moved its tail in order to flee.

Light and air returned to Malada and her mother as they pried apart from each other, their lungs laboring to refill the lost air. Both of them had tears in their eyes, but Eratrea's body language was different. Before, she lay there ready for death and defeated. Now she jumped up and grabbed her daughter.

Eratrea hugged Malada with all her strength. Talking through the tears, Eratrea's voice even sounded different. "I love you, I love you." Malada had longed so often during her childhood for such a moment, but she could only enjoy it for a moment, not nearly long enough for Eratrea.

Malada finally broke free of her mother's grasp and ran straight for Manatado. Cassandra was clenching her wrist and holding her shoulder immobile as she stood over Manatado. Malada came charging in and hugged Cassandra with all her might. At first Cassandra pulled back, angry at the situation, but the warm healing touch of her friend relaxed her body and mind. Malada ran her arms up and down Cassandra's as she closed her eyes and focused. After a minute, a golden glow that wasn't even noticed until it was gone vanished, and Malada fell to her butt in fatigue.

Cassandra felt her arm and moved it, trying to regain confidence in its healed state. Satisfied, she looked at her friends. Manatado was crying but had his arms crossed and his face stiffly looking away from Malada.

"Go away!" Manatado snapped through the tears.

Malada's face grew sad and her body looked fatigued "Manatado, please, I'm sorry."

"Go away. I'm a man. I can handle a little leg pain."

"Manatado, please, I didn't mean it the way I said it." His voice softened from anger but was still sad. "I don't need any help from you. I defeated the monster. I protected the women. I AM A MAN!" Manatado crossed his arms and tried to hold back the tears, but the pain and emotions were too intense.

"I can't deal with this right now! If you're such a man, why are you pouting like a baby?"

Manatado turned his head as if he had something to say but then decided against it. The pain in his ankle was throbbing, and each wave of pain seemed more intense than the last. His face cringed in pain.

"Just let me heal you already!" Malada approached and knelt by his side. At first he turned his body away, but the pain was more than his pride, and with a face full of tears, he turned back and presented his foot.

Malada felt a strange mixture of emotions and was having a hard time concentrating. She grabbed his calf, resulting in a scream of pain. She jumped and felt her heart race. Malada focused as best she could, but nothing was happening. Her eyes burst open as a new thought crept into her mind. What if she couldn't heal him?

Manatado's face again cringed with a new surge of pain. Malada took a deep breath and put all her effort into summoning her magic. Nothing was happening. She had just healed Cassandra's wrist, but now she couldn't do it again. Manatado's foot shook in pain, and Malada felt a twinge of panic creep into her.

"What are you waiting for? Hurry up already. It hurts."

Malada again took a deep breath and grabbed the ankle with both hands. Again nothing happened.

"Hurry up, hurry up!"

Cassandra's face was now full of worry. "Malada, what's wrong? Why aren't you healing him?"

A note of panic crept into Malada's voice. "I don't know. I'm trying, okay?"

Manatado's voice started to turned more toward a plea. "It hurts. It hurts, Malada."

Eratrea came up and placed her hand on Malada's shoulder. "My dear, what's wrong?"

Tears broke through the seal that was keeping them back as Malada heard her mother's voice. Malada's face glistened in the sunlight as the tears ran like water.

Eratrea turned Malada around and placed her head down into her shoulder as she cried. "Mom, can't you please heal him? My magic is brokennnn."

"Please, Eratrea. Please, it hurts so much." Manatado stopped trying to act manly and was gripping his ankles in pain.

Eratrea placed her head on top of Malada's. "My magic cannot heal, only destroy." Eratrea took a deep breath. "Just like me." Together the two stood there crying into each other's arms while Manatado lay on the ground crying to himself, with Cassandra at his side comforting as best she knew how, while Lukinia lay solid in stone, and tied up nearby her was Nicolda, abandoned by his own kind.

Chapter 54

"Mommy, I wish Daddy was here. He would know how to help."

Eratrea felt awful she wasn't more helpful to her daughter. "My dear, your father had been dead for a very long time, most of your life, I'm sure. Unless you mean Redleaf."

"No, Mom, I mean Ciefraf."

Eratrea's face turned white. "How do you know that name? I have never spoken it to you ever."

"Father came to me, Mother."

Eratrea took a step back and then fell to her knee and then to her butt. After the look of shock wore off, Eratrea returned to her knees and held up her hands pleadingly. "You must not believe the awful things he has said about me. I . . ." Eratrea turned and looked away. "I was so young, I hadn't learned boundaries yet. I was mesmerized by his world. I couldn't appreciate the gifts he had given me. Oh, Malada, I've done so many things wrong."

Malada took a deep breath, grabbed her mother's hand, and brought her up for a hug. "You need to understand something, Mother." Malada smiled as she locked eyes with her mother. "You are forgiven."

Eratrea hugged her daughter with a never-before-felt intensity, and it stirred up things inside Malada. Malada felt her heart open new again, and she felt the magic rush out of her. A white light encircled Manatado, who was trying to hold as still as possible to avoid any pain. A strong wind blew through the area, and Manatado raised up off the ground.

Manatado's body shimmered and shined with a bright light, and as Malada and her mother pulled back from their embrace, he was gently laid back down on the ground. Cassandra ran up and placed her hands on his shoulders. Manatado gave Cassandra a reassuring look. Then, after rubbing his ankles, he stood up.

He shifted his weight back and forth until he had fully regained confidence in his ankle. Manatado prepared to run up and hug Malada but then remembered he was mad at her and stopped and turned away. As he did so, there, lying oddly by itself, was a dwarf all tied up. He gave a glance to Cassandra, and together they untied Nicolda.

Nicolda stretched out his aching muscle and then took a step back with a look of astonishment on his face. "I, I, I can't believe everything I just saw."

"My, my, my people, they just left me to die . . . Riftia the destroyer of dwarves, defeated by a teenage boy . . . humans with the ability to control magic . . . Gerterma." Nicolda turned around and walked to a couple of circles before facing Manatado and Cassandra. "I have decided that I will join you." Nicolda fell to a knee and placed one hand over his heart and held the other high in the air. "I, Nicolda of the Clandine Clan, now pledge my loyalty to you, Manatado, leader of the . . ." Nicolda looked around at those assembled and then back at Manatado. "Manatites?"

"Nope, won't be using that name," Cassandra called out and then looked around as if she hadn't.

"So what is the name of our clan?" Nicolda asked.

Manatado turned back slightly and shot Malada a look that said, "Told you." Malada sank her head into her mother's shoulder, while Cassandra thought about what it all meant.

Manatado looked back at Nicolda. "Rise, my friend, we welcome you." Manatado puffed his chest up and spoke as manly as possible. "I, Manatado, would like to welcome you to the Manatites Clan."

Cassandra snickered and rolled her eyes. "Okay, then, great clan leader, what do you suggest we do next, then?"

Manatado raised his hand to his chin and made a thinking pose. Wanting to make a point, he thought of the bravest and dumbest thing he could. "I propose, I mean, we shall pursue and destroy that machine."

Cassandra covered her eyes and looked away in disbelief. Malada and Eratrea raised their heads and dropped their jaws. Nicolda swallowed as he took a moment to think about what he had just done.

Cassandra turned back around. "We've nearly died several times already since leaving the village, and now you want to chase the most dangerous thing on earth! NO NO NO, it's time to go back to the village and let the adults figure this out."

Manatado turned to face her, feeling more manly than ever before. "What? What adult has given you any hope that they can do anything right? Gerterma has betrayed us, the entire dwarven empire gave itself away to a mad man, Eratrea started that machine, and the entire human empire is working for Jalum, and you want to trust them to fix it all?"

Cassandra took a stern look and stepped close to Manatado. "Okay then, great clan leader, how do we destroy that thing?"

"I bet she can tell us." Manatado pointed his finger at Eratrea.

Eratrea released her daughter's hug and took a big breath before answering. "That machine was designed by science to destroy both magic and monsters. I don't know how it can be destroyed."

Manatado snapped his fingers and stepped toward Malada and away from Cassandra. "Well if neither magic nor monster can destroy it, maybe science can."

Eratrea took another step back as Manatado zeroed in on Malada. "Well, okay, yeah, now that I think about it that way, there might be a way."

Manatado raised his hands in victory as he came in close to Malada, so close she could hear him whisper. Yet instead, he spoke loudly and clearly for all to hear. "Can too be manly, can too protect you, and CAN TOO LEAD!" He then raised his head and stepped past Malada.

Eratrea continued after an awkward moment. "But to use science, we have to go to where the machine was first designed. It requires we go to Athenia."

Manatado stood up straight and zeroed his eyes onto Malada. "Then we go to Athenia!"

He spun around, took a few steps forward, and faced off into the distance.

Cassandra quietly approached Malada and whispered into her ear, "What's up with you two? Why is he being so different?"

Malada dropped her eyes like a guilty puppy dog. "When we were together inside my shield, while inside Riftia, I, I kinda said something."

Cassandra's glance begged for more. Malada took a deep breath. "I held him and told him, ugh, that I would always protect my little man."

Cassandra's mouth dropped. "You used the word 'little'! NO wonder he's so . . . wow, what are you going to do?"

"Well, nothing I guess. I didn't mean it like I said it, but I'm not sure he wants to hear that."

Cassandra gave Malada a gentle hug and then turned and walked up to Manatado. She gently coughed, getting his attention. Manatado turned around and gave her a look that made Cassandra blush and stopped her from speaking. Manatado took a big step, standing very close to Cassandra, and tried to kiss her on the lips.

Cassandra rejoiced at first, her eye met Manatado, and they connected. It didn't last long before Manatado's eyes glared directly at Malada's. When Manatado moved toward Cassandra but was eyeing Malada, Cassandra became angry and slammed her forearm into his head.

Manatado recoiled in pain, ducked, stepped back, and put his hand to his head. "Wha—"

Cassandra was fast and angry, and over and over again she hit Manatado on the shoulder, tears starting to form. "How dare you! How dare you try to use me to make her jealous? How dare you!" Again and again she hit him painfully but harmlessly on his shoulder. Cassandra then pushed him away, made eye contact with Malada, and then turned away, crying and running off into the near distance.

Seeing Cassandra angry only made Malada angry at Manatado too. Malada wrapped her arm around her mother's arm, and together they walked off in another separate direction.

Nicolda stood up, dumbfounded at what had also just occurred. He walked up to Manatado. "I just pledged my loyalty to an idiot. This day couldn't possibly get any worse. He then walked off to overlook the canyon. Manatado just moments before had felt like he was on top of the world. Now in only a moment's time, he was alone, and it was entirely his own fault.

Chapter 55

Manatado rubbed his face where Cassandra had slapped him. He looked up and saw everyone walking away from him— except Lukinia, who was trapped in stone. In every direction he looked, someone he cared for or at least admired had their back to him. All he wanted was to impress a girl; all he got was misery.

Manatado cleared his throat, again and again, before he could finally speak up loudly enough for all to hear. "Everyone, everyone, I'm sorry. I've, I've been immature. I've been . . ." His arm raised up to scratch around his ear "Selfish and single-minded on something I shouldn't have been." Manatado glanced in Cassandra's direction, and he caught her head tilting back away as if she had been listening. Manatado took a single step in Cassandra's direction. "Cassandra, I'm sorry I did that. I don't want you to be mad at me, because . . . because I like the way you make me feel. You know stuff about me. You come to my side when I'm hurt. You care about me in a way that makes me care about myself in a better, more responsible way. Please forgive me."

Cassandra turned around and made eye contact. A tear had formed in her eye, but she nodded yes and they came together and hugged. "Why do boys have to be so stupid, and so lovable?"

After they finished their hug, Manatado turned and faced Malada and Eratrea. "Malada, I'm sorry. I know . . . I know you don't think of me as the man I want you to, but that doesn't mean you meant to hurt my feels, and I didn't have to act so . . . childishly."

Manatado took two big steps toward Malada and held out his arms to hug. She cringed for a moment, but then after being prodded by her mother, she stepped forward and let Manatado give her a big bear hug.

"There, I apologized. Now, Eratrea, will you please lead the way to Athenia? I have a mentor to save, you have a machine to destroy, and we have a friend turned to stone, an outcast looking for revenge, and a heck of a long walk. I would like to start before I realize what I just said and change my mind." With that, Manatado stood up straight and started walking off into the distance.

He walked several meters before turning back around. Malada rolled her eyes at him before speaking loudly. "All in favor of a new clan name?"

Ayes came from everyone but Manatado and Nicolda.

"How about the clan of Valentina?" Cassandra offered but got looks of protest from Malada and Eratrea.

Manatado, feeling a little hurt, chimed in. "How about the clan with the magic girls?"

Eratrea stepped forward. "I have a real suggestion and, Malada, it comes from your father. He always used to talk about an unknown being, something greater than us all, something godlike. Ciefraf called his the great creator. He would rave about some all-knowing and all-caring god. Personally, I would never understand how such a powerful being would care about something as insignificant as us. Yet your father believed, and if your father was willing to forgive me, I think it's right we honor him." Eratrea held back her emotions as she spoke.

"I suggest we call ourselves the clan of the unknown creator."

All eyes turned to Manatado, who ducked his head down and nodded yes. After a moment, Manatado's body language realized something, his head picked up, and he spoke with a hint of excitement. "Malada, you found your father! Oh, and your mother! Wow, maybe I am good at this!"

Malada shook her head in disgust at Manatado. "You? You didn't even do anything."

Manatado smiled. "I know, that's what makes me so good."

Cassandra approached and looked at him. "You really are stupid sometimes." She laid her hands down on his shoulder and then laid her head down as well in a semi hug. She then scurried off to Malada and her mother's position. They hugged, and as they pulled back, Cassandra said, "Tell us all about what happened to you."

Malada gathered herself and then motioned her arm to present Eratrea. "Guys, first let me introduce you to my mother, Eratrea." Malada turned to face her mother. "Mom, after we got separated, the defense force found me, but they didn't know who I was, so I hid myself among some refugees. They took us to a village called Valentina, where I met these two, Cassandra and Manatado. Mother, without them, I never would have been able to make it here."

A tear came to Eratrea's eye. "My sweet, I was so, so scared. I wanted so desperately to come find you, but I thought if he had me . . . Jalum wouldn't want you too." She turned to face her daughter's friends. She then stepped forward and hugged them both.

Manatado tilted his head upward to speak. "Malada, what about the vision. Are we so sure which side your mothers is on?"

Malada's face erupted into a fury, but Eratrea pulled out from the hug and held up a hand to calm her. "He's right, my daughter. I've done bad things. I've done things I regret. Maybe he is right. Maybe you shouldn't trust me."

Malada spoke resolutely. "No, Mother, you are forgiven. Whatever happened in the past is done. We trust you know now."

Cassandra and Manatado rolled their eyes but said nothing.

Eratrea couldn't hold back the emotions anymore. "Thank you, thank you, thank you!" She again embraced the two teenagers. After a long moment, she pulled back. "Ah yes, now the way to Athenia." Eratrea looked around in several directions before confidently pointing back down the canyon they had come up.

Chapter 56

Together they set out, back down the canyon. Manatado carried Lukinia and a backpack they had found and filled with supplies. Everyone carried something, and the journey downhill was painful and exhausting.

"Marching through the forest was fun, Manatado. This sucks." Cassandra started to like having Manatado in charge. He was easily offended, awkward, and whiny, but he walked and talked with a new confidence that was reassuring. He was both easy to tease and easy to follow, and Cassandra liked that.

Manatado replied with labored breaths. "Well if we had a boat, a train, or a car, we would use it. You're welcome to try to find us one. I never got to ride in the Socratea tree."

"Well neither did I. Malada, can't you or your mother just magic zap us there? Please?" Cassandra paused to look back, only to find Malada and her mother falling farther behind. "Manatado, stop. This is stupid. We can't continue like this."

"Oh, so I'm stupid now. For someone who has a crush, you're not very nice."

"A crush, you wish. You're just jealous."

"Jealous, jealous of what?"

Cassandra huffed, "That I can move on." She then stopped and walked back to the other girls.

Manatado put Lukinia down and pouted with his face. "Yeah, well I'll believe it when I see it."

Both teenagers muddled to themselves and exchanged glances of frustration at each other. Cassandra sat down with Eratrea and Malada, while Nicolda approached

Manatado. "You know, young man, you're an idiot. But to be honest, when I was an adolescent, I was an idiot too. I think it is just something about the hormones."

Manatado dropped his head, depressed. "Do you have a point other than to rub it in?"

Nicolda said, "No, young man, you misunderstand. You see, there are many gifts in life. Some are natural and given at birth. Some are developed and trained, while others seem to be given from outside in the moment. I see in you what the others see too. You have it. It's your natural given talent. I have also seen you accept the gifts that are given in the moment. Now all we have to do is develop and train you."

Manatado looked blankly at the dwarf. "What do you mean? Given from the outside, I don't understand what you mean."

"When you jumped into that monster's mouth, tell me, was that your doing?"

Manatado looked even more puzzled. "Well, yes, no, kinda sorta? It's hard to explain. It's like I just knew what the right thing to do was and when to do it. I mean, yeah, it was me, but it's not like I planned that out or anything."

Nicolda smiled at him. "A gift given in the moment. Be proud. Not all are willing and able to accept such gifts."

"Gifts, from who? You mean like how Ciefraf gave his power to Eratrea?"

"Yes, but more subtle. Now, as for who is giving such gifts, I leave it to you to find out for yourself. Who the unknown creator is and what it is all about are answers best found personally."

Manatado spoke softly. "Okay, thanks. I'm not sure that helped the situation, but I will keep it in mind."

After the girls had finished a group huddle and talking session, Malada turned and faced the two men and a frozen Lukinia. "Well, Manatado, this isn't working. What are we going to do?"

"Well I had barely left the village before this whole thing started. I have no idea how far it is or how long it will take us. Eratrea, perhaps you could use your magic to get us there faster."

Eratrea shook her head no. "I'm afraid my powers only control the elements of nature."

Malada looked up toward her mother. "But, Mother, Father said that your magic came from him and he could control many types of magic."

"That may be true, my love, but, but the bonding has been broken. This is all that's left, perhaps because it was the first of the powers he gave me."

"The first? What other powers did he give you?"

"Patience, my love, he taught me the power of patience."

"Really, is that why you powered up the death machine?" Something about her mother's attitude toward her father really bugged Malada.

"Don't take that tone with me, young lady! I saved you! You should be grateful, not sassy."

Malada turned around and faced away from her mother. Cassandra came up alongside and wrapped her arm around Malada. Manatado stepped forward. "I have a suggestion." But before he could even spit it out, he was bombarded with a row of, "Shut up, Manatado," from the three girls.

Manatado glanced back at Nicolda, who shrugged his shoulders, questioning. "Like I was going to say, Eratrea, if you can control the wind, I can get us there faster." The three women stopped and glanced over their shoulders as he spoke. "Just like in shell backing, if your turtle is moving too slowly, you throw up a sail. There is plenty of equipment left in the valley. All we need to do is put some wheels on a base and throw up a sail."

Eratrea gave Manatado a glance that showed she was impressed. "You know what? That's a great idea."

Cassandra turned to face them now. "Manatado, we will set up camp here while you go take care of that. Thank you."

Manatado blushed with the compliment and then stayed red with annoyance at being assigned a task even though he was leader. Nicolda, as if reading Manatado's mind, pulled him on the arm. "Come on, I'll give you a hand."

Chapter 57

Manatado's wind cart proved very steady and speedy once they exited the canyon valley. Controlling the wind for long periods of time was exhausting to Eratrea, and try as she might, Malada couldn't summon her magic. Malada's insecurities about her ability to use magic were growing. Her father, Ciefraf, said that her powers were her own, so why couldn't she use them at will?

Manatado's frustrations were growing too. Ever since he tried to kiss Cassandra, she had taken every opportunity to insult him. If he was the leader of this group, he sure didn't feel respected like it. Even Malada would barely talk to him. She would entertain him in conversation just until she saw an opportunity to leave him for her mother or Cassandra.

Cassandra was feeling angry and guilty. She was mad at Manatado, but she could also see herself doing something similarly desperate. Had either of Manatado's best friends been there, she might have been tempted to kiss them just to make him jealous. The thought tickled her but then made her sick.

Nicolda steered the cart as they passed over long, rolling, grassy hills. The mountains were fading off into the distance, but the path ahead was still unseen. They were heading for a small dwarven outpost. The outpost was located along a river that came off the last mountain in its range. By chance, a couple of dwarf brothers fleeing bandits took cover near a high bank, as it turned out that high bank was the entrance to a cave.

The place had been designed to be hidden from those passing by. Nicolda explained that this was the farther outpost they maintained. A large deposit of diamonds had been found by those brothers celebrating their escape in the river. Nicolda explained that this was officially unadministered land, meaning there was no law and order, no doctors, and plenty of bandits. The elven forest was off in the far distance, and they seldom left the forest.

Malada brushed off every attempt Cassandra and Manatado made to converse with her, and she eventually got up and sat next to her mother. Together the two teens sat in silence, unable to talk through the awkward moments or the tasks at hand. Instead, they would make eye contact and then look away, make eye contact and then look away.

Malada waited for the cart to finish cresting a long rolling hill before she started talking to her mother. "Mom, tell me about Father."

Eratrea took a deep breath. "I'm too busy, sweetie, maybe later."

Malada was starting to realize her mother needed a firm hand sometimes in order to do the hard things, so she pressed on. "Mother, now is the time. Tell me about Father."

Eratrea cringed a little. "No, I mean, what do you want to know?"

"Nothing, really. I mean, everything. How did you meet him? What was he like? Why did you break the bonding? There is just so much. Why did you lie to me as a child?"

Eratrea looked down and away. "Ugh, I guess . . . well I guess you should know. I met your father, oh, I would say seventeen years ago. I . . . well I had run away from home. I was lost in the forest." She took a deep breath as she decided what and how to say it. "He saved me. I was lost, and I mean more than just lost in the woods. I . . . well now that I'm older, I can say I was depressed and angry, and it had gotten so bad I was . . . well I was ready to do extreme things, like even running away from home."

Malada had a million questions to ask, but she simply nodded and tried to absorb every bit of what her mother was saying. "It was there he found me. He was nothing more than a small little . . . benign being. Kind of a cute creature, very unintimidating. He asked me what was wrong. He was a great listener. Never once did he ever say to me, 'You should have done this,' or, 'You should have done that,' and once he understood, he showed me I was wrong. Together, together we did some amazing things. I could never understand how he did it, but he always seemed to find someone in distress, and he never failed to help. Together we . . . we saved lives . . . one at time. And as we saved their lives, we saved my own, as I found a reason worth living for again."

"Oh, Mom, that sounds amazing."

"Oh, it was, but it wasn't enough. You see, there were hard times going on in the world. Humans were expanding, ever more clashing with the other species. I wanted your father to stop the war. He chose not to. That's, that's all you need to know about your father."

Malada wasn't sure she agreed, but Nicolda whistled and broke her train of thought.

Nicolda brought the cart to a halt. To the right of the cart was the river. To the left was a very strangely arranged pile of rocks. He jumped off the cart and paced the river's edge. After some time, he found what he was looking for and signaled for the others to follow.

The path, barely worthy of the name, was clustered with rocks, foliage, and debris. Nicolda was able to navigate the path with ease while the teenagers constantly struggled to make forward progress. Eratrea decided to stay back and rest in the cart while they checked out the outpost.

Nicolda wound, slid, and hopped along the riverbank, jumping to a stop at the entrance to a cave. He stopped cold, which was unusual because he seemed so eager to get there. Nicolda shot Cassandra and Manatado a very nervous look before rushing into the cave. The two teens looked back at Malada, who repeated the worried look and then hurried after Nicolda. Malada turned around and, realizing she was done talking about her father, slowly followed after her friends.

Cassandra rounded the corner to see Nicolda with a sword drawn as he creeped ever deeper into the cave. Manatado felt his heart racing; something was wrong. Oh, how he wished for a weapon, a rifle, a sword, his old hunter's knife, but he had nothing, nor did Cassandra have any weapons with her bow and arrow missing.

Manatado could feel not only his own anxiety but Cassandra's as well. He reached out, grabbed her hands, and made eye contact. "There are three rules for combat."

Cassandra smiled at him, gently mouthed the words "shut up," and then stood behind him and pushed him forward. Together they followed after Nicolda. The cave sparkled brightly. The sunlight from the cave's entrance was being recast and spread out from a collection of diamonds placed strategical about.

Water dripped off in the distance, and the cold smell of animal musk filled the air. It was damp and cold with no decoration along the walls, only scar marks from mining. Nicolda had come to a stop in the center of the main area. There, he stopped to examine a large pile of recently mined diamonds.

Manatado tried to whisper but didn't do a very good job at it. "Why do you think something bad happened here. Why couldn't it just be empty, as if they left to join the others in the canyon?"

Nicolda spun around and gave a stern look. Then he pointed to the large pile of collected diamonds. "Who would leave that much behind? Nobody, that's a fortune."

Nicolda's explanation made Manatado gulp as he spoke. "Bandits? Invaders?"

Nicolda shook his head no to each.

Manatado and Cassandra then made eye contact as they came to the same conclusion. "Monster." Then, as if on a play's cue, Eratrea let out a horrific scream.

Chapter 58

Together they ran back up the ravine to where the cart was. Loud crackles of thunder roared about, deafening their approach. Manatado was the first to crest but immediately stopped and fell back. "Oh my god, oh my god." "What, Manatado, what is it?" Cassandra asked hurriedly.

Manatado's hand pointed as it shook. "Spi . . . spii . . . . spider!"

Cassandra grabbed hold and went with Malada as they crested the mound. There, above the cart, reaching aggressively to grab Eratrea below, was a giant spider. It had a van-sized thorax that shined black on top and burned red on bottom. Its head held pincers large enough to grab a human by the waist, and eyes that spanned the entirety of it. At this moment, it was using them to try to chew through the cart as its legs reached around.

Cassandra grabbed some rocks and started throwing them at the spider. The spider turned and shot a large amount of web, knocking Cassandra back and ensnaring her at the same time. Malada ran under the cart and joined her mother.

Nicolda grabbed his blade and charged at the spider. He sliced the tip off one of the spider's legs, but it quickly adjusted and grabbed the dwarf with another leg. With an amazing swiftness, the dwarf was covered with webbing and placed aside for later consumption.

Malada screamed out for Manatado as the spider again pounced down on the cart in pursuit of its prey.

Manatado shined brightly as he charged up the mound with an armful of diamonds. Handful after handful, he chucked them as hard as he could at the spider. Diamond after diamond bounced off the creature with little to no effect other than to pause the monster as it turned to attack him.

Cassandra screamed at the top of her lungs. "Use the light, use the light . . . you idiot, use the light." Her words dropped off into tears.

At first, Manatado had no idea what she meant, but as he turned, a bright shining light flashed across Cassandra, blinding her, giving him the idea. Manatado held the largest diamond up as high as he could and wiggled it.

Luckily, it took only a moment for him to find the right angle, blinding the spider. The monster let out a hiss as it buckled its head in reaction.

"Charge, charge," Nicolda screamed. "My blade is next to the cart."

Manatado swallowed, emptied his mind, and went. He ran on instinct and reaction. His hand held the diamond high as he tried his best to keep the blinding light on the spider. He hurled the diamond right into the spider's mouth as he slid like a baseball player, grabbed Nicolda's blade, and slashed the nearest leg in half. The spider cried out in pain, and Manatado ran.

He ran and ran, and finding a nearby boulder, he jumped behind it. The spider limped back to the cart and was once again after the girls; however, this time it seemed less able.

Manatado felt his chest pounding and his heart racing. He couldn't believe what he had just done. Nor could he think of what next to do. "What do I do now?"

There was no answer, so he called out again, only louder this time. "What do I do now?"

Again, after no answer, he looked over the boulder and his heart sank. There, being spun together in a web at a dizzying speed, were Malada and her mother. "What do I do now?" He asked the question, but there was no answer. Fear and guilt overcame Manatado as he cowered behind the boulder. "What do I do now?"

Chapter 59

Flaming arrows flew across the sky over Manatado's head. "Leave it to us, young human!" A shirtless well-toned elf slammed his staff into the ground behind Manatado, sending dust all around.

Manatado coughed. "Who are you?"

The elf never acknowledged the question but waved his other arm forward, summoning a small band of elves to charge at the monster spider. Two arrows with ropes attached flew in from the tree lines and dug themselves into the creature's thorax. An elf zip lined down each with blades in hand.

The spider dropped Malada and hunched back, spraying a huge amount of web at one of the elves zip lining toward it. The web encased the elf and, using a good leg, batted the encased elf off into the distance. The second elf zip lining detached itself and flew high up into the air. The elf came down and slashed its blade down into the head of the spider.

The spider screamed out in pain, shook for a moment, and fell to the ground. Manatado jumped up in excitement and pumped his fist in the air. The shirtless elf gave him a stern look and then faced back toward the spider. The thorax was shaking and wiggling. The band of elves all took up weapons and readied themselves.

"Grab your friends and drag them to safety, hurry." The shirtless elf barked his command at Manatado, who hesitated. "Now." Again Manatado hesitated. The elf now shot Manatado a very scary look, and he began running toward the shaking spider. Manatado grabbed Malada and

Eratrea by the webbing and turned. Yet as he turned, the spider's thorax burst open with a sea of rat-sized spiders. Manatado screamed out in fear and ran as fast as his feet could move. They were fast. One of the spiders launched itself at him. Manatado could feel the wind from the elf's staff as it flew right by his head, sending the flying spider backward. Manatado had never been so scared in his life, and he kept running and pulling until his body collapsed.

The elves sliced, slammed, and stomped at superhuman speed, but the spiders were too many. The shirtless elf paused for a moment, and Manatado thought it was over, but another elf saved him as he placed his hands together over the staff. After a moment, the staff began to spew fire from both ends.

The elf was masterful with his weapon and magic. Fireballs rang out from the staff, as did large plumes of fire. His feet were deadly, too, as he twirled through the air, dodging, smashing, and burning every spider he could find.

The action came to a halt as the air smelled horrible. Manatado lay curled up next to the girls for a long moment before sitting up. Tears had obviously been rolling from his eyes. The whole area was still for a long time, when suddenly the whirling sound of an arrow in flight flew right past his head. The squeal of a spider being hit dead center pierced Manatado's ears. He slowly looked over in the direction from which it had come, and there, smiling with bow in hand, was Cassandra. Manatado smiled briefly before falling to the ground and passing out for a moment.

Chapter 60

The shirtless elf cut Malada free from her web and then freed Eratrea as well. As he cut Eratrea out, he clutched her tightly in his arms and, when she smiled at him, kissed her passionately.

Manatado spoke without thinking and didn't realize he was staring. "Whoa."

Malada looked down at him, scowled, and gently kicked him. The elf and Eratrea finished their kiss, and Eratrea's faced flushed deep red, as did Manatado's, as he was still staring, followed by Malada, who was growing very angry.

The elf placed Eratrea upright, turned around, walked two steps, and then cleared his throat. "WHAT HAVE YOU DONE? YOU HAVE SCREWED EVERYTHING UP! YOU WERE TOLD VERY SPECIFICALLY—NEVER, NEVER, NEVER START THE MACHINE! THIS IS ALL YOUR FAULT!"

Malada erupted. "Shut up, Redleaf! You weren't there! You have no right!"

Before she could get another word in, Redleaf spun around and barked over her. "Don't you sass me, young lady! You aren't supposed to be here at all! We sent you away. We sent you somewhere safe! You are just like your mother, never listening to instructions!"

Malada puffed up her chest as she prepared to bark back but decided against it and instead seethed inside. Manatado could tell she didn't like this elf, and he took up a defensive position right next to her.

Eratrea, with a tear in her eye, spoke. "I know, I know. I'm so sorry, but I couldn't. I couldn't let him harm her."

"I told you this is much bigger than one family. That's why we sent her away. Now that machine is destroying all of the great forest of Bashan. Many, many elven families have lost their homes, and that machine is devouring our entire culture.

Eratrea's hand went to her mouth. "Of course, even after I started it, he would still need fuel to power it. Those ancient magical trees will power that machine for our entire lifetimes."

"Human lifetimes—we, we will have to deal with these consequences for many years yet still after."

"What do we do now?" Eratrea's voice carried the sound of guilt and fear.

Redleaf stood up and spoke for all to hear. "Tonight we will take you to our camp. Tomorrow the children will be sent off to safety and you, Eratrea, will use every last magical power left to help us defeat that machine."

Malada motioned again as if she was going to yell out in argument but again backed down. The group conferred quietly as they organized everything needed for the hike back to their camp. The cart was abandoned over the gentle protest of the teens, and they were forced to carry everything, including the frozen-in-stone Lukinia.

The march was long and exhausting. There was little energy for talk or songs along the way, and it probably would have been discouraged by the elves anyway. When they finally dragged their tired feet into the camp, they were impressed with how hidden it was. Even in the middle of the camp, it could easily have been mistaken for any other part of the forest. Nicolda received some instruction from the elves and then led the teens to a flat spot under a massive tree. This is where they were to set up camp but, being so tired, they instead opted to simply roll out some sleeping bags and lie down. Malada was saddened and nervous as her mother went with the elves, but she was too tired to argue about it and went to sleep.

Chapter 61

Malada woke with a start. Her body was upright and her arms ready for a fight. Her chest pounded and her adrenaline rushed, but as her eyes scoured the area, she saw nothing. She heard nothing. She waited.

After a long pause, a gentle snore from Manatado broke the silence. Malada could sense something, or someone, was there but couldn't see or hear them. Finally, she got up and started walking toward her gut feeling. She paused, turned back, and grabbed a blade the elves had given Manatado. She put her shoes on and stepped out into the forest.

She walked several meters, and then several more. After she was far from the camp, she found him. The benign little being was sitting on a log, resting peacefully.

"Daddy!" Malada squeaked out in excitement, waking the little being.

"Wha—whoa, oh." Ciefraf was looking weaker than last time. "Oh, my love. I'm so glad you found me. I was coming for you, but I seem to have lost some of my strength these past few days."

Malada embraced the benign little being. "Oh, Daddy. Are you okay?"

"I'm fine, just showing my age a bit, I'm afraid." He paused as if trying to remember something. "Ah, yes. How did things go with your mother?"

"Oh, Daddy, you would be so proud of her. I told her she was forgiven and now, now all she wants to do is help us."

Ciefraf smiled. "Oh, my love. I-I-I'm glad she is trying. But please be cautious. Your youthful optimism might set you up for a big letdown."

"No, no, no, Daddy. She is good now. Really."

Ciefraf looked as if he was going to argue the point but changed his mind. Malada took advantage of the pause in conversation. "Daddy. Mommy said something."

Ciefraf nodded for her to continue.

"She said that you could have stopped the war. She said that she left you because you refused to . . . well she didn't say that part."

He took a deep breath. "Well she isn't totally wrong. I could have stopped the war between man and orc. Yes, it would have saved many lives, but it would have come at the cost of one of my strongest vows."

"Daddy, I don't think I'm understanding."

"Having great power doesn't mean one gets to wield it as they please, for if they do, they quickly become slaves to the master of self. I vowed never to use my powers to harm, or force my will upon, anyone. Even if done in the name of a greater good, it would be wrong. Let me see if I can think of an example." Ciefraf paused for a moment before an idea came to him. "Ah, yes. You have been to visit the fairies. You learned of the forest queen Ankinia defeating the evil wizard Malgamar. Did you not?"

Malada gave a less-than-confident nod yes. Ciefraf rolled his eyes before continuing. "Malgamar was a powerful comrade of mine, but he eventually came to believe that our powers should be shared with the other species of this world. So he set out to find those in need. He came across a tiny group of forest creatures, too big for a bug and too small for a rodent. He soon learned these small animals could think.

Malgamar trained, shared, and enhanced the creatures until they became something close to what they are today."

"I don't understand. What happened?"

"Patience, my child. I'm old. It takes me a moment to gather my thoughts."

Malada gave a childish guilty look and then nodded for him to continue.

"Not all of the elves wanted the changes and powers he was giving them. Malgamar became infuriated that they would reject his gifts. Eventually he became so obsessed that the fairies turned against him and kicked him out of their forest."

"Oh, so he wanted to do something good and ended up doing something bad. But why tell me this story?"

Ciefraf didn't speak and instead prodded Malada to think it through. She waited patiently for an answer and then collapsed her eyebrows as she thought it through. "You mean, you think Mommy will do something bad when she thinks she is really doing good?"

"Has she not already, my love? Ugh. I grow so weak and weary. Go, my love, and fight for what is right. But beware your mother—her intentions may be right, but she will not be."

"I don't understand. What does that mean? How will I know?"

"Follow him."

"Redleaf, that jerk. I don't like him."

"No, follow him."

Malada paused and took a deep breath. "But he's an idiot!"

Ciefraf smiled. "Even in my youth, I might have been called as such. Look beyond and you will see it in him."

Malada didn't like where the conversation ended, and she could see the body of the benign little being starting to fade away. "Daddy, don't go. I need you."

"Be to him what he can't be, and allow him to be to you what you can't be."

Malada felt tears falling down her face. "NO, Daddy, don't go. No, Daddy." The words did nothing, and the body of the benign little being faded away into nothing. Malada fell to her knees and cried until a startled and wild-eyed Manatado came charging in with his fist flying in the air.

"NO, no, NO," she said.

Manatado had no idea what he was attacking or doing, but he was doing it bravely. Cassandra came charging in out of the bush, tackling Manatado down to the ground.

"I got them, I got them!" Cassandra yelled as she held Manatado facedown into the ground.

Malada hopped up and helped Cassandra stand up, off of Manatado. Then, as the three of them faced each other in the dark woods, Malada threw her arms around them both and squeezed. "Thank you. Thank you, my friends."

Chapter 62

The teens were woken up early to the sound of barking commands. "On your feet, children." Clapping followed each command. "Today you have much to do, on your feet!" Manatado tried covering his head with some large leaves, but that only drew the commander's attention. At last, the three finally found themselves upright and standing side by side, being eyed by a short stout elf. "My name is WaterWakes, and I will be preparing you for today's mission."

Malada was instantly cleared of any sleeping fog when she barked back, "Take the machine away from Jalum."

"Negative, that is not your assignment today. Leave that to the adults." WaterWakes paused and gave a stern look toward Malada, preventing any objection she might have. She took a deep breath as if preparing to yell but instead mumbled under her breath as she spit the air back out. "Today you will be seeking out the potion master."

WaterWakes snapped his fingers and another elf brought in the rock that was Lukinia. "The three of you will seek out the potion master and do whatever she deems necessary to retrieve a potion that will restore your fairy friend here. Any questions?"

The three teens looked at each other, each with a hundred questions they wanted to ask. WaterWakes didn't wait long before he continued. "While the path through the forest is safe, we are giving you arms to protect yourself, as these are dangerous times. The second elf now rolled in a cart of various weapons. Cassandra was now clearheaded and very eagerly reached out for a slick, sleek all-black bow, with metal arrow tips. Malada was handed back her shield and given a staff.

WaterWakes then walked up to Manatado. "What weapons have you been trained to use, boy?"

Manatado swallowed. "Um, um, I, uh."

"Spit, it out, boy. What do you know how to use?"

Manatado gulped and then pointed to the far-left corner. The second elf motioned to grab a large-barrel high-caliber rifle. WaterWakes smiled and brought his hand together in pride, when Manatado shook them off and pointed again. This time with raised eyebrows, the second elf held up a medium-sized hunting knife. WaterWakes tilted his head so his eyes looked down at Manatado and shook his head as he handed it to him. Manatado grabbed the blade and his holder and slunk away from the group.

The second elf then handed each of the teens a small bag with an assortment of snacks and water. WaterWakes wasted no time. As soon as the third bag was handed out, he started barking. "This way, I will see you to the trailhead. I will then take my leave of you and join the adults as we battle to capture Jalum's machine."

WaterWakes started walking off in the direction he wanted them to follow, when Malada finally spoke up. "Where, where is my mother?"

WaterWakes only paused and then continued walking as he answered. "Your mother is the lynchpin to our plan. She has been given great responsibility. She doesn't need to be worrying about a child at this moment. Remember that if your thoughts start to drift as you walk." The elf stood off to the side as a sign marker appeared behind him, showing the way.

Cassandra now spoke. "What will the potion maker want from us?"

WaterWakes rolled his eyes. "The potion master is a strange creature. No one can say for certain what she will ask for in return. It could be a simple lock of hair, or it may require a perilous path up a mountain to retrieve a rare flower. Either way, by the time you return, we should know the outcome of the battle."

Cassandra looked as if she wanted to ask another question, but WaterWakes put his arm on her side and gently pushed her toward the path. WaterWakes then gave a bow, as was elven custom, turned, and left.

The three teens again found themselves alone in the forest at a crossroads. Cassandra and Malada exchanged nervous looks, faced Manatado, and spoke in unison. "Manatado, what do we do?"

Manatado enjoyed being stared at by two girls and lost himself in the moment. Memories of him hanging out with his friends Roger and Tamack had long ago stopped crossing his mind. Yet now he thought of them and how he longed to brag about being the center of attention of two girls. Manatado had no idea what they were saying, nor could he stop the blushing and the smile that radiated his face.

Cassandra finally slapped him hard on the arm. "What do we do?"

The jolt brought him back to the moment, but he was still behind.

"Wait, what do we do about what?"

"Ugh." Cassandra and Malada exchanged frustrated glances. "What do we do about this situation?"

"Oh, well, um, yeah, I say . . . Lukinia was kind of annoying, and scary, and crazy, but she still is . . . and she needs us. The adults, well I don't trust them. I really don't trust that Redleaf, but I also don't have any clue how to battle that machine. I would also say the idea of sitting this one out is okay with me."

Malada didn't like his answer. "You coward! You are just afraid of that machine. You don't care about my mother, or me. You just care about yourself!"

Cassandra was now mad and came to Manatado's defense. "You can't say that! He defeated Riftia, not you or your mother! And might I say, your mother doesn't seem too concerned with anything she is being asked to do. If she didn't want to do it, why was she coming with us after it! No, Manatado is right. This time, we just do what we are told. How can we even trust you after you didn't even tell us the truth?"

Malada's face expressed shock. "What! How dare you call me a liar after everything we have been through?"

"OH yeah, Redleaf said they sent you away. You told us your mother was captured."

"You've seen Redleaf. No one can say no to him! She was a captive!"

The two girls faced off so close they could smell each other's breath. Manatado wrapped his arms around both of them and squeezed hard. At first they both pulled away, gently hitting at him to let go. After a long moment and realizing that he wasn't going to let go, they relaxed some, then more, then they started to cry, and then they embraced. For a long time, the three of them hugged, but Manatado couldn't help himself. "This is nice. Now I think we should all kiss . . . and, um, make up."

The two girls strongly pulled back, hit him on his arms in protest, locked arms with each other, and turned away from him. They then looked at each other and started walking down the path.

Manatado paused, with a sad puppy-dog look on his face. "Wait, what?"

Chapter 63

It was several hours' hike before they came upon the potion master's hut. The forest darkened as they approached. The sounds of the birds and the bugs died away. A foul-smelling breeze crossed their path. Malada and Cassandra came to a stop several yards away. Together they made eye contact. Then, in unison, they stepped behind Manatado and nudged him forward.

Manatado felt the warmth of the girls' hands on his back and drifted away, enjoying the closeness. The potion master's hut was dark with neon-yellow lights tracing the rim of the roof. It stood seven feet tall and as wide around. The front door was solid dark wood with gargoyle statues flanking the entrance sides.

Manatado leaned back into the girls, who continued to push him forward. When they neared the door, Cassandra leaned forward, her face brushing up against Manatado. She then grabbed the metal ring, pulling the door open. Malada placed the frozen Lukinia statue in his arms. Together the girls pushed Manatado into the dark hut and slammed the door behind him. They then raced to the window to watch.

Manatado felt like he had woken from a dream into a nightmare. The room smelled of rotten things and soured milk. Several small fires kept cauldrons on the far shelf at a low boil. A black bird flew across the far side of the room. Manatado gulped and reached for his hunter's knife. The blade shook as he kept hold of Lukinia and used her as a shield. He then backed up against the door and tried to pull it open.

An aged and rough voice cried out from somewhere in the darkness. "Who dares to enter my house and raise a weapon to me?"

Manatado screamed, "AAAA, I'm sorry, I'm sorry, I'm sorry. I'm just scared. I mean no harm." He held Lukinia tightly as he tried to hide behind it.

"Then drop the blade!"

Manatado screeched again as he fumbled the blade, dropping it to the ground.

The same voice from before spoke but with a different pitch and tone. "He drops his only defense. He leaves himself open to the darkness."

The first voice returned. "He braves the darkness, and not for himself."

The second voice replied, "Do you come alone?"

Manatado paused, not realizing he was being spoken to, causing the second voice to call out again. "Well, boy, talk or have your tongue taken from you."

"AAAa." Manatado let his eyes glance over his shoulder at the window, hoping to see his friends. "Um, I, um, come first!"

The first voice from the darkness spoke again. "This one seeks the middle ground. He will compromise away everything."

The second voice replied, "The middle ground is where the lukewarm water is. Lukewarm water doesn't know if it is hot or cold, so it thinks it's fine."

"What?" Manatado said, "I'm not water, and I'm not lukewarm. Now I'm here to see the potion master."

A white moonbeam suddenly pierced down from above, illuminating a two-headed witch. The heads pulled as far apart as their necks would allow as the body stepped forward. The witch's arms extended out and grabbed Lukinia. Manatado pulled back at first but then relinquished after one of the heads snarled at him.

The two heads examined Lukinia in every detail. "Hmm, most powerful magic this be. Very few who can do this. Tell me, how did this happen?"

"So you are the potion master?"

The second head rushed toward and got face-to-face with Manatado. "Does its brain have damage? Does this creature not think clearly? Maybe its hormones are too much for its brain."

"Hey," Manatado blurted out in protest, but he wasn't quite sure what they were saying. "What do you mean? What is a hormone?"

The first head tilted back in laughter that speared their ears. "Sweet innocent youth. Bring in your friends. We have something to discuss." The witch then turned around and sat down in a rocking chair in the corner of the room. She sat Lukinia down next to her and signaled for all of them to come and sit. Malada and Cassandra, who had been peeking in through the window, now gracefully entered and tiptoed up behind Manatado.

Again the witch signaled for the teens to sit. Cassandra poked Manatado gently in his ribs, startling him as they approached. Manatado smiled at her and then, together, they sat cross-legged like kids around a teacher.

"Now, first tell us how your friend became stone," the first head asked.

Manatado raised his hand to his ear as he spoke. "Well we aren't entirely sure. You see, we think it was Jalum, as he is the one who gave her back to us."

The witch's second head shook left and right. "Tsk, tsk, was not Jalum. Jalum has no magical powers, just science. No, this was the work of extreme power."

The first head continued. "You can't mean . . . even Jalum wouldn't be stupid enough to get in league with the dark master."

The three teens listened closely and spoke together. "Dark master?"

The first head jerked back and hissed. "Do not mention the evil one again."

Malada seemed almost relieved. "Jalum has a master too?"

The second head spoke. "We all serve a master. Even a master of self is still a master."

Cassandra stood next to Manatado and gently grabbed his arm. "Who is the dark master? I've never heard of them."

The two heads looked at each other. "Innocent youth." The second head turned to face the teens. "When creation turns its back on its master, what does the master do?"

There was a very long silence before the first head spoke. "Boy, we asked you a question."

Manatado was startled, as his focus had moved to Cassandra's hand on his arm. "Oh, um, so what does creation do when its master turns its back on it?"

The witch's cane thumped Manatado on the head, bringing about a single tear. Malada pinched Manatado. "No, what does the master do when its creation turns its back on them?"

"Oh, destroy and start again?"

The witch's two heads let out a gentle laugh. "Whew, be thankful you are not the creator." The heads then switched off speaking in turns. "The creator looked at what he had made and it was good. Yet it was empty and served no purpose, so the creator filled the lands with all the creations and everything they needed. Yet existence alone wasn't enough for his creation, and soon the creation longed to become the creator. There was one who led the way. But the creator is forgiving, generous, and kind, and no matter how far apart the creation could get from its master, it could never get free of the master's gifts, nor could it ever surpass the master. So it grew spiteful, arrogant, and cruel. Now it has gone so far it exists only to work against the creator's will."

Manatado's mouth dropped. "And now Jalum is in league with this creature who turned Lukinia into stone."

The two witch heads looked at each other in astonishment. "Truth comes from its mouth! Astonishment!"

The girls looked at each other and then reluctantly gave a nod to Manatado, who proudly smiled back at both of them. His smile only lasted a moment before he swallowed. "Whoa, so what does that mean for your mom, who is going to fight him right now?"

Malada's face froze before she raced toward the door.

The witch raised her cane and slammed the door shut. "You will only fail, unless you are ready."

Chapter 64

The witch banged her cane against the ground three times and then signaled for Malada to return and sit down. The second head stared eagle-eyed at Malada. "Come all this way for nothing, have you? Willing to throw everything away to protect her? No, she is not the one."

The first head responded. "Agreed, but her haste is not without merit. Much happenings are afoot. The one is needed to point them the way."

Manatado made eye contact with Malada. He fought back the urge to give her a great big hug. "Perhaps you can give us the potion we need to fix Lukinia. Then we can get back to whatever it is we are going to do next."

The witch pinched her noses. "Whew, does your entire species stink of such hormones?"

Manatado tilted his head. "You used that word before, 'hormone.' What does it mean? And I don't stink, do I girls?" Manatado looked at Cassandra and Malada, who giggled at each other and then pinched their noses childishly.

The witch's second head raced to full extension in Cassandra's direction. "Who are you to laugh? You stink too!" This brought a giggle from Malada and then the scorn of the second head as well. "And you, young miss, have you never bathed in your life?" Malada's jaw dropped in embarrassment.

"Hormones, to teach such innocent youths, are what make you change from boy to man or girl to woman." The first head finished while the second continued. "They also have the unfortunate side effect of—"

"Making a horrible stench," the second head blurted out.

"Cough, cough . . . making one's brain foggy, unfocused, and . . ." The witch raised her cane to Manatado's face, which had moved in the direction of staring at Malada. The witch gently thumped him on the head before the second head spoke. "Impossible. He is too saturated. We cannot acquire the ingredients needed to save your friend."

Manatado frowned his eyebrows. "Hey now, we came a long way and we are in a hurry. Now tell us what you need so you can save our friend, then get back to the adults, and maybe save them too." He put on a manly face and tried to give Malada a manly look.

Another gentle tap from the witch's broom brought his attention back to the witch. The first head replied, "Pure evil turned her to stone. Only pure intentions can bring her back."

"What does that mean?"

"It means you are too hormonal to give us a pure tear."

Cassandra stepped closer to Manatado. "Pure tear?"

The second head shook its head no. "Only a tear free of hormones can prove pure intentions and thus make a pure tear."

Malada put her finger to her mouth. "So all we have to do is make Manatado a girl?"

The two witch heads looked at each other. "NO, the boy must prove he has only the desire for what is best for your friend, not what is best for him."

Cassandra now walked over to Malada. "It means all we have to do is get the hormones out of him."

The two witch heads nodded at each other.

The two girls then looked at each other. "How do we do that?"

Chapter 65

The two girls whispered secretly toward each other. They then stepped up to the witch and, after a short discussion, were handed a large handful of small bottles to catch the tears in. Manatado could feel a nervous twist forming in his stomach over the girls, and the witch plotted a way to make him cry.

Manatado took a small step, then a medium step, and then started running for the door. He pulled on the handle as hard as he possibly could, but nothing happened. He turned around and pressed his back against the door. There before him, Cassandra and Malada stood ready to pounce on him.

Cassandra went first, grabbing him by the head and pulling out ear hair after ear hair. She collected some tears and ran them over to the witch while Malada moved in. Manatado put his hands over his ears while Malada grabbed his nose and pulled out a nose hair. Malada collected some tears and then ran them over to the witch.

The witch tried the tears that Cassandra had but shook her head no. Cassandra charged at Manatado, passing by Malada, who was on her way to the witch. Cassandra slammed her foot down on Manatado's and kept pressing, collecting more tears. Malada, having failed, swapped places with Cassandra and twisted his nipple, collecting more tears.

After a few attempts each, the girls again met in a huddle. Once they broke apart, they stood in a line and all stared at Manatado angrily. Then, one after another, they hurled insults and frustrations at him.

"This is all your fault!"

"Can't you do anything right!"

"You're such a failure. People are going to die because you are a failure."

"Your father would be ashamed of you!"

The witch held out her cane, as it had a bottle attached to it, from which she collected Manatado's tears of sorrow.

Again after several rounds, the three collected together in another huddle. Manatado had never hated anything so much before, so when the girls came back with more insults, he had had enough. He had never yelled and vented so hard before in his life, and it brought tears of anger to his eyes. Cassandra rushed in and tipped Manatado's head, collecting the tears as he screamed. Again the witch shook her head in disappointment.

Instead of huddling this time, the girls just spoke ideas out loud. They went round and round until they landed on one they liked. "Maybe he needs to sweat the hormones out." They never gave Manatado a chance to reply before they had him in a large pot of nearly boiling water. Cassandra found some candles and started placing them around Manatado while Malada gathered some wood and started a small cooking fire.

Manatado felt worse and worse, and he finally started pleading, "Please, please stop. I'm so hot I can't take it anymore." Again the tears were collected and failed to be pure tears. At last the girls dragged Manatado out of the pot and laid him flat on the floor, breathing deeply and in distress.

"I'm out of ideas, so, like, what? I'm almost willing to try kissing the hormones out of him." As Malada spoke, Manatado bolted upright and looked flush again. "Wait, what?"

Cassandra and Malada looked at each other and then shook their heads no. "Seriously, what do we do?" This time, the girls approached Manatado and knelt beside him. "Manatado, this is serious. What do we do?"

"I liked the kissing idea."

"Be serious!"

"Well, I'm trying. Can you just will your hormones to your control?"

Cassandra grabbed Manatado's hand. "Thank you for trying, but we need more. Here is what I want you to do. First, close your eyes."

Manatado reached out and held Cassandra's hand back, only he started rubbing her with his hand. Cassandra pinched him and placed his hands together in his lap. "Now take a deep breath."

Manatado's chest rose and fell, but he kept peeking his eyes open and puckering his lips just on the hope they were going to go back to the kissing idea.

"NO one is going to kiss you, Manatado. We are your friends only. Malada's boyfriend is with the elves, and I'm in love with Tamack." Malada shot Cassandra a questioning look, but the strong reaction of disappointment and rejection crushed Manatado's spirit.

"Malada, that's not true. You would have said something."

"I'm sorry. Manatado. I, I just needed your help so badly I couldn't stand to disappoint you." Malada was quite sure where this was heading, but she followed Cassandra's cues.

Manatado shook his head back and forth. "No, no, that's not true."

Cassandra nodded her head further, encouraging Malada to go on.

"Manatado, please try to understand. I didn't want to hurt you."

At first he didn't believe it, but Manatado's face was easy to read and the two girls sat and watched as his heart broke in slow motion, followed by Cassandra's, as she realized it wasn't because of her that his heart was breaking. There were times when Cassandra just wanted to kill Manatado, but there were other times he made her feel special too.

Cassandra carried on. "Now, Manatado, I think the time has come for us to separate." A genuinely sad tone came through in her voice. "Saving Lukinia is your task. Saving Eratrea is ours now. We are going to have to leave you now."

Manatado's face turned white. "Wait, wha-wha-what do you mean?"

Cassandra and Malada grabbed each other's hand and stood up. "This is where we say goodbye." Together they stood up, leaving a dumbfounded, sad young man alone on the floor. They grabbed their bags of supplies and headed toward the front door. They paused for a second, looked back at Manatado, and then walked out. Manatado ran to the door and pulled hard, but it wouldn't open.

He ran to the window like a puppy and watched them walk back down the path and out of view. After some time, he turned around and faced the witch. Her heads stared deeply at him but didn't say a word. Manatado waited for the witch to do something, but all she did was stand there tending to a pot of boiling broth.

Manatado walked up and picked up Lukinia. He took a moment to examine what had become of her. He noticed something for the first time, even after all that time caring her. Yet now it was all he could think about. It was his harsh words that had sent her running off into the forest. Lukinia had been very afraid as she was frozen. What did it mean? Did Lukinia cross paths with Jalum's master? How come Gerterma never mentioned Jalum's master?

Manatado started to think about what had scared Lukinia so intensely. He could imagine her tiny body shaking in fear at the power of the enemy—alone, spying on the enemy, only to be capture, tortured. A new feeling of guilt started creeping up into his soul. It was he who lashed out at her. For what? Wanting him—it was the fairy way for girls to pursue the boys. Now he felt horrible. It was his petty desire for Malada that had caused him to act so nastily. What if he had been gentler in letting her down? Could he have avoided all of this? Now he had lost everything, and it was all his own fault.

Manatado sat cross-legged on the floor, holding the frozen-in-stone Lukinia. His body slowly dropped down over it, and soon the sound of sniffling came. The witch attached another bottle to her cane and held it across the room. She bumped against Manatado's face and a tear rolled down and into the dropper.

The witch had a small jump in her step, and as she added the tear to the boiling cauldron, a poof of yellow light burst out across the room. The witch jumped up and down. "Most inconceivable . . . it worked, it worked."

Cassandra and Malada burst back into the room, pulled Manatado up from the floor, and had him give Lukinia to the witch. The witch placed Lukinia on a small table in the corner. Then, using her cane, she gathered a large quantity of the broth and poured it over Lukinia. Lukinia was bathed in a golden light that crumbled the stone away, and as it did so, Lukinia's voice came across. "But I did what—" Lukinia didn't finish the sentence before realizing she was somewhere new. She paused, looked around slowly, and then paused again as her heart skipped a beat while the three teenagers were eagerly looking at her. "Oh, look at that. It's you guys, yeahhhhhhhh," Lukinia less-than-excitedly squeaked out.

Chapter 66

The three teens stared big-eyed and directly at Lukinia as she straightened out and gathered herself. She raised her hands as if she had a wand, but without one, she didn't know what to do, so her hands flailed about awkwardly before clasping behind her back. "So, um, where are we? What happened?" Lukinia looked at Manatado as her memory returned. "Manatado, I thought you didn't want me, um, around."

This time, Manatado blushed, as he had forgotten that when Lukinia was awake, he had been cruelly blunt. "Hi, Lukinia. I, I, I owe you an apology. I guess my, um, hormones had me focused on the, um, wrong things." He shuffled his feet around and looked at the floor as he spoke.

Lukinia was slightly taken aback, and her eyes scanned the room intensely for hidden dangers. Even though the girls were there for the event, Manatado had no desire to speak what had happened out loud. Lukinia finished scanning the room, and her attention returned to Manatado. "Yeah, um, thank you. I guess I owe you an apology, too, as I have no idea what human dating customs are. Perhaps it is best if we just move on. What are we going to do now?"

"Jalum has the machine and is using it to attack the elves." Manatado wrapped his arms around the two girls and smiled. "We are going to go after them as they go after Jalum."

"Jalum has the machine . . . so then . . . all is lost." Lukinia's voice trailed off. "I can't go back to him again."

Manatado, misunderstanding, stood up tall. "Don't fear Jalum, Lukinia. This time, you are with us, the clan, the clan of the unknown creator."

"What?" Lukinia's reaction was of instant dislike, but she bit her tongue. "I think I missed something with that whole clan thing."

This time, Malada stood up straight and spoke. "After Manatado defeated Riftia."

Cassandra slid up next to Manatado, squeezed his arm, and smiled at him, making him blush intensely.

"Nicolda was so distraught by his clan behavior that he denounced them and vowed to join ours. But you know, since we didn't have one, Nicolda felt it appropriate to form a new one with"—Malada rolled her eyes as she pointed with her head at the blushing Manatado—"this guy as the leader."

Lukinia looked dumbfounded. "So some random dwarf gave you all a name, and now you're, what, like a band of brothers? A family? I don't get it."

Cassandra responded as she backed off from Manatado. "No, you get it." She took a few steps toward the path. "Now, shall we get moving?"

Manatado was able to breathe again as Cassandra stepped off. "Lukinia, why don't you join us? That is, at least until you decide if you want to be a permanent member."

Lukinia relaxed at the new invitation, too distracted to take any offense. "But I have no want, no ability, to control my magic. I don't think I would be much use to the clan."

At this, the two-headed witch coughed with the first head while the second head said, "Another who looks but does not see."

Lukinia turned around. "Oh my, yes. Potion master, do you have any wands available?"

The witch looked Lukinia over very thoroughly. "Unfortunately, yes I do, but I'm afraid you will be most disappointed in both the quality and the price." The witch turned, bent over, and picked up something out of a dusty box. She blew the dust off and gave it a whirl with her hand. "Elves, you see, do not use wands. This is the only one I have. Traded for it from a weary traveler. Twenty gold bits."

Lukinia approached the witch, looked at the wand, frowned, and waved it around, amplifying her frown. She gulped. "Um, you mean I can't just have it?"

The witch laughed a horrid chuckled laugh. "Free, ah ha ha ha. In fact, you kids still owe me. I believe your total will be twenty gold bits, for a new total of forty bits. Now, before you leave, pay up."

Lukinia looked at the teens. None of them had expected to need money. The girls all looked at Manatado, who, once again the center of attention, started to beam. He looked at each of the girls and, in an unspoken way, said, "You need me." With a swagger, he reached behind him and into his money pouch, or where his money pouch should have been. Manatado's face was easy to read, and without any words being spoken, the four bolted for the door.

The witch raised her cane and slammed the door shut as Manatado ran into it. "Deadbeats, I should have known they would be deadbeats." The second head scolded the first, who replied, "Now, now, they are only innocent youth. I was prepared for this."

The teens and Lukinia turned around and stood with guilt-laden faces watching the witch.

"Wages are ten bits an hour, and I do believe there are four of you. That should be just enough time to get it all done." The second head now laughed with understanding. The witch moved over to a dark spot in the back of her hut and opened a large unseen door. There behind the door was a massive pile of dirty pots and pans. "Now, get to it."

The four looked at each other, gulped, lowered their heads, and walked through the door and into the pots and pans.

Chapter 67

The film of ickiness covering the witch's pots and pans was formidable. Manatado dulled his blade by chipping away at it. Cassandra's face dripped with sweat as she pounded away with a pointed rock. Malada and Lukinia zapped, blew, and thundered the grime off. Malada smiled as she felt like once again she had some control over her magic. Yet in the pit of her stomach, she still worried whether it would always come this easily. For a very long hour, the teens scrubbed away.

Cassandra asked, "Lukinia, when we were in your village, I didn't see many male fairies, and the ones I did see didn't have any wings. Um, what's up with that?"

Lukinia at first felt annoyed at having to interact, but the more she did so, the more comfortable she seemed to become. "Oh, well yeah, male fairies are mostly useless."

"Oh, so not unlike human boys." Cassandra gave Manatado a glance that let him know she was kidding, but he still humphed.

"So the story behind that is, well, um, you see, male fairies were the first to rebel against Malgamar. As punishment for their act of rebellion, he took away every power he had given them, except knowledge. That way, they could always understand what they had given up. But in the end, the women rebelled, led by Queen Ankinia and aided by the men. Malgamar was, um, removed."

"Oh, so that's what happened. What do they do now?"

267

"Well, I mean, what can they do? They run our shops, grow select foods, raise the children. Why, what do human men do?"

Manatado jumped in before the girls got another verbal jab at him. "Everything, human men can do everything."

"Poorly," Cassandra whispered just loud enough for everyone to hear but then whistled and looked away.

A gust of wind blew across the workroom and the sunlight grew dull and dark. The witch yelled for the kids.

"Come, come quickly and grab your things."

The teens scrambled to gather up their gear and headed out the front door. The sky overhead had grown dark, and in the far distance, a massive amount of lightning came raining down from the sky.

A large explosion of green energy erupted from the same location.

The first witch head spoke. "The battle has begun. Debt has been paid. Go now." The second head continued. "Yes, go to your deaths. Only greatness can overcome, and you alone are not great enough."

Manatado paused and looked back at the witch. "You're right, but we are not alone. We are together, and together we are a clan. "

The witch's heads looked at each other, smiled, and then waved goodbye. The teens set out at a run but soon realized the distance was too great to run, so they settled into a marching speed. There was little talk, and a nervous feeling clouded over them. The clouds above continued to whirl, thunder, and darken the area around them. The smell of fire at first lofted into their noses, only to morph into overpowering. The heat from the fire would rush over, bring sweat to their skin, and be blown back toward their destination by a frozen breeze.

As they crested a small mound, the fire seemed to charge at them. Branches above them ignited as the wind from the heat erupted everything around them. Malada and Cassandra grabbed hold of each other and sat down. Manatado lost his breath as the wind was once again about to change. He grabbed the girls and yelled for Lukinia to follow. Together they raced with the icy wind past a tree engulfed in flames and scrubs that were bursting into balls of fire.

Manatado pulled them as hard as he could. His feet pounded while the girls leaned forward, desperate to keep up with him. The air once again left his breath, and he lost the strength, sending all three to the ground. A roar of flames rushed over the teens, and Manatado could feel them burning every hair on his body. The fire roared loudly, and crackling branches exploded. The three teens huddled together, struggling to find clean air. The heat seemed to engulf them. Then, just as quickly, the fire seemed to move away. The temperature lowered and the air cleaned.

The teens sat upright in total disbelief. They watch as the fire raged on, ever outward, ever away. The teens checked all around, and there behind them, flying idly in the air, was Lukinia, and she looked like hell. The corners of her clothes and the collars were burned, the stray hairs on her head smoked, and she had an overall dark, smoky look now. There was a long pause before she broke out into a grand smile. "I, I, I did it. I did it. I withstood the raging inferno." She then reached behind her, pulled out her caliphate, and held it up high with both hands. "Caliphate, I have achieved. I have survived a great inferno." The caliphate shined brightly, and then a new symbol burned itself to the outside of it. The symbol was of a fire with the center of it glowing green. Lukinia had never appeared or been as proud, and she looked at the teens with a new look, one of respect. Then something else happened. A new image appeared. It was Lukinia rescuing Manatado from the Chasm of Eternity. The second image seemed to change something inside Lukinia.

The girls then caught their breath before they looked at Manatado. They made eye contact with each other and then shared the biggest smiles and snickers.

"What? What? Why are you looking at me like that?" Manatado looked around for a reflective surface but couldn't find one. Cassandra, with a smile on her face, motioned her hand over her head and pointed at Manatado. He slowly put his hand on his head, and as he did so, the burned ashes of his hair fell into his hand. He raised his sad eyes to the girls. Malada now used her hands to run across her eyebrows and pointed at him. Manatado moved his hands to his forehead, but there was nothing. His eyebrows had been completely burned off. Lukinia now appeared next to the girls, and together the three erupted in laughter.

Chapter 68

The fire had cleared all the branches and leaves, leaving behind a clearer sight of the battle in the distance. In fact, the farther away the fire got, the more clearly they could hear the battle. Lightning bolted, jolt after jolt, from the sky. Walls of fire collided with fireballs, exploding into thunder, and mechanical whining mixed with screams of pain. And there in the middle of it all was Malada's mother.

The group marched as fast as they could manage, but it had been some time since they last slept and ate, and they were all exhausted and tired. Their breath had become so labored and their fatigue so strong that they didn't even notice when things went silent. In fact, it wasn't even after the sun came back out that they noticed. It wasn't until Manatado whipped off his backpack and dunked his head in a small stream that they noticed.

"Listen, guys . . . it's silent. That must mean the battle is over." Cassandra spoke with labored breaths. She then let out a screech as Manatado pulled his head out of the stream. It had been covered with black soot.

Lukinia's mood had become much better, and without insult, she simply created a cloud and washed him clean. She then flew up close to Manatado and looked him in the eyes. "See, I can take care of my men." She then pinched him on the cheek and flew on.

Malada and Cassandra glanced at each other before looking back at Manatado. "Made for each other." The two then snickered and laughed as they walked past him.

Manatado stood there frustrated and tired of being everyone's punchline. As he marched behind them, he couldn't help himself from thinking of things he could have done or said that would have put those girls in their place.

Lukinia suddenly rushed up ahead to a small sapling. It had taken root down deep in between some rocks, which had shielded it from the fire, and now Lukinia was tending to it. She ran her wand gently up and down the baby tree. She summoned a cloud and gave it some water, and for what felt like a long time, she tended to it. It was a new side to Lukinia, to see her being so helpful. After she had finished, the small tree seemed to almost look a little bigger. The teens approached and surrounded Lukinia, who was very nervous.

Malada asked first. "What's wrong?"

Lukinia looked directly at Malada. "The tree has something it needs to show us, and I don't think you will like it, Malada."

Malada now had a very nervous look about her as Lukinia waved her wand and, as before, a circle now appeared and a vision displayed. It was an image of Eratrea and Redleaf. They had Jalum tied up and bound on the floor before them. The image zoomed out and the three of them were atop the machine. A few stories below them on ground level was a large crowd of elven warriors.

Cheers went up from the warriors, many of them looking awful, bloodied and bruised. Redleaf stepped forward to the edge and looked down at his fellow elves. Eratrea stood behind him, off to the side. Redleaf raised his hands and quieted his warriors. "Today, my brethren, we have saved our civilization!" Uproarious cheers again erupted from the elves. "Time and time again, the elves have shown they can do what the other races cannot! The dwarves fell to the power of the human science, and it cost them everything! And what did the human do in return? Did they defeat the monster they said they would? NO! The orcs fell to the power of the human science, and they were enslaved. But not the elves! We have taken instead the science for ourselves, and we shall now use it against them!"

Another round of applause and cheers came from the elven warriors. "Today, today is a day that history will remember. Today is the day we turn human science back on them!" Redleaf paused for effect. "Today we take control of the human machine, and we will do with it what they would have done to us. Destroy them!"

Malada gulped and held on to Cassandra's arm tighter and tighter, and she whispered under her breath, "No, Mother, no."

Redleaf kicked Jalum over to the edge of the platform and held him from falling with his foot. "This man, this is the man who led the human effort. This man is the one who attacked us. This man is the one who did it all. For him, there can be no mercy!" With that, Redleaf kicked Jalum off the edge. The image panned down only enough to watch him fall some. The image cut out, and Lukinia looked at Malada sternly.

Malada shoved her head into Cassandra's shoulder and started crying. Cassandra awkwardly held her back, but she, too, was feeling emotional. Manatado stepped forward and placed one hand on each girl's shoulder. "Malada, I'm noticing that adults make a lot of terrible choices. I hope we never become adults."

Malada pulled her head out of Cassandra's shoulder and brought them all together in a hug. "I don't know what I would or could ever have done without you guys." Cassandra and Manatado caught eyes before Manatado got nervous and looked away. Cassandra herself was feeling upset and was frankly getting tired of being the support person.

Lukinia spoke. "You humans are very complicated. I'm finding myself missing the simplicity of the boys back home. I mean, look at you three. Each of you is in love with one another, but none of you are in love with each other. It's crazy complicated. Fairies do it right—when you find a man you want, you take him. If he's already taken, you buy them or fight for them. Easy."

Cassandra looked slightly revolted. "What about love?"

Lukinia's head titled down while her eyes looked up. "Seriously?"

This time, Cassandra and Malada spoke together. "Seriously!"

"Fine, but waste your time some other time. We have to decide what we are going to do." Lukinia pointed in the direction of where the battle was.

As if on cue, everyone looked at Manatado, who looked back blankly. "Yeah, um, so fine. Let's get going. We will just have to do what the adults forgot how to do."

Cassandra asked, "What does that mean?"

"It means, well I don't know exactly what it means, but I know adults seem to make all the wrong choices. So we're going to do what they are not—the right thing—even if that means doing things the hard way over the easy way. I think, well, um, that means I think it's best to help individuals and let the rest sort itself out."

Malada froze, stricken by what she saw as similar between her father and Manatado.

"So by that thinking, we need to . . ." Cassandra intentionally trailed off, probing Manatado to say more.

"Oh yeah, so it means, um, we . . . we go back to our original mission, save Malada's mother." Manatado gave Cassandra a big smile, as he felt more confident around her.

"Now let us head out." They grabbed all their gear and, with great fatigue, carried on.

Chapter 69

With weary, tired feet, the teens finally approached the battle scene. Pockets of trees still stood surrounded by now-desolate burned ground. A nasty-smelling smoke filled the air around them. They hopped over bomb craters, passed through hollowed-out trees, and went around boulders used as roadblocks.

There was no life there. They could hear no birds or see even a bug. The area was totally silent, dead, waiting for life to return. They walked slowly. Lukinia went first, her wand at the ready. Cassandra held her bow and arrow at the ready while Manatado took out his knife. At last they came to a clear-cut path, a path leading away from the battle.

Malada looked around and recognized this place from the vision. "It was here. This is where Redleaf and my mother killed him."

"Look, Malada, I think it's great and all that you care about life, but let's be real. Jalum was an evil dude, and I think he deserved it." Cassandra was tired of playing the comforter.

Malada was taken aback. "But, yes . . . but no. I mean, I don't know what to think."

Manatado spoke proudly. "Hey now, we don't want to be like the adults. Adults always make decisions they think help everyone, and in the end, they only end up hurting others. No, I say we do it right. Gerterma chose to help his brother save humanity—didn't work. The dwarven empire chose to build a weapon—didn't work out. Eratrea chose to help Redleaf—now we need to make sure that doesn't work out. So I say we don't need to save everyone from everyone.

We just need to save certain ones from themselves. And that's how we are going to be different than the adults." Malada looked like she wanted to argue back but decided against it. Cassandra gave Manatado a look that made him feel even prouder, and a great big smile broke out. Malada then stepped forward. "You remind me of my father." Manatado's face soured, as being compared to her father wasn't the comparison he was hoping for.

Lukinia called out from the distance. "Over here! I've found someone."

There was a commotion as they all ran to Lukinia. There before her, lying in between berry shrubs, was a pale and sickly Gerterma. Manatado knelt beside him and grabbed his hand. "It's lukewarm, almost cold. That's not right. Gerterma, can you hear me?"

A shallow groan came out from Gerterma, but his eyes still wouldn't focus. Manatado started freaking out. His head looked left and right, up and down, but wasn't really seeing anything. Manatado's face paled as he prepared to pick him up.

"Manatado, wait. First we need to check and see if he is bleeding." Cassandra could see his panic below the surface. She knelt beside him and grabbed his forearm. "Do you feel any warm liquid?"

Tears came to Manatado's face and he nodded yes. Cassandra reached out and pulled up Gerterma's shirt, and sure enough, he was injured badly. Malada let out a small scream as she saw and then looked away. Manatado reached out and pulled Malada closer. "You have to heal him. You HAVE to!"

Malada's breaths became rapid, and panic overcame her composure. She screamed again as her hand felt the blood cover her hands.

"Malada, save him. You have to!"

Malada again screamed out, this time in a full panic. "I don't know, I don't know!"

"Yes you do!"

"Stop it, stop it, both of you!" Cassandra had never had such authority in her voice before. "Manatado, we need a bandage fast. Find the plant known as Indian toilet paper, GO!" Cassandra now looked at Malada. "Get ahold of yourself. Now, when I pull the stick out of him, you need to press down as hard as you can on both, BOTH SIDES!"

Malada took a couple deep breaths and prepared herself. Cassandra counted down from three, and Gerterma let out the faintest, weakest whimper she had ever heard. Malada was quick and forceful. She looked away and cried as she could feel the blood pushing against her with force.

Manatado arrived with a large handful of soft, smooth leaves. "More," Cassandra demanded as she placed them over one of Malada's hands. Cassandra had Malada pull her hand out as she took over applying pressure. They did the same for the other hand. Malada then cleared a spot for Manatado as he arrived with a large armful of leaves. They made a bed, grabbed some rope, and tied the leaves as a bandage around his wound.

The action ground to a halt as Gerterma lay near death but still breathed. The three teens covered in blood looked at each other. They then came together in a hug. Manatado pulled back with teary eyes and looked at Cassandra. "Thank you, thank you, thank you." Cassandra held him back tightly. "You saved him. You always do what I can't. Thank you." Cassandra now let out a tear of her own.

Chapter 70

Malada ran off into a large group of trees and hid behind some scrubs. She cried, feeling like a failure, and was so mad at Manatado. It didn't make any sense to her, none of this did, and she cried for a long time.

After a bit, she felt a gentle tug at her side. She pulled her head back and raised her arms to fight, but all she saw was a small benign being. "Daddy." Malada wrapped her arms around the small being and hugged him so tight. The small benign being coughed and she let go. As she pulled back, she again became sad. "Daddy, what's wrong? You look so weak, and pale. Quick, sit down. I should get Cassandra. She can help you."

"Stop." The voice was very weak. "Don't go."

Malada stopped. "But, Daddy, I can't help. She can."

"No she can't."

"Oh, Daddy, what's wrong? I'm so scared."

"It was never fair to you, having a father so old. I wanted to be so much more of a father than I was. Now tell me, my child, why do you cry?"

"I failed, Dad. I failed at so much."

"We all do, my dear. Every one of us, it's part of life. You must learn to forgive."

"But I can't even use my powers. You said they were mine, but I can't even use them. I can't save my friends when I want to, and I can't . . . I can't do so much."

"The powers are yours. The will is not."

"What does that mean?"

Ciefraf took a deep breath. "You and I are bound to the creator. He gave us power to accomplish his will, not ours."

"I don't think I understand. Is that a good thing or bad?"

"It's a wonderful thing. Our creator is the creator of good. Follow his will and he will let you do no evil."

"What about Mother?"

"Ah, Eratrea is bound to me. That is why I must suffer each time she uses my power."

"I hate Mother!"

"Never say such a thing!"

"But, Daddy, she, she . . . she . . ."

"She needs forgiveness."

"I gave it to her and she betrayed it."

"Then give it to her again, again and again, as much as it takes."

"Takes to what?"

"Save her."

"From what?"

"Oh, oh . . . cough, cough. My child, there is still so much for you to learn. There is so much I failed to teach you. But I'm proud of you. You have done so much good, and I know I leave you in the hands of good friends."

"Leave? OH no, Daddy, you can't leave."

"Time decides otherwise. I have for you one last present. A pet. Promise me you will take good care of it and it will take good care of you."

"A pet?"

"Do you promise?"

"Yes, Daddy, I promise to take care of it."

The benign little being started to fade away. "That's a good girl. I love you." With that, Ciefraf faded away.

"I love you too, Daddy."

There was a long deep silence. Then, as if echoing from all around her, a horse neighed. Again the horse neighed, this time sounding closer. Malada looked around and around, but she couldn't see anything. The ground around her began to gently shake. A rumble from the sky above drew her attention as a puff of clouds broke off and started traveling away. The cloud turned downward and toward Malada. Again the sounds of a horse echoed all around her, and as the last of the cloudy billow fell away, a Pegasus horse emerged. The Pegasus swooped down right above Malada before rushing straight into the sky.

The Pegasus looped, twisted, and acrobated in the sky. It flew so fast jets of air followed its path like clouds from an airplane. Then, like a meteorite, it slammed down into the ground right next to Malada. The Pegasus let out a powerful neigh before opening its wings to the fullest and bowed before Malada.

Malada's mouth dropped open. The Pegasus nodded with its head for her to hop on. She instantly complied as she gleefully threw her leg over the animal's head. Malada felt the world rise up as the Pegasus stood fully upright. She rubbed her hands into the Pegasus's fur, and as she did so, handles magically appeared. Malada squeezed her legs together and, magically, stirrups appeared.

Malada gripped tightly, and even if the animal wasn't speaking, she seemed to know exactly what the animal was thinking and feeling. As soon as she was ready, they burst straight off into the air at great speed, quickly achieving great height. The animal then opened its wings and began a gentle glide downward. Malada could see almost everything from this height. There, in the far distance, were the foothills to the dwarves' canyon. In between, she could still see the smoke rising from the forest of Bashan burning.

The animal gave Malada a mental flash of what it was preparing to do, and as soon as Malada grabbed a firm hold, they dropped. At first they fell as if out of control, but with amazing grace, the Pegasus broke off and did a double loop. It then dove down into a remaining groove of trees and expertly navigated through it. The animal then told Malada to hold her breath as they dove straight down into a small lake.

The Pegasus folded in its wings, and together they dove down deep into a small lake. The animal switched motions and began swimming at great speed. They dove down deep past the light, for just a moment, and then burst out into the air. The Pegasus landed perfectly, opened its wings again fully, and then bowed to let Malada off.

Cassandra and Manatado were not far away and came rushing over. "Oh my god, oh my god, is that, is that a . . ." Cassandra couldn't help but let her voice be filled with childish excitement. As Cassandra and Malada made eye contact, they spoke together in a scream. "Pegasus!"

Cassandra's face turned back and forth between her friend and the animal. Malada blushed some before speaking. "This, um, is, um, my new pet."

Cassandra's face went pale and then turned red, and the more excited Malada seemed, the angrier Cassandra became. Malada turned around to start petting the animal, when Cassandra couldn't take it anymore. "You get a pet Pegasus. What? I don't understand. Why do you get everything?" Malada's face suddenly turned pale. Cassandra's tone sharped. "You get everything. You get the magic powers, magic shield." Cassandra's eyes pierced Manatado as she spoke next. "You get the boy. YOU get to travel the world and . . . and you get a pet Pegasus! What about Cassandra? Don't I get anything? Oh, I know what I get. I get a wet shoulder from everybody crying on it. That's all Cassandra gets, is used."

Malada was taken aback. "Wha-wha-what?" Malada now stepped forward and was face-to-face with Cassandra. "Are you kidding me? You have everything I wanted. Who taught you how to shoot that bow and arrow? Who taught you how to save Gerterma? My father, my father is nothing more than a withered benign being. My mother, well my mother is a source of all these problems. I, I wish I were you, and no, I don't get the boy."

Manatado's face saddened. "Wait, what?"

. The two girls' eyes were locked into a furious staring contest. A long moment passed before the two once again seemed to speak at the same time.

"Can I ride your Pegasus?"

"Can I have a hug?"

Together they embraced for a long time.

Manatado inched closer. "I want a hug too."

"No!"

"No!"

Chapter 71

After Malada and Cassandra made up, they went for a very short ride on the Pegasus. They returned and, after dismounting, jumped around in circles, screaming in excitement. Manatado, feeling left out, tried not to pout but only ended up doing so. Malada saw the disappointment on his face and gave him a friendly hug. "Thank you for waiting." He reveled in the attention but noticed how much faster the feeling faded this time.

The three walked back toward Lukinia and Gerterma, who lay next to a small fire. Lukinia looked up with a little bit of pride. "See, I took care of him, while the three . . . wa-wa-wa—is that a Pegasus?" Lukinia immediately flew toward the creature and embraced it with a full hug around its neck. "But, but, but how? This is impossible. The fairies have searched everywhere for your kind." The Pegasus neighed loudly before Lukinia paraphrased. "Oh, your kind went into hiding when man started the war with the orcs." Again the Pegasus neighed loudly, this time with several variations. "Slow, slow down. That's quite an amazing tale. Apparently at the start of the war, a very powerful wizard sent out a warning—'Man has betrayed the natural order. Flee.'" Lukinia gave the teens, and particularly Manatado, a scowling glare. "In return for his warning, you have pledged to serve, his offspring?"

Lukinia's jaw dropped. She slowly turned around and looked at Malada, dumbfounded. "YOU? You are the daughter of this most powerful wizard?"

Malada looked down at the ground. "Ah, yeah, so that's, um, why I, um, have magic powers."

"But you can't even control them! What, what does this all mean?"

"I'm learning. I'm working on it. They are my powers, just not my . . . will. I don't quite know what that means yet."

Lukinia looked at Malada, awaiting more, before Manatado broke into the conversation. "It means, Lukinia, that we still need each other. It means we have to stick together. It means . . . huh, well I guess it means clan before self."

Lukinia now looked dumbfoundedly at Manatado. "You're the leader? Doomed, doomed I say . . . doomed." She then flew up to Manatado, made herself human-sized, kissed him, and spoke as she pulled back. "But you're cute, and for a boy . . . there is something about you I like. And there is much about you I don't like. Still, I was tasked to help you, so I will, at least until you're dead and I can take the shield back home."

Lukinia then turned herself invisible again. The two girls looked at Manatado, who couldn't help but blush. Malada broke out laughing at full volume, while Cassandra scowled at him. Manatado shot Cassandra a look back and raised his hands like he was asking, "What?"

"Are you kids done fooling around?" The voice was weak, faint, and dull in life.

Manatado exclaimed out in frustration at himself for getting distracted. "Gerterma!" The three teens rushed to his side. Manatado grabbed Gerterma's shoulder and forearm as he lay nearly motionless.

Gerterma labored intensely as he spoke. "There is so much to tell you, and I fear I don't have the . . . time."

Malada got down on her knees and grabbed Gerterma's other arm. She gently pushed back Manatado. "I think I'm beginning to understand." She placed her other hand on Gerterma's head and spoke under her breath. Manatado wasn't sure, but he thought she said, "Your will be done." A white glow started to shine from Malada's hands. The glow flowed up and down her body twice before traveling through her hands and across Gerterma's. Gerterma's body stretched out and seemed to hover as the shine covered the whole of his body.

The shine gently dulled as Gerterma's body came slowly back down to the ground. His eyes opened wide with excitement. He started to jump up, when he suddenly screamed out in pain. Malada jumped back and screamed at the reaction. Gerterma continued to scream out in pain as his hair and nails grew out white, at great speed. Wrinkles appeared across his face, his muscles seemed to fade, and his body now looked thirty years older.

Malada shouted out in fear and ran into Cassandra's arms, where she cried heavily. Manatado ran up and knelt next to Gerterma. Gerterma opened his eyes and reached out his hand to Manatado. Manatado grabbed the arm and helped Gerterma to a sitting position. Gerterma shook his head a few times, thoroughly examining his body for himself. After regaining his awareness, he made eye contact with Manatado and Cassandra. "Thank you, thank you, all." The voice was healthier, but weaker too.

Manatado composed himself before speaking. "What, what happened? Are you healed?"

Gerterma ran his hand up and down his body before speaking. "Well, yes, if not perhaps a little worn for the wear."

Malada poked her head out from behind Cassandra. "What happened? I don't understand how I hurt you."

Gerterma again ran his hands up and down his body as if making sure it was all there. "Well, well, um, young lady, you did not. In fact, I am very thankful to you for helping me."

"But, but, but you're old now!"

Gerterma put his hand to his chin. "Well when you go against the creator's will, there is a penalty to be paid. This is nothing more than my penance, my punishment for betraying my . . . well for many things. Let's leave it at that."

Malada poked her head out from Cassandra's shoulder. "What does that mean? I still don't understand how my magic hurt you."

Gerterma looked very kindly, grandfatherly at Cassandra. "Young child. You healed me. Death was knocking at my door, and you ushered him away. No, what you see here is the truth. This, this is my true self."

Manatado shook his head back and forth. "What are you saying? Speak clearly. No riddles."

Gerterma smiled that same look toward Manatado. "You see, this is how old I am supposed to be. My natural age. You see, at the start of the orc wars, we found our age to be cumbersome. So we made a choice, a bad choice. We told ourselves that only we could bring victory, if only we had our vigor of youth."

Cassandra broke in. "Gerterma, who is 'we'?"

"Oh, yes, by 'we' I mean Jalum and myself. You see, when I told you that after our first battle the officers sent Jalum away, I was being intentionally vague. You see, our first battle didn't go like I said it did. In fact, we got our butts kicked. We knew we had the skills, but instead of accepting our place, which would have been to teach, we sought out our own glory.

"We were derided by our officers, scolded in a way that Jalum took very personal offense to. So that very night, he snuck into the officers' office. There, he found something, something perfect for us. We took the book and headed out in pursuit of our new . . . desire."

Manatado asked, "What was it you went after?"

"Found. Guarded by a terrible wolf-like beast in the deepest cave of the dwarven mountains. Here again is where I . . . well I lied. The dwarves captured us on our way out. The leader of the dwarves knew what we had taken, but Jalum was cunning and hid it so well none could find it. It was the dwarves' belief that our stealing of the potion awakened Riftia. However, they couldn't find the potion, and we had yet to take it, so they ended up releasing us, with Nicolda's help."

"So was the dwarf king really killed by Riftia? Or was it Jalum?" Manatado asked boldly.

Gerterma's head dropped down low, and he took a deep breath. "It was Jalum, by controlling Riftia. You see, as we quested for the potion down in the caves, we came upon a most unusual tomb. Jalum was certain that only treasure would be guarded by so many warning signs, and I was unable to convince him otherwise. Nor was I of any help when Riftia awoke and attacked us. I was . . . knocked out by the first blow. I'm not certain how he defeated the monster so as to gain masterhood over it. It was his control over Riftia that let Jalum destroy Athenia."

Manatado repeated from memory, "The city of Athenia has been swallowed whole by a crater. Jalum destroyed Athenia by using Riftia to dig it out from below. How diabolical! He is a crazy, evil madman!"

Manatado stood up and slammed his hand into his fist. He then paused as if struck by something. His face changed, as he had come to a realization, a realization that upset him. "And this madman is who you betray us for! You led us right to him, time and time again . . . as a test . . . as if we were some sort of research project. Tell me, Gerterma, was it an accident that the Aradoro just happened to attack the village while we were leaving? Was it a coincidence that we ran across the magic monkey? How did Jalum catch up to Malada in the Socratea tree? And just how did we end up in the custody of the dwarves who just happened to be working for Jalum?"

Manatado was furious, and he was waving his finger angrily at Gerterma, who looked like a guilty dog. Gerterma waited for Manatado to finish before he replied calmly. "I made many, many bad choices. I made them thinking I could justify them by, in the end, saving many more. I see now I was only making choices for my own glory. I don't expect your forgiveness, nor do I ask it."

Manatado broke in, speaking with authority. "Well too damn bad. You are forgiven. You are still one of us. Now tell us what we need to know. Because it seems like only we can do what you adults can't, and that's the right thing. Now that Eratrea has regained control, she is doing exactly what Jalum did. So you are going to tell us exactly how to regain control of that machine so we can stop Eratrea and Redleaf from destroying humanity."

Everyone took a deep breath and looked at Manatado. He seemed to stand a little taller and looked stronger than ever. Gerterma took great pains to stand up. Manatado . watched, too emotional to help. Gerterma slowly approached Manatado and wrapped his arms around him. "I'm so proud of you. I would be proud to call you son. Now let me help you so maybe someday you can be proud to call me father."

Chapter 72

Lukinia announced her discovery as she approached the group. "Jalum's body is not here. Either it has been removed or—"

Gerterma finished the sentence for Lukinia. "Jalum's body is not here because Jalum is still alive. And yes, he still has his youthfulness and athleticism."

Cassandra protested. "But we saw his body fall in a vision from the trees! He couldn't have survived that."

Gerterma shook his head. "Never underestimate his desire to live, and conquer. It's a relentless unquenchable thirst that he can never satisfy. It has changed his morals, it has changed him to evil, and it has changed him into something to be feared. I, I, I was also too fearful of him. I convinced myself that I had no other choice than to follow him because I knew his desires outweighed his humanity and his love for me."

Manatado again had that determined look about him. "You said he is still just a man. A man can be stopped." He looked at Malada. "A stepfather and mother can be stopped." He looked at Cassandra. "Adults who value their causes over life can be stopped."

Manatado now looked at Gerterma. "Now tell us how to defeat that machine."

Gerterma gave Manatado a thorough looking over. "You will need every bit of courage, strength, and perseverance to accomplish it."

The three teens and Lukinia came together and focused on Gerterma as he spoke. "There are only two ways into the machine now that it has been activated. The easiest way would be through the standing platform, which is where you saw Jalum fall from. They will know this and be ready for it. The second way is to enter a secret code to open the roof hatch."

Cassandra blurted out, "Do you know the secret code?"

Gerterma shrugged. "I knew the last code Jalum was using. I'm uncertain if Eratrea and Redleaf will be knowledgeable enough to change it. The last I knew, the code was an ancient phrase. I don't know what it means. 'Arkatu marti oudiso.'"

The three teens looked at each other and spoke it out loud in turns. Manatado then paused and looked back at Gerterma. "Wait a minute. You said now that the machine has been turned on, there are only two ways. What would have been the third?"

Gerterma gave a look of surprise and then smiled. "Well that would be through the furnace. That machine has gobbled up some of the most powerful and ancient trees from the elven forest. No one could survive those fires."

Manatado looked at Lukinia. "What about a fire fairy?"

Gerterma looked surprised again. "Oh, well yes, maybe a fire fairy might."

Manatado stood up straight, holding his head up high. It was the kind of look that made Cassandra blush and Malada groan, "Ugh." Manatado spoke confidently. "We have our plan. Malada, you drop Cassandra off on top with the Pegasus and then make your way for the platform." He then looked at Lukinia. "The fire fairy and I are going in the hard way."

Lukinia began to protest. "You can't be seriou—"

"I am, and I am counting on you." Manatado tilted his head down slightly and gave Lukinia a stern look.

Lukinia looked around before taking a deep breath. "The things I do for boys, ugh."

A distant rumbling could have been mistaken for thunder had there been any clouds. Manatado turned to face the distant noises of battle. "Come, then, clan of the unknown creator."

"I object!" Malada interjected.

"Wha—?" Manatado was taken aback.

"We are not the clan of the unknown creator anymore. I am proud like my father to serve a creator who cares for his own creation. We are now the clan of the creator."

Manatado nodded and turned back toward the distant noises. "Well then, clan of the creator, let us do what others can't. What's best for all, not what is best for some."

With that, they loaded Gerterma up onto the Pegasus and set out for the machine.

Chapter 73

The noises of battle ebbed and flowed as they marched as fast as possible. Some of the noises were recognizable, such as Eratrea's lightning attack and the machine slamming its arms down into the ground. Cries of fury and pain mixed with thuds and clacks as the machine's armor held.

They were approaching the edge of the forest when a new sound they didn't recognize came over and over again. Fast, repeating, and powerful, the sounds came in waves. Cassandra and Manatado made eye contact and told the others to pause while they checked it out.

Manatado and Cassandra pulled out their weapons and took a path through the remaining forest. They carefully made their way past trees, scrubs, and the river, when they came to a small opening just before the forest ended. There, they could see the entire battlefield. It was covered in destruction. Every army had been assembled to defeat the monsters and build the wall. Now every army had been defeated by the machine.

The valley slowly ran downhill from where they were out into a massive plain that was littered with destroyed vehicles, burning wreckage, and abandoned equipment. There in the middle of that vast plain was a large fence surrounding a massive sinkhole.

Cassandra very quietly whispered, "That must have been where Athenia was. Look at all the roads. See how they all lead to that fence surrounding the hole."

A stream of laser lights shot out from one of the human encampments as the laser blast erupted into small explosions at their destination, the machine. Manatado reached out and grabbed Cassandra's hand reassuringly. "I think we found help."

"I think we found some traitors!" A gruff middle-aged man, a man they knew as a former deputy of Gerterma's, walked out from behind them and held up a gun. The two froze, totally dumbfounded. The former deputy signaled for them to raise their hands up to the sky. They slowly complied, fear filling their faces.

"Hey, I know you two, don't I? Oh yeah, now I remember. You two were the draft dodgers who stole something out of Gerterma's office. I don't know what you stole, but you cost a good man his career."

Manatado tried to speak, but each time he tried, nothing happened. A voice called out from the group of people they were watching. "Sarge, Sarge!"

The deputy shook his head. "Now what?"

A smaller-statured silhouette approached the deputy and saluted. "The laser gun has overheated. We need your assistance."

The deputy pounded his foot to the ground in frustration. "Fine, come here. Take this, and don't you dare let either of these two escape."

"Yes, Sarge!"

With that, the deputy handed off his gun and ran for the group.

The silhouette of the statue stepped forward into the light. "Are you kidding me?" The voice sounded very familiar to the teens. "Manatado? Cassandra? Is that you two?"

Cassandra and Manatado kept their hands up in the air as they turned around. The voice of the silhouette was Manatado's village friend Tamack. Tamack looked absolutely dumbfounded. He lowered the gun and put it away in a holster. Then, after a long pause, the three embraced.

Malada jumped out from the brush and tackled the three to the ground. Another voice joined in. "Don't worry, buddy. I'm on the way!" That voice then jumped into the ever-growing pile of bodies. For a few chaotic moments, the group wrestled about before they became aware of who they all were.

The newest voice had Manatado restrained, with his hands behind him.

"Rogers, what are you doing? It's us!"

The newest voice answered back. "Manatado? Is that you?" The voice let go his grip, and as Manatado turned around, he saw Tamack's best friend Rogers. Rogers now looked around at each person. "Manatado! Cassandra! Ugh, girl from another place."

Manatado filled him in. "This is Malada. What's going on. What is happening here?"

"Dude, are you kidding me? Where have you been?" Tamack started talking, but Rogers continued on. "Seriously, man, like, ever since you three checked out, things have been total chaos. Whatever you did, things are bad."

"Tell us, what happened since we left?" Manatado spoke with a serious tone that surprised Tamack and Rogers.

The two looked at each other, and Tamack spoke first. "Well damn, like, everyone important seemed to be at that big event in Athenia when, well . . ."

Rogers took over. "Crash down into that giant hole out there."

Very excitedly and without pause, Tamack continued. "Then all of these monsters started coming out."

Again almost without pause, Rogers continued. "Then all the armies started showing up. All of them."

Tamack continued. "Elves, dwarves, goblins, our army, and even what was left of the orc army showed up."

Rogers continued. "And everyone was like, boom, blast, destroy, and we beat back the monsters."

Tamack said, "Yeah, all except one, a really big worm that could dig underneath us."

Rogers said, "So after we all corralled the monsters back into the crater, we built that huge fence."

Tamack said, "Then, like, totally from out of nowhere comes this giant robot, with laser guns for eyes, arms that seem to attack from every which way."

Rogers now continued. "Yeah, that things goes total bonkers and starts smashing all our vehicles."

Tamack said, "But it doesn't attack the elves, so we are like, what the heck is going on?"

Malada sheepishly chimed in. "Oh yeah, that would be my mother. She, um, yeah, seems to be on a rampage."

The two village boys looked at each other. "Your mother?"

Malada looked down at the ground. "So after we defeated Riftia, she, I mean my mother, and stepfather seem to have, um, gone amok."

Tamack exclaimed his question. "Wait, what are you guys doing here?"

Manatado answered, "We're here to defeat the machine."

Rogers laughed. "No offense, dude, but come on. Really, what are you doing here?"

Manatado looked at the girls. "Plan still stays the same, only now maybe he can have some help with a distraction."

Tamack and Rogers looked at each other, surprised by their friend. "Okay, dude, what do you need from us."

"What do you have over there?"

The two boys had a hint of an excited squeal as they answered. "A freaking laser machine gun, dude!" This time, as he had so often watched the girls commune in ritual, Manatado now grabbed his friend's forearm and exclaimed, "A laser machine gun!" The three then jumped around in small circles to express their excitement.

Malada and Cassandra made eye contact. "Idiot boys." They then started off into the brush. "Give us a signal when you're ready." They began to set off, when some rustling in the bushes silenced everyone as they all drew their attention to the new sound.

"Get your old wrinkled hands off me!" Gerterma was hand slapping Mr. Marks as he escorted Gerterma along.

Mr. Marks smiled as he yelled out, "I caught him. I caught the spy in the woods."

Manatado questioned out loud, "Gerterma?"

Mr. Marks smiled. "You, I know you, boy, don't I? Ah, and this is Gerterma?" Mr. Marks moved his face in closer. "Ha, it is Gerterma, an old wrinkled version. I knew it! I knew it! I knew you were hiding something."

"Let go of me, you old man! I've done nothing to you!" Gerterma tried pulling away but wasn't strong enough anymore.

"You stole some kids and fled the village when we needed help the most! That's treason in my book!"

"No, you don't understand. Let go of me!" Again Gerterma started hand slapping Mr. Marks.

Manatado looked around. "Lukinia! Lukinia, you were supposed to be watching Gerterma!"

After a long pause of silence, Lukinia appeared out of breath and scared. "Run!" The word came out weak, as she was out of breath.

Cassandra asked, "Run?"

Lukinia waved her arms as she again tried to yell, winded, "RUN!"

Cassandra nodded her head, understanding but not complying. "Run."

There was a short pause of silence before the sound of cracking trees and a roaring engine came barreling through the forest right at them.

In almost-unison, the entire group screamed, "RUN!"

Chapter 74

The group spread out running in a variety of different directions. The machine rolled to a halt directly in front of the laser gun. The machine raised its arm up high and then smashed it down, destroying the weapons holder and defenses as the sergeant in charge waved his arms wildly, indicating for everyone to flee.

Tamack, Rogers, and Manatado all headed off in the same direction. Tamack yelled as they ran. "So, like, you have been traveling with the girls this whole time?"

Manatado replied in between breaths. "Yeah."

Tamack was in obviously better shape than Manatado, who was getting winded. "So did you . . . kiss her?"

"Who?"

Rogers replied, "Don't play stupid, the girl you like, Maflada."

"Malada! And, um, well no, she kissed me."

Rogers and Tamack screamed out in jealous glee. "Dude!" They made small bowing motions as they ran. "Wait, so you were traveling with Cassandra too. Did you kiss her?"

Manatado grew frustrated and found it harder and harder to breathe, so he came to a halt. "Well, um, no, she kissed me, then Lukinia."

Again Tamack and Rogers screamed out in jealous glee, bowing playfully. "We're not worthy, we're not worthy."

Manatado's face tightened and blushed as he looked around. "Uh, uh, uh, oh, shut up, you idiots." The three paused as they looked around the forest. They had no idea where they were now. "Oh, great, all your military training and you get us lost in the forest."

Tamack shot back, "Oh yeah, all your grand travels and you get us lost in the forest."

The two squared up as if ready to wrestle, when an arrow flew between them and stuck in a tree. A little flag unrolled as they approached it. As it unrolled, it simply said, "Run." The three looked at each other stupidly. Nothing happened for a moment, until a red beam activated on the tree the arrow had hit. Again the three stopped and stared at the red beam. After a moment, the tree erupted in flames as a laser bolt impacted it. The three boys again ran as the machine came busting through.

Manatado screamed like a little girl as the machine chased after him. Cassandra came swinging across on a long vine, pulling him to safety. The machine shot out another burst of laser, chopping the vine and sending the two flying off into midair. They reached the top and Manatado felt his stomach sink as they began to fall back down to the ground.

Malada came bounding in on her Pegasus, catching the two, one with each arm. Manatado screamed as he desperately tried to climb up Malada's arm. Cassandra gracefully shifted her weight, threw her leg over the back of the Pegasus, and was riding perfectly in place behind Malada. The Pegasus struggled as Manatado kicked his leg out in a panic, striking the animal.

The Pegasus shifted hard, shaking the riders as it flapped its mighty wing, rebalancing itself. Manatado lost hold of Malada but found himself in the arms of Cassandra. She interlocked her arms around his, and together they spun around and now sat face-to-face.

"I have never kissed you, you liar!"

Manatado blushed, dumbfounded. Cassandra then kissed him. She kissed him hard and long. "There, now you're not a liar anymore." Cassandra then turned her head and yelled at Malada. "Okay, let's throw him in."

Malada yelled back, "Is Lukinia ready?"

"She knows the plan, so yes."

"Wait, what? Throw me in where?" he asked.

Malada and Cassandra both pointed at the front of the machine. Its large metal doors had opened, and it was busy harvesting and collecting trees to feed its fire.

"Remember, it's your plan." Cassandra poked Manatado on his nose playfully. She then twisted him around and placed her arm under his. The Pegasus came around and was now flying directly at the machine. Its huge blazing inferno spilled out from its raging furnace.

"Wait, wait, I changed my mind, new plan. NEW PLAN!"

Cassandra made eye contact. "You can do this. You will do this."

"Wait, that's what I say just before."

Cassandra lifted hard on his armpits, and Manatado flew through the air alongside the Pegasus. They sped through the air directly at a blazing inferno at the base of a machine of war. Manatado screamed in pure terror as Cassandra let go. "Cassandra!" Manatado flew totally out of control. A flash of light caught his eye, and there at the base of the machine was Lukinia. Lukinia was moving her wand in a circle, and there before it, a barrier was forming.

Manatado realized there was no stopping it, so he brought in his arms and legs and curled up into the fetal position. The heat from the furnace grew quickly as he approached, and Manatado closed his eyes. He could feel the heat all around him when, for a split second, he felt cool. The sensation lasted only a second before he landed on a scalding-hot metal pad at the back of the furnace. Manatado's hands and butt touched the hot surface, and he jumped up, hitting his head on a panel. The impact caused the panel to fall, revealing a ladder up and out. Manatado fell back to the hot pad, jumped up again in pain, and grabbed hold of the ladder. His hand and butt hurt, but he started climbing. Lukinia flew in and grabbed him, pulling him to the top of the ladder. He fell to the floor, totally disoriented. She crashed into the ceiling and rolled off to the side.

Together the two lay in pain on the floor in silence. After a long moment, Manatado spoke. "Lukinia, are you okay?"

Lukinia ran her hands over her body again and again. "Yes, yes, I have done it again." She reached back and grabbed her caliphate. She tried to stand up but immediately fell down. "OH, I'm hurt. Oh, it hurts, it hurts."

Manatado rolled over to his stomach and crawled on his elbows toward her. "I'm here, I'm here."

Lukinia placed her caliphate on Manatado's chest, over his heart, and spoke.   "Caliphate, I have sacrificed for a love I won't receive in return."

The caliphate started to glow, and Manatado could feel his chest warming. The shine wore off and the caliphate formed a cocoon around itself. After a moment, the shell shed off and the caliphate had a new symbol on it. It was a picture that symbolized love before self, a heart standing before a fairy symbol for self. Lukinia looked longingly at the caliphate, gave it a big hug, and put it away.

"My leg is broken. Help me get to a safe place, and then you can go on. Go on to help your Malada."

Manatado smiled. "Thank you, but the clan of the creator doesn't leave anyone behind." He gently picked her up, cradling her in his arm. Lukinia resisted at first but quickly relaxed and tucked herself in. He stood up, looked around, and found himself surrounded by machinery, a fire pit, and no obvious way to go.

Chapter 75

Cassandra held on tightly to Malada as she held on tightly to the Pegasus. The animal seemed to dance in the air as it evaded the machine's attacks. While she couldn't talk to it, Malada did seem to be able to communicate with the Pegasus. "She can't get us close enough. We need a distraction." Malada called back to Cassandra, asking for ideas.

Cassandra squeezed a little tighter as they took cover and landed in the trees. "We need to find the boys, Tamack and Rogers. I think they can help us."

"But where do we find them now?" Malada asked.

Cassandra looked around, getting her bearings, when two voices came screaming and running their way. It was Tamack and Rogers, and they were trying to run but were very winded and fatigued.

Cassandra and Malada exchanged a look before Cassandra verbalized it. "Why do boys always run and scream?"

Malada giggled, shrugged her shoulder, and then yelled and waved for them. "Over here, over here."

The two boys hurried over, very winded, and tried to say something, but Cassandra was fast and had the four of them riding the Pegasus before they could even catch their breath. The machine burst through the tree line as the Pegasus was already off the ground. The Pegasus struggled with the weight, but it worked hard and, with a jostle of their stomachs, the four were suddenly circling the machine from above.

"Oh, thank you. Oh, thank you," Tamack started to say.

"We really appreciate it," Rogers finished.

Cassandra gave the two a stern look. "Now we need your help in return. We need you to distract that machine so Malada can drop me off at the back door and make her way to the front."

Tamack and Rogers looked at each other and then at Cassandra. "No!"

Malada started to tilt the Pegasus. "Fine then, we can let you off here!"

"OKAY! Okay! Okay!" Tamack screamed out in fear as he held on ever tighter.

"At least give us the laser machine gun, please!" Rogers begged.

Cassandra and Malada immediately began scouring the ground, when they found it hanging from a tree. Malada placed her hand on the Pegasus, and together they communicated a plan. Malada turned back and relayed the plan to Cassandra. Cassandra spun herself around and came face-to-face with Tamack. He leaned in for a kiss, and Cassandra quickly deflected and grabbed both Tamack and Rogers by the forearms.

The Pegasus dropped down out of the sky, and Cassandra couldn't help but smile as the boys screamed out in terror. They neared the ground, the machine's laser bolts chasing after them. The Pegasus twirled around and was now flying upside down. Cassandra's shoulders strained as the boys now hung on desperately to her.

The boys collided with a thick branch and had to let go of Cassandra as they now clung to it. There between them, hanging from the tree, was the laser machine gun. The Pegasus twirled around again and landed on the ground. The animal took cover and lay down, panting heavily with fatigue.

The animal needed a moment of rest, but the machine was in full pursuit. Cassandra and Malada nodded an unspoken plan to each other and then ran in opposite directions. The machine halted as it decided what to do. A large burst of laser beam shot out at Cassandra, exploding the trunk of a nearby tree, crashing it down in front of her.

The machine then stopped and started turning toward Malada, who was ready and stood tall and proud on the top of a tree. She brought her hands together and a bright light started forming between her hands. The machine paused. Then it reached out its arm as if to grab Malada. She let loose the burst of light, and it sent a shock wave through the machine.

Electricity exploded throughout the machine. The exterior lights all burst with Malada's power. Small explosions and sounds of grinding machine came and went as the machine then went dark.

Malada dropped down from the tree and sprinted to Cassandra's side, letting out a huge sigh of relief that Cassandra was not hurt.

"What kind of magic was that? I've never seen anything so powerful. It took out the machine in one shot!"

Malada and Cassandra hugged, yet as they did so, a new sound came from the machine as it restarted. Sounds of mechanical whirling resumed as the fire for the furnace once again ignited.

Malada sighed in disappointment. "Not powerful enough."

Cassandra grabbed Malada's arm and pulled her in the direction of the Pegasus. "No time, get me up there now while the machine is resetting."

Malada nodded and together they ran for the Pegasus.

Chapter 76

The engine room went dark. Manatado still hadn't found a way forward or out, other than through the furnace again. The light from the fire bounced around and gave the room a gentle red-orange glow.

Lukinia, with her broken leg, sat uncomfortably and unhappily in his arm. As the lights went out, she grabbed on tightly to him and grimaced. "Powerful magic is coming. I can feel it."

Manatado stepped back as panels from the far side of the room burst down from the ceiling. A bright-white shining light traveled through the metal of the machine, with lightning bolting out. A bolt of lightning shot out at Manatado. The very tip of the bolt struck him in the chest as Lukinia raised her wand in defense.

Together they tumbled to the floor. Bolts of lightning shot out and traveled through the machine. The light continued down through the floor, and a massive explosion erupted in the furnace. The entire room shook violently as pieces of the machinery started breaking and falling apart.

The rocking of the explosion stopped, and the room became totally dark as even the light from the inferno below went dim. Lukinia lay painfully on the floor. Its warmth felt nice in the deep darkness. Manatado whispered out into the darkness, "Lukinia, are you okay? I think I'm blind."

Lukinia sat up but couldn't see anything either. She reached out with her hands, and panic set in as she realized that she had dropped her wand. "My wand, my wand. I've lost my wand. You must help me."

"Lukinia, I'm blind. How can I help you?" Manatado spoke with great self-pity.

Lukinia didn't find her wand, but she did find a small piece of machinery. She raised her arm and aimed for the sound of Manatado's voice.

"Ouch, what was that? Something's in here. I'm over here. Come and take me. Kill me first."

Lukinia rolled her eyes even in the dark. "This is no time for a pity party. Now reach out your damn hands and start searching."

Manatado complied but muttered under his breath, "Manatado do this. Manatado do that. Oh, Manatado, tell us what to do. Oh, Manatado, you're an idiot. Stupid bossy girls."

"What was that!" Lukinia snapped at him. She waited for a reply and, after getting none, muttered under her breath, "Stupid boys, never do anything useful."

"What was that!" Manatado snapped his hand, just happening to find her wand at the same time. "Can't do anything useful, huh. Well guess who just found your wand. Oh wait, this useless boy just dropped it. Oh my." He crawled toward Lukinia.

The machine began to vibrate, and the sounds of small explosions brought back the light from the inferno. Manatado landed on all fours directly above Lukinia, who landed face-to-face with Manatado. The two locked eyes, both frustrated with each other. The lights kicked on and the engine room was flooded with light again. The two stared each other down, when a large object came down from one of the burst panels.

It was an elf, and he immediately had his spear to Manatado's throat. "Now then, who do we have here? A fairy and a . . . whatever that ugly creature is." The elf moved in closer to Manatado's face. "What are you, like, a half-dwarf, half-orc creature?" The elf took a sniff. "A human? Only the human kind can smell that horrible. Now drop the fairy."

Chapter 77

Together Malada and Cassandra mounted the Pegasus. Malada laid her hand down on the animal to communicate their new plan.

"Malada, that was such powerful magic. How did you do it?" Cassandra asked.

Malada blushed. "I'm still not entirely certain, but I think I'm starting to figure it out. It's as if I can tell the magic what to do and how strong to be, but it's like the magic has a veto and sometimes just won't let me do it. I don't know, does that make any sense?"

"Not having any magical powers, I wouldn't know."

"Magic doesn't always come in the form of spells or potions. Your magic, well, your magic is people."

"Wait, what?"

"We don't have time. Just know I wouldn't be here if it wasn't for you. Now get ready. I see lights turning back on in the machine."

Cassandra gave her friend a hug and then threw her leg over and prepared to jump off. The machine was regaining functional usage of its parts fast—so fast, in fact, that as the Pegasus turned to approach the machine, its laser gun shot directly at Cassandra. It happened so fast the Pegasus didn't know what to do. Cassandra paused in fear. The beam was deadly, and it was coming straight for her.

Malada was the only one who saw it coming in time. She thrust her shield out in front of Cassandra but had to reach too far, and as the laser beam disappeared into the shield, together they fell from the Pegasus.

The Pegasus neighed and paused, hovering in flight. Cassandra nearly fell as well, barely sliding onto her stomach in time to prevent falling. They were too late to save her. Their breath froze as they were too late to chase after and catch her. Time seemed to move in slow motion.

As they fell, Malada moved her shield below her, and instantly Cassandra knew what she was doing. Just before they hit the ground, Malada moved the shield into place, and as they hit the ground, Malada disappeared into it.

Chapter 78

"I said, drop the fairy!" The elf was very direct.

"I can't. She's injured. She has a broken leg." Manatado protested in defense.

"Are you dull, boy? She's a fairy. She can fly. Down drop the fairy with your left arm and hold out her wand with your right!"

Manatado looked down at Lukinia, who shrugged. "I've never felt so safe with a boy before. I guess I just like the feeling."

The elf jabbed the tip of his spear into Manatado's thigh. "I gave you an order, human."

Manatado's arms flew up in response to the pain. Lukinia took to flight, but the elf instantly had her trapped inside a container. The elf held up the container and looked at Lukinia. "Fairies. What a waste of magic." The elf sealed the container, stuffed it into Manatado's belly, and took hold of the wand.

The elf then took his spear and signaled for Manatado to start walking. Manatado reached a wall and could go no further when the elf called out, "Turn around, face the wall, and stay still." Manatado turned, but not fully, allowing him to see the elf reach into a chest pocket and grab a key card. The elf walked up to the wall and used the key card in a slot next to the door.

The wall slid upward and the elf signaled for the two to walk through it. Manatado limped with every step, crying out with muted protests. "Ouch, ouch. Ugh, ugh." Manatado held on to Lukinia's container tightly, and it was some time before he noticed how desperate she was to get his attention.

They started to climb a long set of stairs before Manatado was able to discreetly twist the container around so he could make eye contact with Lukinia. She was desperately upset about something, but somehow Manatado didn't think it was because of their situation.

Lukinia was bouncing around like a mad girl. It was as if she was trying to break the container. Manatado thought the weight of the container indicated it was glass, but it was darkly tinted and too heavy for glass. Lukinia had no chance of breaking it. Manatado tried sneaking words to Lukinia in between his groans as they spoke. "Ugh, what, ugh?"

"Ouch, not, oh oh oh oh, under—ugh, ugh, ugh—standing."

"What did you say?" The elf poked Manatado with his spear.

"Oh, only that I don't understand." He said the words directly at Lukinia, who was relieved to have his attention.

"You don't have to understand anything, boy, other than this. Quit your limping and walk your lazy butt up those stairs."

They were approaching the top of the stairs, and the lighting was beginning to turn more natural. Manatado limped along one stair at a time as Lukinia got frustrated at not having a wand. She made a circle with one of her hands. Manatado shook his head, still not understanding. Lukinia waved like she had a wand and then made a circle again. Manatado thought about it, but he couldn't make a hole with a wand. In the end, he shrugged his shoulders and shook his head.

They rounded another flight of stairs with even more natural light now. Lukinia took a deep breath and tried again. This time, she motioned as if she was riding a horse. Manatado nodded his head, finally understanding. She then flew around pointing at her wings. After a moment, Manatado called out, "Pegasus?"

The elf guard was quick, slapping Manatado on the head with the handle of his spear. "Shut up already!"

Manatado recoiled his neck and slowly started back up the stairs. Lukinia clapped and then immediately began to act as if she was falling. Manatado was beginning to understand. "Somebody fell off the Pegasus?" He saw her start to clap as again the elf slapped Manatado on the head. This time, however, he was ready. Manatado dropped the container and it rolled directly between the elf's legs. The elf's spear pierced directly into Manatado's butt.

The elf pulled the spear out, bent over, and reached out between his legs but missed. Manatado ran backward and hit the elf as hard as he could, sending the elf over the railing. The elf grunted in pain as he landed a few flights below. "I'll get you for that!"

Manatado didn't hesitate. He grabbed the container and started running up the stairs. The clanking sounds of the elf in pursuit overpowered the pain in his leg and butt. As they approached the final set of stairs, a hallway went off to the side, and there at the end was a window. Next to the window, Manatado saw another key slot indicating it was a door. Manatado paused. Then, with the elf right behind him, he jumped for the door.

Lukinia and the container went flying as Manatado's chest passed them, toward the window. The elf grabbed hold of Manatado's ankle and dragged him backward forcefully. Manatado was spun around like a doll. The container crashed against the window but didn't break. Manatado felt his body slide toward the elf.

The elf's face looked furious. His free hand held tightly to his side, indicating he had been injured. "Redleaf he can do without. I think I shall kill you now!"

Manatado was terrified. He screamed at the top of his lungs, over and over again.

The door at the top of the stairs opened. The elf raised his spear high and held it with both hands. The look on his face told Manatado that he was not joking. Manatado continued to scream.

The elf began to thrust down when the spear was taken from his hands. "WaterWakes, what is the meaning of this? You were told to bring them to me, not to kill them, and most certainly not to let the fairy get away. The three together looked at the container. While it was still intact, the top had now been screwed off.

Manatado relaxed enough to breathe again. His lungs labored to recover from the lost air from screaming so much.

"But Redleaf, he attacked me. Sent me down the stairs, over the railing."

"Enough, I have had enough of your excuses. I never would have expected a pathetic human child to get the best of you. Eratrea has left us. I need you in the control room. NOW!"

WaterWakes turned his head back and forth before stepping back and heading up the stairs, with a very angry look on his face. Redleaf now held the spear to Manatado's throat. "He is correct, you should be killed." Redleaf took a long look at him. "I know you. Yes, you are that boy traveling with Eratrea's daughter. Tell me, what are you to her?"

Manatado closed his eyes and swallowed hard. "Um, um, um, I, um . . . I don't know?"

Redleaf moved in close. Stress and fear ran down Manatado's face. "Very well. Stand up. If I can use you to control the girl, I can use you to control the mother." Redleaf then used the spear to signal Manatado to stand up.

Chapter 79

Cassandra watched as Malada fell toward the ground. At first her arms flailed about, wildly out of control, yet after a moment, she composed her, reached out, and grabbed the shield. Cassandra wanted to dive after her, but it would have been too late. Cassandra and the Pegasus both held their breath as Malada neared the ground. Malada skillfully enlarged her shield and then twisted it so she was on the outside.

The shield hit the ground and bounced around, but Malada fell straight through. Cassandra held tightly to the Pegasus. "After her!" The animal folded its wings in tightly and took a deep dive downward. Cassandra opened her eyes, and to her great amazement, they were not the only ones falling. Eratrea was in the full dive after her daughter. At first Eratrea didn't seem to be moving at all, but as they neared the ground, her body got bigger and closer. There was no way they would all fit.

Cassandra pulled back on the Pegasus, calling off the rescue. Together they watched as Eratrea fell directly into the shield. The Pegasus made low, slow flying circles around the shield and the area became oddly quiet. The machine rumbled and hummed, spewing out black ash and smoke, but it didn't move or attack.

Cassandra and the Pegasus waited for what seemed like a long time. Neither of them had any idea what to do. Then, when Cassandra came up with her idea, she immediately regretted not having done it sooner. They landed next to the shield. Cassandra grabbed a long length of rope and tied it to the end of an arrow. She ran around to the front of the shield and took aim. The arrow fired but hit the shield and bounced off.

The Pegasus neighed in protest, or explanation—Cassandra couldn't tell. Again she stood back and fired the arrow, only to have it bounce off. Cassandra couldn't understand. The Pegasus rose on it back legs and neighed loudly. Again Cassandra had no idea what the creature was saying. She tried throwing the arrow in, but that, too, bounced off. Panic was growing in her, and the Pegasus's constant protesting wasn't helping. At last Cassandra stuffed the arrow into the Pegasus's mouth just to shut it up.

The Pegasus grabbed hold of the arrow and dove into the shield. Cassandra stood dumbfounded, alone. Again nothing around her was happening. Again panic started to grow inside Cassandra. "What if there is something I'm supposed to be doing. What if they all die and it's my fault?" She raised her hands to her head and fell to her knees.

Cassandra's torso fell forward and she rested on her hands. She hoped. She waited. She rejoiced.

The Pegasus burst forth from the shield, diving high into the sky. Cassandra looked at the rope. It was tugging. It was tugging. What does that mean? She did the only thing she could think of. She grabbed the rope and pulled. The rope was long and each tug exhausting.

Cassandra felt the rope tighten, and it became very hard to pull. She wrapped the rope around her and ran around a thick tree. She placed her thigh against the tree and pulled. Sweat dripped down her forehead, and as she pulled, the rope gave way.

Eratrea held her daughter in her arms. A white glow around them evaporated as they came back into the world. The two landed and rolled in the dirt before the shield, while

Cassandra fell backward into some small scrubs. Again silence filled the area.

It took a moment for Cassandra to brush herself off and get out of the bushes. She immediately ran to Malada's side. Cassandra fell to her knees and grabbed Malada's hand and held it to her face "I'm sorry, I'm sorry."

Malada coughed and smiled. "I feel like we have gotten off plan. Not your fault." She sat up and immediately started surveying the situation.

Eratrea was a little more shaken. "What? What just happened? Wait, what plan?"

Malada stood up and hugged Cassandra. "Thank you for saving me. Now we need to help a boy." Malada grabbed Cassandra's hand and they ran for the Pegasus. Malada called back to her mother. "The plan, Mother, was to stop you and Redleaf."

"But why? I'm fighting for you."

Malada looked back and gave a stern glance. "No, Mother, you were fighting for yourself."

Eratrea shook her head as she watched her daughter and best friend mount a flying horse in an effort to take something away from her. "But I saved you, didn't I?"

Chapter 80

Manatado moved slowly. He took one step at a time. He had no idea where Lukinia was. He had only a bad feeling about what was going on outside. He felt depressed because it was his plan. His inability to follow through made him angry. He closed his eyes and tried to think of something happy. Redleaf slapped him on his injured butt, hurrying Manatado along. That's when an idea came to him.

"This really wasn't the way I wanted to bring this up, but, well, before we start to dislike each other, um, well . . . Dad, I just wanted you to know that I have only good intentions for your daugh—"

Redleaf slapped him on the head.

"Shut up. Why would I care?"

"Well, she is Eratrea's daughter, and aren't you her, um, boyfriend?"

Again, another slap hit Manatado on the back of the head. "My relation is no concern of yours."

He took a step up the first stair. "I mean, don't you want what's best for your—"

This time, Redleaf pressed hard on the wound, forcing Manatado to walk faster. "I decide what's best for them. NOT YOU!"

"So, um, I didn't want to tell you this way, but you're going to be a grandpa!"

Redleaf poked his spear into Manatado's knee, grabbed him by the throat as he fell, and held his face upside down, facing his. Redleaf looked deep into his eyes. "Nice try, kid." Redleaf then slid open the door at the top of the stairs and threw Manatado onto the floor.

The control room had WaterWakes and two more elves manning the controls. A large screen displayed a scene on the ground. Cassandra was shooting an arrow at Malada's shield. Manatado couldn't understand why, but he was greatly relieved to see Cassandra okay. Display panels lined most of the room but one entire wall was missing, opening out into a large platform. Manatado recognized it as where Jalum had fallen from. No one could have survived that fall, he told himself.

"Are we up and running yet?" Redleaf yelled out to his crew.

"Almost, but this human technology is very foreign. For example, sir, it's asking me if I want to reset the oscillating gyros? I don't understand what that means."

"Oh, who cares about this stupid human technology. Just say yes," Redleaf commanded as if annoyed.

"Ah, yeah, now, sir, it's asking me to begin alignment process. I don't know how to do that."

"Yeah, fine, just let me see." Redleaf walked over to the display panel. "Oh, I hate technology. Look, here is a back button. Just skip it and get this thing moving."

"Yes, um, sir." WaterWakes continued to push buttons on the monitor while Redleaf took note of the display. Eratrea and Malada had just popped out of the shield. "Oh, so, Eratrea, you do live. Uh, well, I guess it is always good to have a fallback plan."

Manatado felt his blood boil as he heard how heartlessly Redleaf spoke. Manatado felt like now was his chance. He braced himself for the pain and lunged at Redleaf. Manatado felt his shoulder crash right into Redleaf's gut. Redleaf hunched over in pain but held his ground. Redleaf then grabbed Manatado by his ankles and held him up high. "Pathetic. You could never protect

Malada. Accept the fact that humans without science are simply pathetic."

Manatado winced in pain as Redleaf held him up high by his injured leg. Tears ran down his face, but he still threw a few punches. They barely affected Redleaf as he tossed Manatado like a doll into the corner.

"Sir," WaterWakes called out urgently, "the girls are taking flight. What do you want me to do?"

Redleaf turned his attention to the screen as Malada and Cassandra took flight. "I've had enough of that girl's insolence. No more warning shots. Take them out with the laser."

"Yes, sir." WaterWakes began pushing display buttons. "Should I remind you Eratrea would strongly object."

"Do as you are told!"

Relief seemed to come across WaterWakes's face as his screen flashed red before him. "Sir, the laser isn't calibrated and won't fire."

"Blast it all!" Redleaf slammed his hand down on a panel. "Just get rid of them, then!"

"Yes, sir!" WaterWakes moved to a new display and started using joysticks as controls. The machine jostled and shook as it turned to begin its attack. Another red light started flashing across a display. A new sound could be heard as well, as if the metal was groaning.

"What is that?" Redleaf barked out. The screen turned to the image of Rogers and Tamack. They were now using the laser machine gun to attack the machine.

"Sir, should I attack the new target?" WaterWakes asked.

"Show me Eratrea." The screen changed over, and Eratrea was now charging off in the direction of Rogers and

Tamack. "That's a good girl. Loyal to the end. Never mind that new target WaterWakes. Get the girls."

"Sir, one of the girls is missing!"

"Show me." The screen image switched over, and there on the Pegasus was Malada. "Where did the other girl go? She is the only one of the three with any real skills. Find her!"

"But, sir, look at Malada. I believe she is getting ready to use her magic again!"

"Slap her out of the sky! Now!" The screen turned over to Malada, and she was standing on the Pegasus, her hands held high to the sky. A large white light grew in strength, but before she could use it, the machine swung at her. The Pegasus ducked, knocking Malada off her perch, but this time they stayed together.

The machine swung again at Malada. The Pegasus again dodged, but both times were scary close and the animal now backed off quickly. "Again, after her! We have destroyed the armies of the world. We have destroyed the monsters. I will not be beaten by a little girl!"

"But, sir!" WaterWakes began to protest, but Redleaf was fast, and before he could finish, he had been removed from the display.

Redleaf tripped WaterWakes down onto his back. Redleaf then grabbed the spear and, for a moment, held it at WaterWakes's neck.

The two exchanged very tense looks before Redleaf handed WaterWakes the spear. "Find something you can do. Go and find that fairy! You caught it once. Failure this time could only mean insubordination."

WaterWakes scurried backward a few steps before jumping to his feet and rushing out the door. The door had just barely closed when it reopened with WaterWakes walking backward, his spear at the ready. Redleaf looked up from the display. "What now?"

Redleaf burned in anger, first at WaterWakes, but his fury quickly switched over to a new intruder. Jalum now held a knife to Cassandra's face as her hands were bound behind her and tears came down her face.

"Cassandra!" Manatado burst out with a genuine sense of caring in his voice.

"Shouldn't you be dead? Oh no, wait, I must have left that to Eratrea, for the job didn't get done, again." Redleaf moved in a warrior stance, darting for his staff, but Jalum's blade was faster and Redleaf found his staff pierced into the wall.

Redleaf paused, took up his warrior stance, and showed he was ready. Jalum smiled a wicked smile and then casually threw Cassandra onto Manatado as if stacking objects. Jalum then walked to the center of the command room. Redleaf crunched his knuckles and charged at Jalum.

Chapter 81

Cassandra landed directly on Manatado, her chest crashing down on his shoulder, and lost her breath. Manatado rolled over got to his knees and reached out for Cassandra's hands. He lifted slightly, bringing the blade up, but in doing so, he hurt Cassandra's shoulder. She cringed in pain, cutting herself on the blade. Manatado jumped back. Cassandra gave him a scolding look before he cut the restraints.

Cassandra raised one arm, her hand flat toward Manatado, as she bent over gasping for breath. After several big deep breaths, she labored out a short sentence. "Stop helping." Manatado threw the blade off to the side and sat back and wrapped his arms around his bad knee as he leaned onto the good one, his facial expression one of both hope and guilt.

Cassandra took another moment, but when she stood up, she nearly tumbled over in pain. "OH, it hurts, it hurts."

"What, what is it?"

"My shoulder, Jalum really twisted it as he snuck up behind me."

"What happened?"

"I was using the code to get in, and the moment I entered the code, he was on me."

"Well thankfully he is well distracted now. Can you move?"

Cassandra tucked her arm tightly to her wrist. Her face winced in pain, but she nodded yes to Manatado. "This is your plan. What's next?"

Manatado sure didn't feel like this was his plan, but once again Cassandra made him feel better about himself, and that rejuvenated him. Manatado smiled in a way that warmed Cassandra's heart. "Now we take control and destroy this thing."

"What? You say that like it's easy. What if there isn't a giant red button that says, 'self-destruct'?"

"Oh, don't worry about that. I will let you take care of it." Cassandra gave him a stern look. He rolled his eyes and replied, "Fine, we can, um, drive it into the whole of Athenia."

Cassandra gave him a long look. "Well, I don't have any better ideas, and you somehow seem to get it done. Lead the way."

Manatado hopped onto his good foot, but as he stood to turn around, he found himself with an elf and a spear at his throat.

"I'll give you this, Manatado, you sure are consistent. Not one step further into the plan and it's already in shambles," Cassandra sassed.

The elf, however, had the majority of his focus on Redleaf and Jalum. Jalum threw several small knives at Redleaf as he changed course to avoid the blades and ended up on the defensive. Jalum was amazingly quick as his boot struck Redleaf's defense, which absorbed the blow but sent him backward.

Jalum charged, hoping to take advantage of Redleaf's backward momentum, but Redleaf was an experienced fighter and increased his backward momentum by backpedaling, causing Jalum's attack to fall short. Redleaf pounced onto Jalum's back, and the two wrestled aggressively on the floor.

Cassandra watched the elf with the spear rather than the fight, and at the moment when she thought he was most distracted, she charged into Manatado, crashing him into the elf. Together they rolled around several times. Manatado's flailing proved difficult for the elf to deal with, and Cassandra wound up at a control display.

"Manatado, I can't read it. It's all in elf!"

Manatado was now latched around the elf, hanging on desperately as the elf tried to pry him off. "I'm a little busy!"

"Oh, he never paid attention in school anyways." Cassandra concentrated on the display, hoping to recognize anything.

Lukinia appeared out from her hiding realm. I can help. What are we trying to do?"

Cassandra smiled at Lukinia. "I'm so glad you're here." Even if Lukinia didn't really like Cassandra, hearing her appreciation was really gratifying. "We need to destroy this machine."

"What? you think they're just going to make a button for that or something?"

Cassandra nodded in understanding. "Then set a course for the hole of Athenia."

Lukinia gave Cassandra a look of disbelief but then turned to the display, and after several entries, the machine began to turn. The machine's new movement jostled the two warriors, Redleaf and Jalum, and as the machine turned, the momentum swung the two combatants into Manatado and the other elf.

Redleaf roared as he stood up from the bottom of the pile holding Manatado like a doll. "I have had enough of you!" He threw Manatado out of the open area and off onto the platform edge. Manatado screamed as he streaked across the platform uncontrollably and started freefalling. Manatado screamed, but for only just a second, as he soon landed in the arms of Malada.

Manatado grabbed on to Malada as tightly as he possibly could. She felt the warmth of his embrace and the trust the two had built together. The Pegasus circled around and landed on the platform. Jalum was exchanging blows with Redleaf and his fellow elf. Malada wasted no time, and as she dismounted, she raised her arms and a bright-white light began to form over her head.

The three warriors had no recourse. Malada's magic would be too powerful for them. Two of them braced for the pain, but something happened and she fell sideways, her arm landing hard into her ribs. WaterWakes hurled his spear around in a display of skill, its dull end crashing into Malada.

"Hey, that's my friend!" Lukinia shouted. Her face raged with anger as she started to feel something new, something better. She felt like she was beginning to belong to this strange group. Her anger was strong and focused. She charged directly into WaterWakes's lower back and pushed hard.

WaterWakes moved several feet, stopping just near the edge. He dug his foot in deep and they reached a stalemate. Lukinia grunted out in effort when the Pegasus charged to her rescue, tumbling the three of them off the platform together.

There was a moment of silence before a strange noise of metal stretching could be heard as the sound of laser blasts struck the machine. There was no time to lose as Jalum skillfully dropped Redleaf to his backside with a sweeping kick. Redleaf's final companion was quick to counterattack Jalum, but his skills were inferior. Jalum gracefully dodged the spear and pulled it and the elf close. Jalum slammed his forehead down on the elf's. The elf, stunned, took a step back and fell to his knees.

Manatado and Cassandra crawled to Malada's side. "Are you okay?" he asked.

Malada held her hand over her side, where it was very tender to the touch, but she wasn't hurt too badly. She crawled over to the edge but saw nothing. Both Lukinia and the Pegasus can fly, she told herself. The three huddled together.

"Manatado, this is awful." Cassandra couldn't help but sound distressed as she spoke. "I don't want to be here anymore. I want to go home." She laid her head on his shoulder and cried. Malada put on a brave face, but when she saw Cassandra cry and felt the pain in her side, she cried too.

Manatado wrapped his arms around his friends and thought to himself, this is all my fault.

Chapter 82

Jalum was a man on a mission. Redleaf was a skilled and experienced fighter. The two exchanged and dodged each other's attacks and counterattacks. The first fighter to make a mistake would lose the fight. That loser was Redleaf. It wasn't much, a slight overextension on a kick, but it allowed Jalum to land a gut-wrenching blow that sent Redleaf down to the ground hard.

Jalum rushed to the control display and stopped the machine. Manatado looked around. They were not far from the edge of the hole that Athenia had fallen into. Smoking, charred war vehicles scattered the countryside. The elven forest still burned in the distance. Damaged and pockmarked road and tracks now stopped abruptly at the great fence. It stood meters high, solid at the bottom, weaved at the top. Monsters jumped up and shook the fence that surrounded the great hole, desperate to escape.

Manatado had never seen the great city. He had never even really left his village before. Now it seemed everywhere he had traveled to had been destroyed. "This is all my fault, isn't it?"

Cassandra looked up from her tears. "No, you could never have done all this. You're just a cute boy. You never could have done anything to stop this."

"Wait, what?" Manatado sniffled.

"She means we can't stop all the adults!" Malada fumed.

"Wait, what?" Manatado sniffled.

Cassandra took a deep breath. "We are just a bunch of kids. We should have realized that."

"Wait, what?" Manatado asked.

Frustration came across in Malada's voice. "She means we never had a chance. We never should have tried."

"Wait, what!"

"Whatever the adults are going to do, we can't stop them," Cassandra bemoaned.

"What!" Manatado jumped up, cringed in pain, gave the two girls a very determined look, and limped toward Jalum, who was quickly pressing buttons until a panel next to him opened.

A control stick rose up and filled the open panel. Jalum gripped the control and the entire machine moved with it. "Let's see, first let's take care of that bothersome Pegasus." Jalum smiled a wicked smile and slammed his hand down on a button.

The panel beeped in protest. "You broke my laser gun!" Jalum glared at Redleaf, who was regaining his composure and was up on his knees. Jalum moved over to him, and Manatado slipped unnoticed into his place. Manatado looked at the display, and while it was in human, he still couldn't understand it.

Manatado pressed the first button, labeled "operations." A long new list of options came up. Jalum picked up a spear and approached Redleaf from behind. Redleaf was more ready than he let on and released a volley of knives as he spun around. Jalum spun the spear, deflecting the knives, and the two were reengaged in battle.

Malada and Cassandra now rushed to Manatado's side, and together the three began pressing buttons. Something went wrong and the display suddenly turned back into elvish. Cassandra hit Manatado on the arm as if it was his fault and then went back to the display. Manatado threw his arms up in frustration.

Redleaf reached out and grabbed Manatado's hand. Redleaf lifted him up and threw him across the room. Malada raised her arms up as if to begin magic, but Redleaf was quick, moved behind her, and held a blade to her backside.

"Now, girl, move away from the controls!" Redleaf then poked the blade just enough to make Malada squeal out.

Cassandra screamed and backed away from the controls.

"Now that's a good—" Redleaf was cut off by a swarm of laser bolts all around the two of them.

Eratrea now stormed in as she jumped off the Pegasus, laser machine gun in hand. "Get away from my daughter!"

Redleaf threw up his hands and backed away."Malada, my love. It wasn't what it looked like."

Eratrea let loose another volley of laser blasters, all directly around Redleaf. "I told you to protect my daughter, not slap her out of the sky with your machine. I didn't say attack my daughter's friends, and I most certainly did not say you could hold my daughter hostage. Consider yourself dumped!" Another long stream of laser blasters erupted until Redleaf scurried out the door and fled.

Cassandra and Manatado took up fighting positions and approached Eratrea. Eratrea smiled and threw down the laser machine gun. "I'm sorry. Kids, I'm so, so, so sorry."

Malada instinctively ran to her mother's side and hugged her. "Consider yourself dumped? Seriously, Mom, that's the best you could come up with?"

Eratrea sighed heavily. "It wasn't like I had time to think about it. How about a thank-you instead of sass?"

"A thank-you! You want a thank-you! You should be the one giving the thank-yous!" Malada screamed out in protest to her mother's response.

Cassandra moved in next to Manatado. "What do we do?"

Manatado answered, "What we always do." Manatado moved between Malada and her mother and held out his hands to them both. "Forgive."

"What?" Malada and Eratrea exclaimed. Then, too tired to fight, they let down their guards and embraced.

"What a touching moment. Too bad it will all be your last." Jalum grimaced as he grabbed the controls and bent the machine over.

Chapter 83

Manatado could barely breathe as Malada and Cassandra held on to him so tightly. The machine bent over, tipping the entire room downward, sliding the group out toward the open balcony. Manatado tipped the group's body weight, altering their course, and they crashed against the edge of the wall. They held together, but Eratrea didn't shift enough. She reached out her arms and managed to grab hold of Manatado's foot as her body started falling.

Eratrea's moment changed Manatado's positioning, and the group was now tilting toward falling. Manatado reached out, straightening his legs out as far as possible with the pain. Eratrea reached up with her second hand as the first slipped, sending his shoe plummeting to the ground. Eratrea wrapped her arms around his legs. Manatado felt his pants slip, but his hands were wrapped around Cassandra and Malada. There was nothing he could do, and his pants slipped off. Eratrea fell, screaming, as she held on to Manatado's pants.

Malada's Pegasus swept across the sky and rescued her as she fell. Cassandra now found her footing and pulled her friends back away from the edge. Together the three fell backward against the side wall. Jalum raised the machine back to level and the kids dropped to the floor.

"There, now that we are alone, it's time for you to decide." Jalum's voice was terrifying.

Manatado jumped up and raised his fists toward Jalum. "We choose to stop you."

Jalum let loose a gut-bursting laugh. "Boy, are you not even wearing pants?"

Manatado blushed. Then he jumped. He placed both hands on the control stick and charged the machine toward the hole of Athenia. Jalum was stunned but only for a second, and with a single hand, he grabbed both of Manatado's wrists and squeezed so hard he had to let go.

Cassandra was right behind him, and as soon as Jalum lifted off with Manatado's hands, her good arm took over. Jalum grunted, "Damn kids, just stop!" Jalum then took his second hand away from the control panel to grab Cassandra's hand. She screamed out in pain as Jalum squeezed so hard.

Malada walked up behind Jalum, readied her magic, and yelled, "Damn adults, just stop!" She then flung her magic into the center of Jalum's back. His body shook as the white magic ran down and shook him in his entirety. Manatado and Cassandra fell to the floor, as did a smoking Jalum.

The room fell silent as, for a long moment, nobody moved. Once the three teens had made eye contact, they jumped up and ran to each other. Cassandra finally spoke first. "Manatado, how much more? I want to go home."

Manatado looked her in the eyes. "Me too, I want to go home too." He then turned and walked up to the control panel. He looked out through the balcony. There before him, just beyond a fence, lay the black hole of Athenia. "This machine is big, but that hole is bigger. This machine is tall, but that hole is deeper. This machine is strong, but that hole is—"

"Not where this machine is going!" Eratrea, unarmed this time, again swooped in from the Pegasus. She looked at her daughter. "Where did you get a Pegasus?"

Malada looked around, surprised. "Oh, um, Daddy gave it to me."

"Well that is way too dangerous a pet. I'm taking it away from you! Only your father would be so reckless!"

Malada's jaw dropped in protest. "You can't do that! He's done more for me than you ever have!"

"How can you say that? Everything I have ever done has always been for you!"

"Oh, you mean like sending me away on my own?"

"Yes, I mean like sending you away to be on your own. I was in a dangerous situation. It was to protect you!"

"Oh, just like it was you trying to protect me when you started the machine?"

"Yes, I mean like when I started the machine. Jalum was an evil man who would have hurt us!"

"Oh you mean just like when you took over the machine to attack and destroy the human army!"

"Yes I mean like when I took over the machine to destroy the human army. Jalum was too powerful already. He couldn't control the world's strong army too!"

Malada backed away and looked at Manatado. "She's confusing me! I, I, I don't know what to do!"

Manatado nodded. "I do!" He then pushed the machine at full speed toward the hole of Athenia. Eratrea rushed at him and tried to push back. Manatado had never been more sure of anything before in his life, and he pushed with all his might. The two tussled back and forth at the controls.

The machine jostled, tilted, and bounced, but Manatado won and the machine crashed at full speed into the fence. The sound of metal crashing against concrete echoed about the control room before the room began to tip over again. The four stood together as the blackness filled the whole of their sight and the pits of their stomachs sank.

Chapter 84

Manatado was so determined to do what he had set out to do that he didn't have a plan for what came next. The darkness of the hole of Athenia was a deeper shade of black than any other he had seen before. Once the light from the rim of the hole passed, they seemed to descend into darkness forever. None of them were restrained, and they could feel their bodies become almost weightless. A bright-white light flashed just before the machine touched the bottom.

The machine slammed down into the ground. The arms detached, smashing into a thousand different pieces. The sound of metal twisting, screeching, and tearing echoed about the control room, as did sparks and loose equipment.

Then it was all over.

The air no longer moved. No sounds could be heard. The great and terrible machine had come to a halt.

The white light vanished, and the group fell to the ground. A chorus of coughing and gasping erupted as the group desperately breathed in the stale, dusty air.

Manatado was the first to cough out any understandable words. "Is . . . ever . . . un . . . okay?"

Cassandra reached out her hand and grabbed Manatado's unclothed good leg. She pulled herself forward and Manatado down. They were side by side when she finally spoke. "Manatado, you have hair on your legs!"

Manatado blushed, opened his mouth to speak, and then closed it without saying anything.

Eratrea called out, "Malada, Malada, where is Malada?"

Manatado and Cassandra both sat up and started feeling around them. Calling out was useless, but so was feeling around in the dark. The three searched as best they could until a groan called out from seemingly between them all. The three all reached out at once. Manatado grabbed a leg, Cassandra the other, while Eratrea slapped her hand down on Jalum's face.

Jalum tried to bite her but found his leg restrained. Manatado and Malada held on as best they could, but Jalum was strong. He pushed away Eratrea and flung himself backward. A squeal of pain was barely audible over Jalum's grunt as he fell, but they all recognized it. Together they all crawled after him. The sounds of Jalum's feet shifting things along the ground guided them in the dark.

Jalum made it to his feet but only got a little ways before running face-first into something in the dark. Eratrea felt her first and pulled her daughter in close. It wasn't hard for a mother to know her daughter, and Malada was faceup in her mother's lap.

Malada coughed. "Mother, are you okay?"

"Yes, yes, my love, I am. All thanks to you."

"Good, I'm glad." Malada coughed again and again. "And my friends?"

"Yes, yes, they are here too. You saved them. You saved everyone."

"No, not quite everyone." Malada moved her hand down to her side.

Eratrea moved her hand over her daughter's. Malada was bleeding, bleeding badly. "My love, what do I do?"

Cassandra moved in closer. "Eratrea raised her hand and readied her magic. "Get back! Get back!"

Malada coughed. "You must trust him."

"Him!" Eratrea exclaimed. "But he's the one who ruined everything."

Malada shook her head. "No, he's the one who saved everyone."

Eratrea felt the weakness of Malada's words. Eratrea looked at her daughter—then Manatado, Malada, Manatado, Malada—and then when she looked back at Manatado, she spoke. "What do I do?"

Manatado said, "Whatever Cassandra tells us to."

Cassandra smiled so brightly it could be seen in the dark. "Place your hand here and press." Even if she couldn't see him, Cassandra turned toward Manatado. "Manatado, I need you to find a way out. I suggest grabbing some stones off the ground and keep heading in one direction until you find a way out or can't go anymore."

Manatado nodded. No one saw it, but yet they all seemed to feel it. Eratrea applied pressure while Cassandra ripped off a piece of clothing to make a bandage. Cassandra placed her hand on Malada's forehead. She was sweating profusely. Cassandra placed her hand under Malada's back—she was bleeding there too. Cassandra applied pressure with her own hands but had no idea what to do next.

"Manatado!" Cassandra tried not to sound panicked. "Um, so yeah, could you, um, you know, hurry some?"

Manatado felt the urgency in her voice. He also felt the pain in his leg and butt. He resigned himself to the pain and, for Malada's sake, limped boldly into the dark. He guessed Jalum had only made it a few meters before running into something, so when he passed that mark, he felt encouraged. When a blue light appeared before him, he felt relief. When the blue light grew in strength to reveal a scary and large set of teeth, he screamed.

Manatado turned and limped as fast as he could away from the monster. The light revealed the lip of the balcony exit. It was only a few feet before him. Manatado jumped as the teeth reached out to grab him. He felt the wind and breath on his bare legs as he jumped. The monster crashed against the balcony exit, bending it further.

Manatado crawled backward, running to Cassandra. She yelled into his ear, "This is helping. Now there's a monster attacking us."

"I know, I know!" he said.

"So now what?"

Manatado shrugged his shoulders. "Pray?"

Cassandra looked down at her friend Malada. Even in the blue light, she looked pale. Out of ideas, Cassandra took his advice and prayed. The monster roared and slammed against the dead body of the machine. Cassandra looked back at Manatado. "I prayed. Now what?"

Manatado again shrugged. "I don't know, wait?"

"Wait, wait for what?"

Chapter 85

They didn't have to wait long before finding out what came next. The whole area shook with a very gentle bounce. A deep throbbing noise came from the corner of the room. It was Jalum, and he was holding something up to his face. It looked like a shell with a hard, natural outer casing, but it sounded like a musical instrument.

Jalum lowered the shell. The monster ceased smashing against the shell of the machine, turning off its blue light as it moved back in ambush, or fear. The ground began to shake more than bounce. A loud rumbling echoed about the cavern. The noise dulled just before Riftia burst through one of the cavern walls. A glimmer of light came with the beast, exposing the blue-lighted monster. Jalum again held the shell to his head and whistled with it.

Riftia lunged out to attack the blue monster. The ground shook as the armored worm Riftia took flight with a walking predator fish. Manatado slapped Eratrea and Cassandra on their shoulders to get their attention. "The shell, we have to get the shell from Jalum!"

Eratrea explained in protest. "No way, he is too powerful!"

Manatado spoke with authority. "She said, listen to me! So stop being an adult and do as you're told. Listen to me!" Eratrea and Cassandra nodded, giving him their full attention. "We need to take that shell!"

Eratrea made eye contact with Cassandra, who looked lovingly at Manatado. She then looked down at a very pale and weak Malada. Eratrea clenched her fist and made a spark of lightning.

The three stood up. Manatado limped over Malada, and together the three stood directly before Jalum. "What's this?" Jalum laughed. "You still haven't found a pair of pants!" Jalum laughed a belly laugh before reaching behind his ear like a magic trick and pulled out a pair of pants. He threw them at Manatado, who, to everyone's surprise, quickly put them on.

The two monsters exchanged blows in the distance as Riftia's body slammed the blue monster. The blue monster clenched its jaws down across Riftia's body, but it wasn't strong enough to break through the armor. The blue monster shook its head and then threw Riftia off into the cavern wall.

Manatado exchanged looks in defense of his actions between Cassandra and Eratrea. He then signaled, and together the three charged at him. Jalum proved just as fast and strong as expected. Jalum's leg was directly into Cassandra's injured shoulder as she cried out in pain. Eratrea stepped in front of Manatado and let loose a bolt of lightning. Jalum was fast and quickly latched on to Eratrea's hands. He guided her hands behind him, sending her attack off harmlessly into the dead control room. Jalum strengthened his grip on Eratrea, and with a spinning move, he sent her flying. Using the momentum from the spin, Jalum reached out and tripped Manatado as he scurried away with something in his hands.

"Stupid, stupid young man. When will you ever learn that you cannot beat me?" Jalum grabbed Manatado by the collar and picked him up off the ground.

Jalum reached out and grabbed the object from his hands. "A rock? Where is the summoning shell?"

Cassandra was standing tall off in the corner. Riftia slammed the blue monster down, knocking it out cold, when

Cassandra blew the whistle. Jalum threw Manatado aside and stepped toward her. "No, no, what did you just do?"

Manatado coughed. "We just beat you, that's what we did. When are you adults going to learn you can't beat . . . US!"

Cassandra blew the whistle. Riftia shook and danced as it accepted its new master. Jalum started to run. Cassandra held the shell to her face, and as she blew the whistle, she pointed at Jalum. The giant worm danced in delight before it jumped into the air. It slammed down, consuming Jalum in a single bite.

Chapter 86

A desperate and weak cough from Malada brought everyone running to her side. "I'll trade you a ride . . . on my Pegasus . . . for a ride on your . . . worm." Malada was weak, very weak.

"Oh, Manatado, what do we do?" Cassandra called out with tears in her eyes as she looked at her dying friend.

Manatado took a deep breath. Everyone always expected him to have the answer. Well he didn't. "I don't have an answer. I don't know what to do." He knelt down beside Malada.

Then, after a long sad moment, he stood up. "But I do know what I can do!" He turned to Cassandra. "Cassandra, get us out of here! Eratrea, you keep us safe from other monsters and, Malada, you stay alive!"

"What, you can't just order me to do something . . ." Cassandra looked down at the shell. "Okay, but how?"

Eratrea chimed in with excitement. "Start collapsing from the outside in, the dirt will slowly build up here in the middle, and when it does, we can slowly climb out."

Cassandra and Eratrea looked at Manatado. "That's what you can do? Boss us around!"

"Well it gave us something, didn't it!"

The two girls looked at each other before shrugging their shoulders. Eratrea let loose a wild swath of small lightning bolts, and with the presence of Riftia, all other monsters had fled. Eratrea and Manatado picked up Malada. Cassandra took a deep breath and blew into the whistle.

Riftia jumped up and down before heading off into the distant dark of the cavern. After a moment, the cavern started collapsing. The far walls of the cavern were falling directly behind the monster as it slowly circled the cavern time after time. Surely enough, the dirt and sand slowly started to bury the once-great machine. Manatado and Eratrea climbed their way up the sand as if going up a mountain as they worked to outpace the falling sand.

The group was nearing the surface when the loud roar of a crowd could be heard. "Oh, look, they're here to cheer us for saving them." Manatado spoke with a true sense of pride that was only overshadowed by Malada's health.

"Get up here!" one of the people yelled.

"Get them out of there!" another yelled.

"One of them is hurt. Get the medics!" yet another yelled.

Manatado was yanked out from the hole, the light blinding him. Cassandra and Eratrea were both pulled and placed beside Manatado while Malada was carted off by some medics. The three covered their eyes from the brightness, expecting the crowd's cheers as they recovered. Instead, jeers rained down upon them.

"Arrest them!"

"Punish them!"

"They destroyed everything!"

The three were aggressively manhandled by a cadre of human duties and soldiers. Fruit was being thrown at the police vehicle as it pulled up to take the three away. They were whisked into handcuffs and thrown into the back seat of the vehicle without delay.

Together the three sat, tired and miserable, as they were driven away. Cassandra said the only thing she could as they went. "Manatado, I hate you." She then laid her head down on his shoulder and slept.

Eratrea gave Manatado a scowling looking that was clearly evaluating the relationship between Cassandra and him.

Chapter 87

The vehicle they were in seemed to drive for a long time. It was Manatado's first time in memory he had ever been in a vehicle at all. Athenia was too far away for school trips, and the one trip the school did take to Maracato was by train, and of course he had missed out on it. He enjoyed the gentle bouncing as they hummed down the black road.

At last they came to a small two-story building. Off in the distance, the office towers and apartment buildings of Maracato reached up into the sky. Manatado sighed as he wondered what a human city was like. He had been able to visit a gnome village, the fairies' home, the deep forest where Socratea trees lived, and the towering branches of the elven trees, but never had he been able to visit a human city. A large group of people were outside the building along with a long line of police and soldiers.

When the police opened the door and they heard shouts—"Punish them!" "Destroyers of the protector!" and "Traitors to the human race!"—Manatado knew he would never be able to see a human town. The police roughly pulled each of them out of the vehicle and rushed them into the building.

Another group of police and soldiers were waiting for them inside. Together the three of them were thoroughly searched, fingerprinted, and properly arrested. After processing, the three of them were moved to prison cells, each to their own. It was a flurry of activity that ended abruptly, and no one had yet to talk to them.

Manatado expected a flurry of insults and blame to head his way, but he got nothing. The two girls very calmly lay down and fell asleep. Manatado was exhausted but unable to sleep. At one point, he couldn't lie down any longer. As he sat up, he jumped with a fright, as there was now a little benign being in the cell with him.

"Wait, what, what, what? How did you get in here?"

"What are your intentions for my daughter?"

"Wait, what?"

"What are your intentions for my daughter?"

"Wait, what?"

The little being growled. "Perhaps you're not as smart as I once thought."

"Wait! What? Wait, I mean, what?" Manatado sat upright and then jumped up. "You're Malada's father? I didn't see the resemblance."

The little benign being scowled at Manatado and erupted in a cloud of red angry smoke. The room went dark and a warm, smoky heat surrounded Manatado. The smoke cleared, and there stood an aged but powerful-looking wizard. His white hair darkened, worn with work. A gruff, unshaven look of vengeance on the wizard scared Manatado. "Are you sassing me, BOY!"

Manatado tried crawling backward as fast and as hard as possible, but he was already at the cell's corner. Manatado shook his head no in fear. The wizard approached and stood over him. Sparks of lightning erupted all around him as the smoke hid everything else. "What are you intentions for my daughter!"

"Don't hurt me! Don't hurt me. She kissed me. I didn't kiss her." Manatado wiggled in place, as his hip and butt hurt.

"She did what?" Eratrea called out from behind the smoke.

"I mean, yeah, I guess. Um, well I'm sorry, I don't know. I certainly like Malada. She is beautiful, powerful, magical . . . but I don't even know if she likes me—you know, that way."

The wizard looked Manatado over. "An honest answer I can accept. Puberty isn't easy for any species. Learning to give an honest answer isn't easy for any species either." A staff that Manatado hadn't even realized was there now helped the wizard as he backed up and let the smoke clear. "So tell me, how did you end up here? Where is my daughter?"

Manatado held back the tears, and now that the smoke had cleared, he didn't feel quite so scared. "Yeah, so, um, we kinda destroyed this machine. I heard one of the police call it public property . . . you know, um, regular teenage stuff. Cops, ya know, always on our backs. So as to Malada. Yeah, I . . . have no idea." He spoke very quickly at the end as he trailed off.

A puff of red smoke filled the room, and the wizard started to grow very large in stature. Ciefraf's face turned into a fury. The heat around Manatado grew intensely hot. "You don't know where my daughter IS!"

Manatado fell backward, nearly fainting. "I'm going to die. I'm going to die."

"Oh, leave him alone. You know perfectly well where she is and how she is doing. He's a good boy. Leave him alone."

Ciefraf returned to his previous stature. "I will make my own evaluation of the young man myself. Good boy or not, our daughter is still kissing . . . and under your watch. And might I say, I am glad you're finally in a place where you can't cause any more trouble."

"Oh, how dare you!" Eratrea was standing at the edge of her cell. "And where have you been? Mr. Father of the Year! No, I had to raise her alone. And where do you get off giving her a Pegasus! Do you know how dangerous those things can be?"

"Don't you lecture me. I do believe that animal saved your life!"

You could have prevented this whole thing! Don't blame me for finishing your work!"

Ciefraf exploded and reemerged in the same cell as Eratrea. "I will never impose my will forcefully on another!"

"Even if it means avoiding all this pain and destruction!"

"Absolutely!"

Ciefraf had now taken human shape, and the two now stared each other down eye to eye. Labored breaths suddenly gave way to the sound of kissing as the two embraced.

Cassandra crawled over to Manatado. "This went from being the most entertaining thing ever to kinda creeping me out."

Manatado turned his head to look at Cassandra, but his eyes were empty like a deer staring into the headlights. "What just happened?"

Cassandra looked at Manatado. "I think I just decided I never want to become an adult."

Chapter 88

The main door to the holding area opened, and a few officers in very formal attire stepped into the holding cell. Ciefraf disappeared into a puff a smoke. Each officer stepped in front of a cell. The first officer opened Cassandra's cell and gently held his hand out, leading the way. Cassandra hesitated, waiting to see if the officer would force her. He did not. The second officer opened Manatado's cell and made the same gesture.

Neither officer spoke, and after a long moment, Nicolda came in through the front door. Manatado and Cassandra ran out of their cells and hugged their friend, the dwarf. "What's going on?"

Nicolda put his hands on his hips. "Well it seems as if people had the impression a few young teenagers were to blame for everything. Luckily, they had a good lawyer and a few good friends." Nicolda waved his hands for someone else to come in. Malada stepped into the room. She looked like she never had before—clean, neat, and tidy. Together the three friends embraced.

Malada spoke first. "Thank you, thank you so much. I asked you to help me find my mother, and you did so much more. I can't thank you two enough. What happened to you two?"

Manatado put his hand to his ear. "Yeah, so um, we met your dad."

"Wait, what?" a stunned Malada retorted.

Cassandra continued on. "Oh, and he knows you kissed Manatado."

"Wait, what?"

Manatado continued. "Your parents interrogated me, asking me what my intentions for you were."

"Wait, what?"

Cassandra very quickly and casually chimed in. "Oh, and then your parents were totally making out."

"Wait, what?"

"You sound like me now." Manatado snickered.

"Wait, what?" Malada looked as if she was about to pass out!

Cassandra changed the subject. "So, Nicolda, do we have to stay in jail?"

"Well there were plenty of people who simply wanted to punish you kids, but you had a few more friends willing to come to your aid." Nicolda waved his hands for the others to come in. Gerterma, Lukinia, Ferninia, Itarus the dwarf, Tamack and Rogers, and the handsome boy from the Socratea all came forward. "We also had some interesting confessions from an elf you might know as Redleaf."

Manatado had a big smile on his face. "So does that mean we aren't under arrest?"

Nicolda smiled. "No, I'm afraid it's even worse than that. I'm afraid you all are celebrities now. There is a big celebration planned in just a few hours, so it's time to get you all ready."

Malada ran up to Cassandra. "I saw the most beautiful dress I thought was perfect for you. I can't wait to show you." Cassandra's eyes opened wide, and together they jumped up and down.

The group started to leave the room, when Eratrea called out, "Wait, don't I get let out?"

Nicolda shook his head. "I'm afraid your part in this whole event will require further evaluation. You will have to stay and be punished for your crimes."

Manatado's jaw dropped. "So wait, wait, wait. After all that, this doesn't feel right. Eratrea helped us in the end. Doesn't that count for something?"

Nicolda paused in reflection. "To the creator, yes. To the world, no."

Manatado frowned. "I don't want to be an adult either. The adult world is awful. Nobody looks out for each other, nobody works for the greater good, and nobody forgives each other. Who wants to be an adult in such a world?"

Gerterma, hearing this now, stepped back and walked up to Manatado. "The world needs more adults like you kids, but you can't change the world, only people. Now that you are famous, maybe you can do just that."

Malada ran up and hugged her mother between the bars. "What do we do, Mother?"

Eratrea ran her hand over Malada's hair. "They are right, I made bad choices. I need to pay for them."

"But, Mother, we did all this to be back together."

"What you did was something even more incredible. Go, go, and take pride in what you did. I will be right here, and I'm sure you can come and visit."

"Okay, Mom, if you think that's best."

"I do, I do."

After a sorrowful moment, the group left. Distant chanting and cheering could be heard in the distance. Cassandra and Malada headed off toward one changing room, while Manatado was herded off to another by Gerterma. An attendant ungraciously helped him into a very formal suit. Manatado hated it instantly. Never in his life had he ever had call to wear such attire.

"Gerterma," Manatado asked, "um, so why aren't you in prison?"

Gerterma looked around before whispering back. "I don't think anyone knows who I am, now that I'm old again."

The attendant rushed up to Manatado and ushered him away.

Manatado was again led off to a large stage. On the other side of a large curtain was a large gathering of people from all species and all walks of life. They were cheering and singing songs. Every time he asked someone what was going on, they would just tell him to wait.

Malada approached and tapped Manatado on the shoulder. "Oh my, how we clean up nicely. You look, um, nice."

Manatado blushed as he looked over Malada. "You look really nice too."

Malada smiled. "Oh yeah, wait until you see this." She waved her hand and Cassandra stepped out. Cassandra looked beautiful. The waves of her dress flowed as she gracefully stepped out. A shiny headband sparkled in her hair. Cassandra walked up to Manatado and smiled a big smile at him. Manatado stood there, stupid looking. Malada elbowed him in the side, prodding him to say something.

"Wow, Cassandra, you look amazing."

Cassandra now blushed. "Thank you, you look very handsome."

The three now stood in awkward silence before Manatado spoke. "So I'm feeling nervous. What are we supposed to do?"

"I think they are going to introduce us, we walk out, wave, and then just walk back," Cassandra answered.

Manatado looked at her. "You are so cool. You just always, well, just know what to do."

Music started and a host now started giving a speech. "Today we are here to honor those who saved us from the renegades!" A big round of applause went up from the crowd. "Those who would attack us are no match for the white wizard, the Valentina archer, and the boy named Manatado."

"What, why don't I get a cool name?" Manatado protested.

"Now let's give it up for our heroes!" the host yelled out as the crowd erupted in applause.

The three kids were ushered out onto the stage. At first Manatado felt very uncomfortable, but as he relaxed, he found this was exactly what he was hoping for. He also realized he hated it.

After a few minutes, the kids were brought back to behind the curtain again. "That was awkward. I thought I would have enjoyed that more."

Cassandra and Malada nodded in agreement.

"It feels weird that they are all so happy about this. All we saw was destruction, and they seem almost happy about it," Manatado reflected.

The kids paused as a new speaker was now addressing the crowd. This man was tall and dark and wore a thick mustache. His presence was overpowering, and his words came with authority. "And as your new leader, I will make sure this never happens again."

"Something doesn't feel right," Manatado insisted.

"I agree," Cassandra answered.

"Me too. Is it this guy who is speaking now? I don't think I like him. I don't even know who he is."

Gerterma approached from off to the side and waved them over. "So what do you kids think?"

"I don't know, Gerterma. Who is that guy?" Manatado asked.

Gerterma shook his head. "He's the next adult in charge."

The three swallowed nervously. "And is that a good thing?"

Gerterma shrugged his shoulders. "All I can say is that I'm glad there are kids like you in this world."

The man on stage yelled out with great applause. "I will lead us into the next great phase of civilization."

A surge of commotion erupted from behind the stage as police, military, and men in suits all ran around wildly. "What's going on now?"

A shout from a man giving orders answered his question. "The woman wizard, she has escaped!"

The three kids looked at Gerterma, who only smiled back. "It's good to have kids like you in the world."

The man speaking on stage finished. When he stepped off, a group of police met him, updating him on her escape. "Find her, arrest her!" the man shouted.

Malada looked at her friends. "Will you help me find my mother?"

Cassandra and Manatado looked at each other and then Malada. "Yes!"